Contents

Editor:
John Gregory Betancourt

Assistant Editors:
George H. Scithers

Copyright © 2008 by Wildside Press, LLC. All rights reserved.

Adventure Tales is published two times per year by Wildside Press LLC.

Postmaster & others: send change of address and other subscription matters to: Wildside Press, 9710 Traville Gateway Dr. #234, Rockville, MD 20850–7408.

Single copies: $12.95, postage paid in the U.S.A. Add $5.00 per copy for shipping elsewhere. Subscriptions: four issues for $39.95 in the U.S.A. and its possessions, $29.95 in Canada, and $59.95 elsewhere. All payments must be in U.S. funds and drawn on a U.S. financial institution. If you wish to use PayPal to pay for your subscription, email your payment to: wildside@sff.net.

Tell us what you think! Visit the official *Adventure Tales* message board at: www.wildsidepress.com

Wildside Press
9710 Traville Gateway Dr. #234
Rockville, MD 20850
www.wildsidepress.com

We invite letters of comment (via email or regular mail), and we assume that all letters we receive are intended for publication (unless marked as "Do Not Publish") and become the

Summer 2008   Vol I, No. 5

The stories in this issue of *Adventure Tales* originally appeared as follows: "Their Own Dear Land" was published in *Blue Book,* January 1943. "The Midwatch Tragedy" was published in *Short Stories,* June 10, 1924. "The Remittance Woman was published in *Everybody's Magazine,* July 1922.

The Blotter

Meet Achmed Abdullah!

I'm not sure when I first became aware of the works of Achmed Abdullah. It must have been in the early 1980s, when I first began collecting pulp magazines, and spotted this curious Arab-sounding byline in issues of *Adventure*. I rapidly became a fan: this Abdullah fellow could write!

Many of his stories deal with exotic locales, usually Oriental. But even his Occidental tales are of interest, well written and fast paced, often with an unexpected twist or two. I began gathering his stories whenever I spotten them, and the result was one of Wildside Press's first original collections of pulp stories: *Fear and Other Tales from the Pulps*, by Achmed Abdullah . . . the first new collection of his work in more than 50 years. (Needless to say, I recommend it highly.)

I could go on about him, but Darrell Schweitzer's scholarship on Achmed Abdullah far exceeds by own, so I will simply quote part of his introduction to *Fear:*

Those who met Abdullah found him very British in speech, manner and ideas. Indeed, he had been educated at Eton and Oxford (and the University of Paris), and had served in the British Army in the Middle East, India, and China, but he was actually the son of a Russian Grand Duke, the second cousin of Czar Nicholas II. His Russian name was Alexander Nicholayevitch Romanoff (sometimes given as Romanowski). His Muslim name was Achmed Abdullah Nadir Khan el-Durani el-Iddrissyeh. While the byline "Achmed Abdullah" was easy to remember and quite exotic, it wasn't, strictly speaking, a pseudonym, and he came by it legitimately. Admittedly "Achmed Abdullah" was more likely to sell books of Oriental adventure than "Alexander Romanoff."

Abdullah/Romanoff was born in 1881 and died in 1945. His birthplace is variously reported as Malta or Russia. What is certain is that after his army service, he embarked on a general literary career, writing novels and stories of mystery and adventure and some fantasy, with much of his work appearing in pulp magazines such as *Munsey's, Argosy,* and *All-Story.* His first novel was *The Swinging Caravan* (1911), followed by *The Red Stain* (1915), *The Blue-Eyed Manchu* (1916), *Bucking the Tiger* (1917), *The Trail of the Beast* (1918), *The Man on Horseback* (1919), *The Mating of the Blades* (1921), and so on, all the way up to *Deliver Us From Evil* (1939). He edited anthologies, including *Stories for Men* (1925), *Lute and Scimitar* (1928), and *Mysteries of Asia* (1935).

Among his fantasy volumes, the story collection *Wings: Tales of the Psychic* (1920) is most recommended by aficionados. His best-remembered and most famous work is the 1924 novelization of Douglas Fairbanks, Sr.'s film, *The Thief of Bagdad*. As it has been reprinted many times over the years, clearly Abdullah's *Thief of Bagdad* is more than a mere typing exercise. It is, after all, the novelization of a *silent* film, which meant the novelist had to be considerably more creative and invent most of the dialogue.

Abdullah's connection with Hollywood did not end with a novelization. He had written plays for Broadway, such as *Toto* (1921) and went on to do a number of screenplays, including *Lives of a Bengal Lancer* (1935), for which he and collaborators John Balderston and Waldemar Young shared an Academy Award. The film was based on the novel by Francis Yeats-Brown, but it is clear that Abdullah was eminently suited to the material.

ACHMED ABDULLAH

Their Own Dear Land

OMAR THE BLACK sighed — and grinned a little too — at the recollection.

"There was Esa, the chief eunuch, yelling at me," he said to his twin brother Omar the Red. "And there was Fathouma, the woman I had, if not loved, then at least left, smiling at me! Ah — I felt like a nut between two stones. Can you blame me that I sped from the place?"

He described how, with the help of crashing elbows and kicking feet, he bored through the crowd; how at a desperate headlong rush, he hurtled around a corner, a second, a third, seeking deserted alleys, while behind him, men surged into motion.

There was then pursuit, and the chief eunuch's shouts taken up in a savage chorus:

"Stop him!"

"What has he done?"

"Who cares? Did you not hear? A

by Achmed Abdullah

Illustrated by
John Richard Flanagan

A Saga of the Two Swordsmen of High Tartary

hundred pieces of gold to the man who stops him!"

"Money which I need!"

"No more than I! Money — ah — to be earned by my father's only son!"

Well, Omar the Black had decided, money not to be earned, if he could help it. He was not going to be stopped, and delivered up to the chief eunuch. It would mean one of two things: an unpleasant death or a life even more unpleasant.

For he knew the chief eunuch of old — knew that the latter, who had been fiercely jealous of him during the days of his affluence and influence at the court of the Grand Khan of the Golden Steppe, had always intrigued against him, always detested him, always tried to undermine him. And here, tonight, was Esa's chance.

A chance at bitter toll!

Either — oh, yes! — an unpleasant death or a life yet more unpleasant. Either to be handed over by the eunuch to the Grand Khan; and then —

the Tartar considered and shuddered — it would be the tall gallows for him, or the swish of the executioner's blade. Or else — and again he shuddered — his fate would rest with Fathouma, the Grand Khan's sister.

And — *ai-yai* — the way she had peered at him through the fluttering silk curtains of the litter! The way she had smiled at him! Such a sweet, gentle, forgiving smile! Such a tender smile!

Allah — such a loving smile!

Why — this time she might be less proud, less the great lady. Might insist on carrying out their interrupted marriage-contract. And what then of this other girl, this Gotha? A girl — ah, like the edge of soft dreams — a girl whom he loved madly. . . .

He interrupted his thoughts.

WHAT, he asked himself, as his legs, one sturdy and sound and the other aching rheumatically, gathered speed, was the good in thinking, right now, of Gotha? First he would have to find safety — from the Grand Khan's revenge no less than from Fathouma's mercy.

Faster and faster he ran — then swerved as a man, whom he passed, grabbed his arm and cried:

"Stop, scoundrel!"

Omar shook off the clutching fingers; felled, with brutal fist, another man who stepped square in his path; ran still faster, away from the center of the town, through streets and alleys that were deserted — and that a few moments later, as if by magic, jumped to hectic life.

Lights in dark houses twinkled, exploded with orange and yellow as shutters were pushed up. Heads leaned from windows. Doors opened. The coiling shadows spewed forth people — men as well as women. They came hurrying out of nowhere, out of everywhere.

They came yelling and screeching: "Get him!"

"Stop him!"

"There he goes!"

"After him!"

The pack in full cry — two abreast, three, four, six abreast. Groups, solitary figures!

A lumbering red-turbaned constable, stumbling out of a coffee-shop, wiping his mouth, tugging at his heavy revolver.

Shouted questions. Shouted answers:

"What is it?"

"What has happened?"

"A thief!"

"No! A murderer!"

"Three people he slew!"

"Four! I saw it with these eyes!"

"Ah — the foul assassin!"

And sadistic, quivering, high-pitched screams: "Get him!" . . . "Catch him!" . . . *"Kill* him!"

Ferocious gaiety in the sounds. For here was the cruel, perverted, thrill of the man-hunt.

"Get him!"

"Kill him!"

"Quick, quick, quick! Around the next corner! Cut him off!"

Swearing, shrieking. Throwing bricks and pots and clubs and stones. *Pop! pop! pop!* — the constable's revolver dropping punctuation marks into the night. And on, on, the sweep of figures. And Omar the Black running, his lungs pounding, his heart beating like a triphammer; darting left, right, left, right — steadily gaining on his pursuers, at last finding temporary refuge at the edge of town, in the old cemetery, among the carved granite tombstones that dreamed of Judgment Day.

There, stretched prone on the ground, he turned his head to watch the mob hurrying on and past on a false trail. He listened to the view-halloo of the chase growing fainter and fainter, finally becoming a mere memory of sound.

Then, slowly, warily, he got up. He looked about. . . .

Nobody was within sight.

So he doubled on his tracks and left Gulabad from the opposite direction, hag-ridden by his double

fear — of the Grand Khan's revenge and of Fathouma's loving tenderness.

To put the many, many miles between himself and this double fear, this double danger — that is what he must do, and do as quickly as possible. His resolve was strengthened by the knowledge that money was sultan in High Tartary as anywhere else in the world; that the tale of the rich reward which had been offered for his capture — a hundred pieces of gold — would be round and round the countryside in no time at all, and so every hand there would be against his, and every eye and ear seeking him out.

Therefore Omar the Black traveled in haste and in stealth. At night he traveled, hiding in the daytime, preferring the moors and forests to the open, green fields; taking the deer- and wolf-spoors instead of honest highways; plunging to the knee — and his rheumatic leg hurting him so — at icy fords rather than using the proper stone bridges that spanned the rivers; avoiding the snug, warm villages where food was plentiful and hearts were friendly. And living — as the Tartar saying has it — on the wind and the pines and the gray rock's lichen!

Footsore he was, and weary; and wishing: "If only I had a horse!"

A fine, swift horse to take between his two thighs and gallop away. Then ho for the far road, the wild, brazen road, and glittering deeds, glittering fame! Yes — glittering fame it would be for him; and he hacking his way to wealth and power; and presently returning to Gulabad.

No longer a fugitive, with a price on his head and the Grand Khan's revenge at his heel, but a hero, a conqueror; the equal — by the Prophet the Adored! — to any Khan.

Omar was quite certain of his ultimate success, and for no better or, be-like, no worse reason than that he was what he was: a Tartar of Tartars — the which is a thing difficult to explain with the writing of words to those who do not know our steppes and our hills.

Perhaps it might best be defined by saying that his bravery overshadowed his conceit — or the other way about — that both bravery and conceit were overshadowed by his tight, hard, shrewd strength of purpose, and gilded by his undying optimism. Anyway, whatever it was, he had it. It made him sure of himself; persuaded him, too, that some day Gotha would be his, so sweet and warm and white in the crook of his elbow.

The imagining intoxicated him. He laughed aloud — and a moment later grew unhappy and morose. Only a fool, he told himself, will grind pepper for the bird still on the wing.

Not a bird, in his case, but a horse. A horse was the first thing he had to have for the realization of his stirring plans. Without a horse, these plans were useless, hopeless — as useless and hopeless as trying to throw a noose around the far stars or weaving a rope from tortoise-hair.

Yes, the horse was essential. And how could he find one, here in the lonely wilderness of moor and forest?

Thus, despondent and gloomy, he had trudged on. Night had come; and the chill raw wind, booming out of the Siberian tundras, had raced like a leash of strong dogs; and hunger had gnawed at his stomach; and thirst had dried his throat; and his leg had throbbed like a sore tooth. "Help me, O Allah, O King of the Seven Worlds!" he had sobbed — and as if in answer to his prayer, he had heard a soft neighing, had seen a roan Kabuhi stallion grazing on a short halter, had sneaked up noiselessly, had unhobbled the animal and been about to mount. . . . And then:

"By Beelzebub," he said now, angrily, to his twin-brother, "it *had* to be yours!"

Again he sighed.

"Ah," he added, "am I not the poor, miserable one, harried by the hounds of fate!"

OMAR the Red looked up.

"Not poor, surely," he remarked.

"What do you mean — not poor?"

"Unless, in your flight, you lost the jewels which you took from the rich Jew."

Omar the Black jumped up.

"As the Lord liveth," he exclaimed, "I had forgotten them!"

Anxiously he tapped his loose breeches. There was a pleasant tinkle, and a few seconds later a pleasant sight as he brought out a handful of emeralds and rubies that sparkled in the moon's cold rays.

Then once more he became despondent.

"What good," he asked, "are these jewels to me? As much good as a comb to a bald-headed man. Why, not even were you to give me your horse —"

"Which, decidedly, I shall not."

Omar the Black paid no attention to his brother's unfeeling comment.

"No," he repeated, "not even were you to give me your horse."

For, he went on to say, Gotha was a slave in the harem of Yengi Mehmet, the Khan of Gulistan. The latter, according to Timur Bek, was as eager for money as a young flea is for blood. Therefore, before Omar the Black had a chance to leave his mark upon High Tartary and return to Gulabad, a hero, a conqueror, somebody else might covet the girl, might offer a great price for her — and Yengi Mehmet would sell her. . . .

He drew a hand across his eyes.

"Allah, Allah!" he cried. "What am I to do? Ah, if you could see this girl! As a garment, she is silver and gold! As a season, the spring!"

"So," was the other's impatient interruption, "you told me before — and bored me profoundly. The question is — you desire this girl?"

"As Shaitan, the Stoned Devil, the Accursed, desires salvation."

"Very well. You shall have her."

"But — how?"

"I shall help you" — Omar the Red paused. "For a consideration."

"There would be," — bitterly, — "a consideration, you being you."

"There is, I being I — or for that matter, anybody being anybody. Therefore, if I help you to get your heart's desire, will you —"

"Yes, yes! Anything! Put a name to it!"

"A dear name! A grand and glorious name! The old palace back home where you and I were born, which I lost to you —"

"In a fair fight."

"Fair enough. I want it back."

"Is that all? Help yourself."

"Thanks. Only — I have not enough money. But you, with a tenth of these jewels, can pay off the old

debts. . . . Listen!" He spoke with deep, driving seriousness. "Far have I wandered, astride a horse and on stout shoes, and too, at times, on the naked soles of my feet, fighting thy own fights — and other men's fights — for the sport of it and a bit of loot. But over yonder" — he pointed north — "is the only place I have ever seen worth hacking sound steel for in earnest. And over yonder the one girl, Ayesha, worth loving. Ah — somebody. once told me there is no happiness in another man's shoes, nor in another man's castle, nor with another man's wife. So — what say you — we go home, you and I, and live there — I with Ayesha and you with Gotha —"

"I — with Gotha? But —"

"Did I not tell you I would help you?"

"How can you?"

"I shall buy her for you."

"What with — since you have no money?"

"But you have the jewels. And did not Timur Bek offer to arrange the matter with the Khan?"

"Yes."

"There you are. Timur Bek will be your intermediary with the Khan — and I shall be your intermediary with Timur Bek. Hand over the jewels. I shall hurry to Gulabad, sell the jewels, talk to Timur Bek, have him buy the girl, then return here with her and —"

"No!" came Omar the Black's loud bellow.

"No?"

"No, indeed!"

"Why not?"

The other smiled thinly.

"Would you leave meat on trust with a jackal."

"In other words, you do not trust me?"

"Neither with the jewels, nor with the girl."

"And perhaps," was the shameless admission, "you are wise. But — well, there is another way."

"Yes?"

"We shall both go to Gulabad."

"I — with a price on my head?"

"On your black-bearded head, don't forget. But who, tell me, will recognize this same head — without the beard?"

"Oh" — in a towering rage — "dare you suggest that I should —"

"Shave off your beard? Right."

"Impossible! Why, by the Prophet the Adored, this beard," — he ran a caressing hand through it — "has been my constant and loyal companion in joy and in sorrow. It is the pride and beauty of my manhood."

"The pride and beauty will grow again."

For quite a while they argued, until finally Omar the Black gave in.

But he cursed violently while scissors and razor did their fell work. He cursed yet more violently when, having announced that the stallion was strong enough to carry the two of them, he was informed by his twin brother that such a thing was out of the question.

For, opined Omar the Red, here was he himself most splendidly clad as became a gentleman of High Tartary. And here was the other, in stained and odorous rags — a very scarecrow of a man. It would seem strange to people, whom they might meet, to see them in such an intimacy, astride the same horse.

Better far, he said, for the other to run sturdily in back of the stallion, with outstretched hand, like some importunate beggar crying for *zekat! zekat! zekat!* — alms for the sake of Allah.

He clapped his brother heartily on the back. "It will be safest for you," he added. "Besides, you will see more of this fine broad world, walking on your two feet, than cocked high and stiff upon a saddle."

Omar the Red laughed.

So, on an evening almost a week later, did Timur Bek laugh, back in Gulabad, when — for at first he had not recognized him, with his beard shorn off — he learned that this smooth-cheeked man was Omar the Black.

"Here you are," exclaimed Timur Bek, "with your face as soft as a girl's bosom!"

He laughed more loudly. "Oh," he cried, "if Gotha could see you!"

Omar the Black swallowed his anger.

"She is still here?" he demanded.

"And pining for you, I have no doubt."

"And — your promise?"

"I have not forgotten it."

Timur Bek went on to say that he was ready to open negotiations about the girl's purchase with Yengi Mehmet. He would do it tactfully and drive as good a bargain as he could.

"I know, of course," he added, "that you have the jewels." He smiled. "The Jew, Baruch ben Isaac ben Ezechiel, made a great ado about it. Swore that nineteen tough Tartars, armed to the teeth, broke into his shop and assaulted him!"

"Nor," said Omar the Black, "did he lie — exactly. For am I not the equal of the nineteen toughest Tartars in the World? Very well. My brother and I shall sell the jewels. Do you know a place — oh — a discreet place where we —"

"Can sell the jewels? Not necessary."

"But —"

"The Khan likes precious gems as much as minted gold."

"Still, he may suspect —"

"He will not listen to the evil voice of suspicion — if the jewels be rich enough. If they be rich enough, his left eye will look west, and his right east. Let's have a look at the loot."

The other reached into his breeches. He poured the gems in a shimmering stream on a low divan; and Timur Bek licked his lips. He said:

"It may take a good many of these trinkets to —"

"Nothing too much to buy me my heart's desire. Here — take half the stones!"

Timur Bek coughed.

"There is also," he said, "the matter of the money which I borrowed from the Khan, giving the little slave-girl, whom I love, as security. You were going to help me pay back the loan — remember?"

"I do. And I shall keep my word."

"The sooner, the better — for you."

Omar the Black frowned. "Eh?"

"This girl, you see, has the Khan's

ear. I need her assistance. Loving me as I love her, she is anxious to return to me. And so, unless I buy her back, I am afraid she —"

"Yes, yes, yes!" Omar the Black interrupted impatiently. "Here — take another fourth of the stones. Surely it will be enough."

"Not quite."

"But —"

"Thirty thousand tomans I borrowed. It will take the rest of the stones to —"

"All right!" with a sigh. "Take them all!"

Timur Bek's hands were about to scoop up the jewels, when Omar the Red cried:

"Wait!"

He touched his brother's knee.

"You are forgetting our agreement," he told his brother. "You were going to use some of the treasure to pay off your old debts, so that we can return home and —"

"I have not forgotten."

"Why —"

"Listen!" Omar the Black winked slowly at his twin brother. "That time I broke into the Jew's shop, I was in a hurry. I took only half the jewels. The other half is waiting for you and me."

He turned to Timur Bek:

"When will you speak to the Khan?"

"Tonight. At once."

Timur Bek left his house. He went round the corner to the garden gate of Yengi Mehmet's palace.

There, while night was falling thicker and thicker, wrapping the streets in a cloak of trailing purple shadows, he whistled: two high, shrill notes, followed by a throaty, fluting tremolo, like a crane calling to its mate.

There was silence.

He waited; listened tensely, then repeated the call — and the gate opened softly; and a small white-robed figure slipped out and rushed into his arms with a little cry of joy.

"O my beloved!"

"O soul of my soul!"

"O king!"

"O sweetmeat!"

They spoke in a whisper, at length. They laughed. They kissed. And presently Timur Bek returned to the rooftop of his house, where Omar the Black was pacing up and down impatiently, while Omar the Red was applying himself to a bottle of Persian wine.

"Well — ?" demanded the former.

"I talked to my girl."

"Not to the Khan?"

"She, as I told you, has the Khan's ear. And it seems that he is willing to sell Gotha. But —"

"Is there a but?"

"Isn't there always?" Timur Bek paused. "He is fond of her."

"What's that?" — excitedly.

"In a fatherly manner. Yes — as if she were his daughter. Therefore he insists that whoever buys the girl must marry her."

"I — marry?"

"Yes. It is part of the bargain. You must marry her at once. Tomorrow evening, at the Mosque of Hassan. A simple ceremony, with no witnesses. The girl, being shy, insists on it."

Omar the Black did not reply immediately.

Marriage, he reflected — as more than once, on his lawless path, his brother had reflected — meant bonds of steel. It meant the orderly homespun ways of life; meant — oh, all sorts of disagreeable things. . . . An end to freedom!

And it was on his tongue to exclaim: "No! Let Yengi Mehmet keep the girl!"

But he reconsidered as he thought

of her — with her full red lips, and her brown hair as smooth as oil, and her gray eyes that seemed to hold all the secret wisdom, all the secret sweet mockery of womanhood.

Lovely! So very lovely!

He loved her. . . . Besides, coming to think of it, marriage was not necessarily the end. Bonds of steel, too, could be broken — by a strong and ruthless man.

"Very well," he announced. "Marriage it will be." And, severely, to his brother: "Let this be a lesson to you — to follow in my virtuous footsteps!"

"As virtuous," remarked Timur Bek, "as mine own. For I too shall take a wife unto myself — the little slave-girl whom I love."

"You have repaid your loan to the Khan?"

"Thanks to you, Great-Heart. To-morrow morning my love and I are going away. Therefore if, for the time being, you and your bride and your brother would care to live in my house, you are welcome. There is food in the larder and wine in the cellar. And after all, with your jewels gone —"

"I shall be poor, I know."

"Only," chimed in Omar the Red, "until Baruch, the rich Jew, contributes another handful of gems."

LATE on the following evening, Omar the Black, arrayed in some of his brother's handsome clothes, went to the Mosque — an ancient and beautiful building raised on a flight of broad marble steps, its great horseshoe gateway covered with delicate mosaic arabesques in mauve and silver and heliotrope and elfin-green.

There the bride, wrapped from head to foot in three heavy white wedding veils, awaited him.

She saw his smooth cheeks. But she gave no more than a little start. For she had been warned of what had happened to his beard; and with or without his beard, she loved him — loved him dearly.

Slowly he walked up to her. He bowed — and so did she.

HAND in hand they stepped before the green-turbaned priest, who united them in holy wedlock, according to the rites of Islam:

"Will you, O son of Adam, take this woman to wife — before God the One, and the Prophet the Adored, and the multitude of the Blessed Angels?"

"I will!"

"Will you, O daughter of Eve, take this man to husband — before God the One, and the Prophet the Adored, and the multitude of the Blessed Angels?"

"I will!"

Silence. . . . Omar the Black stared at his wife.

"Soon to be mine!" he whispered. "Soon — soon!"

Then there was the priest chanting a *surah* from the Koran in nasal, sacerdotal tones:

For the Merciful hath taught the Koran,
He created the male and the female,
He taught them clear speech,
He taught them desire and fulfilment.
An echo of His own creation.
So which of the Lord's bounties would
*   ye twain deny?*
The sun and the moon in their courses,
And the planets do homage to Him,
And the heaven He raised it and
*   appointed the balance,*
And the earth He prepared it for living
*   things.*
Therein He created fruit, and the palm
*   with sheaths,*
And grain with its husks, and the
*   fragrant herb,*

*And the male and the female of man
and of beast.
So which of the Lord's bounties would
ye twain deny?*

"Not I," said Omar the Black to his wife, "to deny this particular bounty."

She gave a happy little laugh; the priest finished; husband and wife salaamed toward Mecca; and then Omar took her to Timur Bek's house, up to the rooftop beneath the stars.

There his brother was. He greeted the couple with loud shouts of:

"Yoo-yoo-yoo!"

But Omar the Black cut him short.

"Enough `yoo-yoo-yoo' for the nonce," he said. "This is the one moment — of many, many moments — when I can do without your company."

So Omar the Red left — winking, in passing, at the bride. And a few seconds later, slowly and clumsily, since his hands trembled so, Omar the Black raised the three wedding veils one by one.

"Wah," he whispered throatily, "you are all my dreams come true!"

Then, swiftly, he receded a step. For, with the moon laying a mocking silver ribbon across her features, he saw that the woman whom he had married was Fathouma, the Grand Khan's sister, and not Gotha.

Omar stood there without speaking. He stared at her.

Even more faded she was than when he had seen her last; more gray the hair that curled on her temples; more sharply etched the network of wrinkles at the corners of her brown gold-flecked eyes. But still the same eyes — with the same tenderness in them, the same sweetness and simplicity, the same depth of feeling. Eyes that lit up as she said to him:

"You broke my heart, years ago, when you left me. But now, the Lord be praised, you have made it whole again."

She walked up to him. And what could he do but take her into his arms?

"Last night," she went on, "when Timur Bek sent me word through Gotha that you had come to Gulabad in search of me, that you wanted me — wanted me for wife — I almost swooned with the great joy of it. And it was so tactful of you to insist on a simple wedding, you and I" — he winced a little at her next words — "being no longer young, lest people ridicule us. Already Esa is on his way to tell my brother the news; and my brother, too, will be so very happy —"

She stopped for breath. She kissed him.

"And," she went on, "I talked to my cousin, the Khan of Kulistan. He will make you a captain in the palace guard, although —" with a fleeting smile curling her lips — "he is a little angry at you."

"Why?"

"Because of Gotha."

"Oh!"

"He liked her, and," she laughed — "more than merely liked her. *Hayah* — the old cat, though blind and lame, still hankers after mice! And you, like the generous soul you are, giving all your jewels to Timur Bek, so that he could pay back to Yengi Mehmet what he owed him, and free Gotha, and marry her!"

He gave a start.

"You said — marry?"

"Did you not know? Very early this morning they went to the mosque and became man and wife. And now they are off to the steppe, the wilderness, to spend their honeymoon. For they are young. They can stand the rigor, the chill harsh winds, the open air. Well" — and again she smiled, while again he winced a little — "we are not young, you and I. But our love is as great as theirs — is it not, my lord?"

He did not reply immediately. He looked at her, with a long and searching look. And then — nor was it altogether because he feared her brother

So he bowed gallantly in the Persian manner, his hand on his breast. He was about to kneel before her, and had already bent his left leg, when suddenly he felt a stabbing pain and gave a cry.

"Why! Oh," was her anxious query "What is the matter?"

"Nothing, nothing."

Gotha, beautiful as a season in Spring

the Grand Khan, and knew that this time he would have no chance at all to get away, but also, and chiefly, because of a queer feeling in his soul, something akin to tender pity — he inclined his head and said: "There was never love greater than mine, O heart of seven roses!"

He was silent; and he thought, with supreme self-satisfaction: *When I do a thing, by Allah and by Allah, I do it in style! It is the glorious way of me.*

"But I heard you —"

"A little pain — in my left leg."

"A wound?"

"No. A touch of rheumatism."

She shook a finger at him.

"Your own fault!"

"Eh?"

"Yes. To be up here on the roof late at night, in the cold, as if you were in your teens!"

"But —"

"You are old enough to have more sense! Off to bed with you — and a hot brick at your feet, and a glass of mulled wine to put you to sleep. Tomorrow we'll leave this draughty house, and stay with my cousin the Khan of Gulistan, and —"

"Look —" he interrupted indignantly.

"Be quiet! I know what is good for you."

Firmly she took him by the arm and led him down the stairs.

He did not resist. They passed Omar the Red's room. And Omar the Black bit his lips and frowned as he heard a faint, "Yoo-yoo-yoo!" heard, a moment later, something which sounded, suspiciously, like laughter.

IT cannot be said that, during the days that followed, Omar the Black was exactly unhappy. In fact, though he hated to admit it, he was enjoying life.

There was his wife. Faded, sure enough, and wrinkled. Not lovely at all, not the one to quicken a man's heartbeat and set his flesh to aching. On the other hand, she was so kindly, so very, very kindly — and so strangely humble when, frequently, she said to him:

"You bring me great happiness. I love you, O best beloved!"

He would kiss her gently; lying like a gentleman, and after a while not lying at all, though he thought he did, he would reply:

"So do I love you, O delight!"

Furthermore — oh, yes, Fathouma was right — he was no longer in his teens, no longer eager to travel the hard road, with ever danger and death lurking around the corner. And it was pleasant to be once more, as formerly at the court of the Grand Khan of the Golden Steppe, a man of fashion, dressed in cloak and breeches of handsomely embroidered, Bokharan satin, and hose of gossamer silk, and boots of soft red leather, and a voluminous turban that had cost fifty pieces of silver — and always a deal of money clanking in his breeches, what with his captain's pay and his wife's generosity — and the work quite suiting his fancy.

Indeed, Omar did no work to speak of. Except that, as a captain in the service of the Khan of Gulistan, he would mount guard at the palace every forenoon for a leisurely, strolling hour or two, swapping yarns and boasts and lies with the other tall captains. And in the afternoons he would whistle to his tawny Afghan hound and stalk through the streets and bazaars, buying whatever he wished, and once in a while getting into a row because of insult real or, more often, imagined.

AND in the evenings he would go on an occasional riotous drinking-bout, rolling home late and noisy — and Fathouma would be waiting for him, would cool his throbbing temples with scented water, nor give him the sharp edge of her tongue, but warn:

"You must be careful, best beloved. A man of your years —"

He would flare up.

"What do you mean — a man of my years?" he would demand. "Why, my heart is the same as ever it was, keen and lightsome! And my soul has the same golden fire, and my joints are still greased with the rich grease of youth, and —"

"Of course," she would agree soothingly. "And yet you look a little tired, and so you had better have your breakfast in bed tomorrow. And here" — stirring a cup that held a steaming, dark, strong-smelling broth — "some tea of bitter herbs for your stomach."

"No, no!"

"Yes, yes! Drink it at one swallow, hero, and it will not taste so bad."

He would sigh — and obey.

He would, to tell the truth, feel better for it the next day, and get up later and later as morning succeeded morning.

And as time progressed, moreover, Omar went on fewer drinking-bouts; and, gradually he became less, eager at smelling out insults and picking quarrels with all and sundry. In fact, the only quarrel which he had — and carefully nursed — was with his brother.

It was the latter, he would reflect, who by persuading him to return to Gulabad, had been responsible for everything: his marriage as well as the loss of his fine black beard. And while, a little grudgingly, he might forgive him the marriage, he could not forgive him the matter of the beard.

It had grown again — and rapidly — oh, yes! But thanks to the shaving, it was not as silky as formerly; and two gray hairs sprouting for each one he plucked out; and he, with his wife knowing it, rather embarrassed at using gallnut dye.

And furthermore, the mocking way his brother, that night after the wedding, had yoo-yoo-yooed and laughed!

No, no — he could not forgive him.

Therefore when Omar the Red called at the palace, asking his twin brother to fulfil his side of the agreement — to supply the cash for settling the old debts and help him get back to the castle and to Ayesha — Omar the Black raised an eyebrow.

"Do you expect me, an honorable Tartar gentleman," he demanded, "a captain in the Khan's service, to take part in such a wicked enterprise as robbing a shop? Ah — shame on you!"

"We don't have to rob the shop."

"Then how —"

"You are rich."

"I am not."

"But —"

"My captain's pay is a mere pittance."

"Your wife —"

"Has plenty. Yes. And," — self-righteously, — "it would never do for a gentleman to accept money from a woman. Surely even you know that."

Then, when the other grew angry and abusive, Omar the Black pointed to the door:

"Begone, O creature!" he shouted.

He instructed the palace servants that hereafter his twin brother was no longer to be admitted; and when Fathouma, who had heard him give the order, argued with him, he told her:

"You do not know my brother. Always, since his early childhood days, he has been a most lawless and sinful person, has always tried to lead me down the crooked road of temptation. He, I assure you, is not the proper companion for the like of me. And his way with the women — to kiss and ride away — shocking, shocking!"

Hypocritical? Not really. Or if he was, he did not know it.

Indeed, somehow, he meant what he said; began to fancy himself as a most sober and respectable citizen.

No longer did his heart leap and skip like a gay little rabbit across the land whenever he beheld a new face, a young face, a pretty face. And one day when Fathouma mentioned that Timur Bek and his bride were expected home from their honeymoon — and what about entertaining them at dinner? — he shook his head.

"No," he said.

19

"But — isn't Timur your friend?"

"He is. But Gotha —"

"Yes?"

"A toothsome morsel, I grant you. Only — inclined to be flighty."

"I don't think so."

"I know. Why, the very first time I saw her, she gave me the quirk of the eye. She asked me, if you want blunt speech —"

"Please! Not too blunt!"

"You are quite right. It would not be fit for your ears. Anyway, I would have none of her. For by the Prophet, I have always followed the white road of honor — naturally, being what I am. Besides, was not my friend Timur Bek in love with the young person? So, as you know, I let him have my jewels, so that he might buy himself his heart's desire."

He smiled benignly; went on in resonant and rather unctuous accents: "The Lord's blessings on them both!"

Maybe Omar the Black believed that he spoke the truth. Maybe Fathouma did likewise; and maybe, being as clever in one way as she was simple in another, she did not — though without letting on.

For she loved her husband. She loved his very failings, and defended them, even to herself. She was happy — and happiest when, more and more frequently, he would spend the night at home and they would be alone; when he would sit by her side, pleasant and jovial and companionable, and tell her tales of his past life, his past prowess and bravery, his past motley adventures, east, north, south, west.

The love in her brown, gold-flecked eyes would enkindle his imagination. And — oh, the clanking, stirring tales he would tell then:

"The pick of the lads of the far wide roads I was, with ever my sword eager for a bit of strife, ever a fine thirst tickling my gullet, ever the bold, bold eyes of me giving the wink and smile at the passing girls, and they — the dears, the darlings! — giving the same wink and smile straight back at me —"

He would interrupt himself.

"That was," he would add, "before I met you."

"Of course."

She would laugh. She was not jealous of the past, being wiser than most women. Also — oh, yes, she was clever — the very fact that his mind was dwelling more and more on former days and former deeds, proved to her that he was getting old and ready to settle down — which was as she wished.

And so late one afternoon when — it happened rarely nowadays — Omar the Black had gone to split a bottle or two with a boon companion, Fathouma decided that she would surprise him, would buy him a present: the handsomest carved emerald to be had in Gulabad.

She put on her swathing street veils and called to one of the lackeys, a Persian, who had recently been hired and who was a most conscientious servant — always present when he was needed and ready to do her bidding:

"Hossayn!"

He salaamed. "Heaven-born?"

"I am going to the bazaar to do some shopping. Come with me."

"Listen is obey!"

Again he salaamed. He led the way out of the palace, crying loudly:

"Give way, Moslems! Give way for the Heaven-born, the Princess of High Tartary!"

He stalked ahead, clearing a path with the help of a long brass-tipped stave.

Fathouma followed. She was excited, elated. Ah, what an emerald she would buy her lord! She tripped along. And she did not know that, as they passed a dark postern, Hossayn exchanged a cough and a fleeting glance with a stranger who stood there hidden in the coiling, trooping shadows. Nor could she know that several days earlier Hossayn had been buttonholed on the street by this same stranger, who had spoken to him at whispered length and taken him to a tavern.

There, over glasses of potent milk-white *raki*, they had continued the conversation. There had been spirited haggling and bargaining. Finally with a sigh, the other had well greased the Persian's greedy palm, giving him whatever gold and silver coins remained in his waist-shawl. He had added, for good measure, a couple of rings and a dagger.

He had leaned across the table, had asked:

"Do you know what I am thinking?"

"Well?"

"I am thinking," — in a purring voice, — "that I have three more daggers, not as handsome as this but quite as sharp — and thinking, also, that, should you deceive me, yours might be a fine throat for slitting."

The Persian had turned pale.

"Do not bristle at me, tall warrior!" he had begged. *"I — deceive you? Never!"*

"Of course not."

"Only —"

"Only?" threateningly.

"I am not the only servant. Nor can I tell when the Heaven-born will —"

"I know. And I do not demand the impossible. All I expect you to do is to be attentive to her, to make a point of hovering near, being watchful."

He muttered instructions; and the Persian inclined his head.

"I understand."

So there was now, in passing, the glance, the cough — and once more:

"Give way, Moslems! Give way for the Heaven-born, the Princess of High Tartary!"

The people gave way as well as they could. But as Fathouma and the lackey approached the Street of the Western Traders, where the jewelers displayed their precious wares, the alleys and squares and marketplaces became ever more packed with milling, moiling, perspiring humanity, not to mention humanity's wives and children and mothers-in-law and visiting country cousins.

For today — and as it turned out, it was a lucky stroke of fortune for the stranger who had left the postern and was following the two as closely as he could — was a great Islamic festival: the day preceding the *Lelet el-Kadr*, the Night of Honor, the anniversary of the blessed occasion when Allah, in His mercy, revealed the Book of the Koran to His messenger Mohammed.

A most solemn occasion, the *Lelet el-Kadr* — it being the night when the Sidr, which is the lotus tree and which bears as many leaves as there are human beings, is shaken in Paradise by the Archangel Israfel, and on each leaf is inscribed the name of a person who will die during the coming year, should it drop.

SMALL wonder that strong, personal interest is behind the prayers after sunset. Small wonder, furthermore, that all lights are extinguished — lest dark and evil djinn find their way up to Paradise and nudge the Archangel, startling him and causing him to shake down the wrong leaf.

Small wonder, finally, that on the preceding day there should be merrymaking — a fit prelude to the Night of Honor, the Night of Fear, the Night of Repentance.

So here in Gulabad as in the rest of the Islamic world, gay throngs were everywhere, people of all High Tartary, with here and there men from the farther east and south and north and west — Persians, Afghans, Chinese, Siberians, Tibetans, even men from distant Hindustan and Burma, come across mountains and plains to fatten their purses on the holiday trade.

Doing well, making handsome profits.

For all were ready to spend what they could — and could not — afford. All were enjoying themselves after the Orient's immemorial fashion, resplendently and extravagantly and blaringly.

The men swaggered and strutted, fingering daggers, cocking immense turbans or shaggy sheepskin bonnets at rakish devil-may-care angles. The women minced along, rolling their hips and, above their thin, coquettish face-veils,, their eyes. The little boys tried to emulate their fathers in swaggering and strutting; to emulate each other in the shouting of loud, salty abuse. The little girls rivaled the other little girls in the gay, pansy shades of their loose trousers and the consumption of greasy, poisonously pink-and-green sweetmeats.

There were jugglers and knife-tossers, sword-swallowers and fire-eaters and painted dancing-girls.

There were cook-shops and toy-booths and merry-go-rounds.

There were itinerant dervish preachers chanting the glories of Allah the One, the Prophet Mohammed and the Forty-Seven True Saints.

There were bear-leaders, ape-leaders, fortune-tellers, bards, buffoons, and Punch-and-Judy shows.

There were large, bell-shaped tents where golden-skinned gypsy girls trilled and quavered melancholy songs to the accompaniment of guitars and tambourines. There was, of course, a great deal of love-making — the love-making of Asia, which is frank and a trifle indelicate.

There were the many street-cries.

"Sugared water! Sugared water here — and sweeten your breath!" would come the call of the lemonade-seller as he clanked his metal cups, while the vendor of parched grain, rattling the wares in his basket, would chime in with: "Pips! O pips! Roasted and ripe and rare! To sharpen your teeth — your stomach — your mind!"

"Trade with me, O Moslems! I am the father and mother of all cut-rates!"

"Look! Look! A handsome fowl from the Khan's chicken coop!"

"And stolen — most likely!"

Laughter then — swallowed, a moment later, by more and louder cries.

"Out of the way — and say, 'There is but One God!' " — the long, quivering yell of the water-carrier, lugging the lukewarm fluid in a goat's-skin bag, immensely heavy, fit burden for a buffalo.

"My supper is in Allah's hands, O True Believers! My supper is in Allah's hands! Whatever you give, that will return to you through Allah!" — the whine of a ragged old vagrant whose wallet perhaps contained more provision than the larder of many a respectable housewife.

"The grave is darkness — and good deeds are its lamps!" — the shriek of a blind beggarwoman, rapping two dry sticks together.

"In your protection, O honorable

gentleman!" — the hiccoughy moan of a peasant, drunk with hasheesh, whom a constable was dragging by the ear in the direction of the jail, the peasant's wife trailing on behind with throaty plaints of: "O calamity! O great and stinking shame! O most decidedly not father to our sons!" — her balled fists meanwhile ably assisting the policeman.

There was more laughter; and Fathouma, too, laughed as she followed Hossayn.

Only rarely she left the palace; and everything amused her. She decided she would tell Omar the Black all about it tonight when she saw him — and she progressed slowly through the throng, with the stranger still in back; then she stopped, a little nervous, as there was a brawl between a Persian merchant and a Turkoman nomad who disputed the right of way.

NEITHER would budge. They glared at one another. Presently they became angry, and anger gave way to rage — and then a stream of abuse, of that vitriolic and picturesque vituperation in which Central Asia excels.

"Owl! Donkey! Jew! Christian! Leper! Seller of pigs' tripe!" This from the lips of the elderly Persian whose carefully trimmed, snow-white whiskers gave him air aspect of patriarchal Old Testament dignity in ludicrous contrast with the foul invective which he was using. "Uncouth and swinish creature! Eater of filth! Wearer of a verminous turban!"

The reply was prompt: "Basest of hyenas! Goat of a smell most goatish! Now, by my honor, you shall eat stick!"

The stick, swinging by a leather thong from the Turkoman's wrist, was two pounds of tough blackthorn. It was raised and brought down with full force — the Persian moving away just in time and drawing a curved dagger.

People rushed up, closed in, took sides.

It was the beginning of a full-fledged battle royal — and Fathouma cried:

"Hossayn! Hossayn! Get me out of here!"

But Hossayn was not near her. All she saw of him, some yards away, was his red fez bobbing up and down in the mob, as if he were drowning.

"Hossayn! Oh, Hossayn!"

Farther and farther floated the fez; the mob seemed to be carrying the man away; and Fathouma became terribly frightened — jostled and pushed about — and everywhere the striking fists, the glistening weapons — everywhere the shrieks of rage and pain.

She wept helplessly, hopelessly. Almost she fainted.

Then she felt a firm grip on her elbow; heard a reassuring voice in her ear: "This way, Heaven-born!"

A MOMENT later, a man, tall and broad-shouldered, tucked her under one arm as if she were a child, while with the other, wielding a sword, he carved a path through the crowd. They turned a corner; reached a back alley; his knee pushed open a door; and she found herself in the shed of a provision merchant's shop.

There, in the dim light that drifted through a window high on the wall, she saw her rescuer: a man with an eagle's beak of a nose, thin lips, small, greenish eyes. A man — she thought with a start — as like to her husband as peas in a pod, except that his beard was red and not black. . . .

She knew at once who he was:

"You — you are Omar the Red! Ah, the lucky, lucky day for me!"

"Luckier for myself!"

"My husband will be so grateful."

"Doubtless. But this time, knowing my brother, I shall make sure, quite sure, of his gratitude." A smile like milk curdling flitted across his face. "Tell me," he asked, "how good are you at the riding?"

"The — riding?"

"Yes. On a horse. A horse, swift and powerful, to carry the two of us, and you on the saddle in front of me, and with one of my arms — wah! there have been plenty women in the past who liked the strength of it — around your waist to hold you steady."

She looked at him.

"Oh," she faltered, "but —"

"Listen!"

He spoke at length. And, he wondered, was that a laugh trembling on her lips? No, no! it must be the beginning of a cry of fear; and, at once, there was his sword to the fore.

"Be quiet!" he warned her. "Or else — and you the woman and I the tough ruffian — here is the point of my blade for the whitest breast!"

So she was quiet; and he went on:

"Come! My horse is waiting for us — and so are the steppes of High Tartary."

He led her out of the shed, walking close to her. A loving couple, people

would have thought; and none to know that, hidden by the folds of the man's cloak, a dagger was pressed against the small of the woman's back.

By this time, the merry-making had ceased. There came the booming of the sunset gun from the great Mosque where, in the west, it raised its minaret of rosy marble. There came, immediately afterwards, the muezzin's throaty chant that the Night of Honor, the Night of Fear and Repentance, was near; and then lights were extinguished everywhere against the malign flitting of the dark and evil djinns, and the places of worship were filled with the Faithful, the streets and alleys became deserted.

Not a wayfarer anywhere. Hardly a sound.

Only, as a sturdy stallion with two in the saddle rode through the northern gate, a sleepy sentinel's challenge:

"Who goes there?"

"A merchant and his wife."

"Travel in peace, O Moslems!"

So Fathouma and Omar the Red were off at a gallop; while at just about the same time, when Omar the Black returned to the palace, there was a Persian lackey telling him a terrible tale — a tale of heroism, showing, in proof, various bruises and even a bandaged shoulder and explaining how he had been attacked by a *shoda,* a rough customer, had been kicked, cuffed, knocked down, sliced and stabbed with a number of sharp weapons.

With a great throng of men, each intent on his own brawl, all about him, he had been helpless; and — Allah! — the cruel, brutal strength of this red-bearded scoundrel. . . .

"Eh?" interrupted Omar the Black. "You — you said red-bearded?"

"Superbly, silkily red-bearded. And hook-nosed. And armed to the teeth. . . ."

"And with an evil glint in his eyes?"

"Most evil!"

THE Persian went on to relate that here he was, prone on the ground, grievously wounded. And there was the other, with the Heaven-born in a faint and slung across his shoulders as if she were a bag of turnips; and the man's parting words had been:

"Take a message to Omar the Black. Tell him to come quickly, and alone, and with a queen's ransom in his breeches. Let him take the *Darb-i-Sultani,* the King's Highway, straight north into High Tartary. And, presently, at a place of my own choosing, I shall have word with him."

Such was the lackey's story; and Omar the Black did not doubt it, since he knew his brother.

What puzzled him later on — and what, indeed, he cannot understand to this day, though frequently he has asked his wife about it — was what she did or, rather, what she did not do.

Why — he wondered — did she not resist? Why did she neither struggle nor cry out?

"How could I?" she would explain. "At first I thought he had come to rescue me. I was grateful."

"Still — after you discovered that he . . ?"

"I was helpless. I am a weak woman — and there was the point of his dagger pressed against my spine."

"Even so — when you passed, on the saddle in front of him, through the gate — a word to the sentinel . . ."

"It would have been my last. The dagger . . ."

"Omar the Red would not have carried out his threat."

"How was I to know? Such a scoundrel, this brother of yours — you yourself used to tell me — and not at all to be trusted."

So, afterwards, was Fathouma's explanation; and we repeat that Omar the Black — and small blame to him — was puzzled.

But, at the time of the kidnaping, the only emotion he felt was worry. Dreadful worry. Why, he loved his wife — and ho, life without her, like a house without a light, a tree without a leaf . . .

As soon as Hossayn told him the news, he took all his money, all his jewels and whatever of Fathouma's he could find. As an afterthought, he went to the shop of Baruch ben Isaac ben Ezechiel, the rich Jew.

Better too much treasure — he reflected — than too little. He told himself — since, after all, in spite of his worry, he was still the same Omar the Black — that loot was loot and would always come in handy. Therefore, courteously, he asked for credit; was courteously granted it — for was he not the husband of a Tartar Princess and a captain in the Khan's palace guard?

The merchant salaamed.

"Do not worry about credit, lord. Take whatever you wish."

Omar wished a lot, took a lot; and, within the hour, followed his wife and his twin brother up the *Darb-i-Sultani,* into the north.

All night he rode and all the following morning.

At first, near Gulabad, the land was fertile, with tight little villages and checkerboard fields folded compactly into valleys where small rivers ran. But, toward noon, the steppe came to him.

The heart of the steppe.

The heart of High Tartary.

"Do not worry about credit, Lord. Take whatever you wish," said Baruch

IT came with orange and purple and heliotrope; with the sands spawning their monotonous, brittle eternities toward a vague horizon. It came with an insolent, lifeless nakedness; and when, occasionally, there was a sign of life — a vulture poised high on stiff, quivering wings, a jackal loping along like an obscene, gray thought, or a nomad astride his dromedary, his jaws and brows bound up in mummy-fashion against the whirling sand grains, passing with never a word of cheerful greeting — it seemed a rank intrusion, a weak, puerile challenge to the infinite wilderness.

A lonely land.

A harsh and arid land. No silken luxury here. No ease and comfort.

The heat was brutish, brassy. His rheumatic leg ached.

Yet, gradually, he became conscious of a queer elation.

It had been long years — he told himself — since he had left High Tartary. Nor had he ever wished to return. Still — why — it was his own land, his dear land. . . . "Yes, yes!" he cried; and, almost, he forgot what had taken him here, almost forgot Fathouma. "Here — rain or shine, cloudy sky or brazen sun — is my own land, my dear land! Here is freedom! And here, ever, the stout, happy heart!"

He put spurs to his horse and galloped on, grudging each hour of rest. And afternoon died; and evening brought a gloomy iridescence, a twilight of pastel shades, a distant mountain chain with blues and ochres of every hue gleaming on the slopes; and a few days' ride beyond the range — he knew — was Nadirabad nestling in the shadows of the old, ancestral castle; and he dismounted and made a small campfire; and night dropped, suddenly, like a shutter, the way it does on the steppe; and out of the night came a mocking call:

"Welcome, brother!"

Omar the Red stepped from behind a rock; and Omar the Black jumped up, sword in hand.

"Dog with a dog's heart!" he yelled.

"I shall fight you for Fathouma!"

"Fight? No, no! You shall pay me for her — and, by the same token, live up to our agreement."

So, since curses and threats did not help matters, there was, presently, a deal of money thrown on the ground and a wealth of glittering jewels — some come by honestly, and some less so.

"Enough," remarked Omar the Red "to pay back the debts to the Nadirabad merchants — and to lift the mortgage on the castle — and for Ayesha and me to live on comfortably for a number of years."

"For more than a number of years," announced Fathouma, stepping into the flickering light of the campfire. "Indeed until the end of your days — if you are ready to do your share of proper toil."

She turned to her husband.

"The soil up yonder, your brother tells me, is fat," she continued, "and the grass is green and sappy and the water pure. A fine chance, in your own country, for a man's hard, decent work — even a man of your years — and there we shall live, the four of us, and thrive — God willing!"

"You," stammered Omar the Black "you said — the four of us?"

"Ayesha and your brother — and you and I. Can you not add two and two?"

Now this — to live once more at home — had been the very thing which, deep in his soul, he had dreamed of and longed for, ever since he had come to the steppe. But it would not do for a man to give in too quickly to his wife.

"Nothing of the sort!" he replied. "We shall ride back to Gulabad and —"

"Listen!" she interrupted.

"Yes?"

She stepped up close to him.

"Would you want," she demanded, lowering her voice, "your child to be born in an alien land?"

He gave a start.

"My — my child?"

"Mine too." She smiled. "Our child, before the end of many months. Oh yes — my hair is gray. But," — blushing a little — "I am not as old as all that."

Then he took her tenderly into his arms. "By the Prophet the Adored!" he cried triumphantly. "Let it be a man-child, a little son, to you and me! A strong little son! The strongest in all High Tartary — "

"Except," cut in Omar the Red, "for the son whom Ayesha shall bear to me."

"Liar!"

"Liar yourself!"

"Drunkard!"

"Unclean pimple!"

Almost, they came to blows.

AND the end of the tale?

The end of the tale is not yet.

But, up there in the ancient castle in High Tartary, live two white-haired men. White-haired, too, their wives. And the latter exchanging winks when, occasionally, their husbands comment naggingly, querulously, about the morals of Islam's younger generation, including their grandsons. . . . 🌐

THE PEARLS OF PARUKI

by J. Allan Dunn

FLEMING strolled contentedly along the main street of Levuka between the flamboyant trees that strewed the white road of coral grit with scarlet blossoms and the lace-edge of the lagoon surf. There are two towns in the Fijis: Levuka, on the island of Ovelau, the capital that was, and Suva, on the isle of Viti Levu — Great Fiji — the capital, that is. To these two comes all the commerce of the group, and Fleming, whose tiny lease-hold islet was nearer to Levuka, was well satisfied to have placed his vanilla crop at an average of three dollars a pound. They called it twelve shillings and six-pence in Levuka, for the government and coinage are British.

Fleming had worked like a dog with that vanilla plantation since he quit trading in copra, pearl, and turtle-shell and in trepang. The big Australian firms with their capital and steamers had, as Fleming phrased it, "knocked the tar out of the small trader." So Fleming had leased an island, sold his schooner, bought a sloop, and set out vanilla. Now he had a pound of dried beans for every cutting of Mexican vanilla that he had planted

three years before. He was twenty-seven thousand dollars to the good, and his plantation was established.

Better than that to Fleming, who was as fond of money and what money would bring as the next man, he had turned the laugh on the scoffers who had predicted failure. He had raised more than a third of the previous year's export of the bean, had put Fiji on the map as a factor in the vanilla market, and had discovered, with a quiet but thorough sense of pride, that John Fleming, successful vanilla planter, was a man of vastly more importance than John Fleming, South Sea trader.

Serene in white linen and white shoes, in white silk shirt, white hose, and white sombrero of bleached hala, he turned up a lane shady with coco-palm and breadfruit, making his way up-hill to the home of the Widow Starkey. When Phil Starkey, a little more drunk, a little more reckless than usual, had gone fishing with dynamite in the tiny bay of his tiny isle of Paruki and, just to show that the devil took care of his own, insisted on crimping the primer cap with his teeth, not many people had lamented his death. Not his native boys, whom he cursed and drove to the limit. They, with all Levuka and its neighborhood, were glad for Helen Starkey, even while they mourned in Fiji style with proper appreciation of the occasion if not of the departed. If the widow shared their feelings she gave no sign but had left the island for Levuka and decorously observed the conventions.

She had been a beauty, with her blond complexion and her slim figure, when she had come out from the States at the summons of handsome Phil Starkey. She was a beauty still, though older and quieter, living on a slender income, too proud, perhaps, to go back home after her matrimonial disaster. That was two years old; and it was time, some said and others thought, that she wiped out the bitterness of failure by a second and happier marriage. Fleming was one of those who thought much along such lines but said little, save as his actions may have spoken.

He was a suitor, though whether he was favored none might say. Whatever the widow thought about a second venture she kept to herself. It looked as if she had determined upon being especially careful, particularly sure of the man. Fleming, feeling that he had proven himself, set up by his reception as a successful planter, had nerved himself to find out where he stood in the lists, for he knew that he was not the only one to aspire to possess the widow's charms.

Nervousness, coupled with a desire to appear unwilted despite the tropical heat, made him walk leisurely. But his pulses quickened as he came in sight of the gaily-variegated crotons that hedged the widow's home. Her dwelling was rather cabin than house, a bungalow of four rooms winged with wide verandas, set in a garden that was a riot of perfume, color, and verdure. The leaves of the crotons and of the climbing vines aped the flowers in their hues; the odor of ihlang-ihlang, plumaria, tuberose, and stephanotis was almost overpowering. But Fleming thought the setting just right for the widow's slender person, sure to be dressed in cool white. He figured her in the shade of the veranda, dainty, feminine, serving him citronade, listening to the tale of his victory. Her place was a little Eden, he fancied. And then he saw the snake.

Harper was a good-looking snake. Fleming did not deny that. But he knew more about Harper than a great many people, a good deal more than Fleming ever mentioned. Harper was tall and dark; and his black hair was waving, close-trimmed to his well-shaped head. He was a good conversationalist and a clever flatterer. He had a blended suggestion of laziness and deviltry that a great many women found fascinating, and at heart he was a cold-blooded blackguard. Fleming knew the sort of things that went on aboard Harper's schooner between port and port, and he had a strong belief that Harper had one woman in Sydney who believed herself to be his wife, and another in Honolulu, not to mention more elastic alliances in Tahiti and elsewhere. To see Harper lounging on the widow's veranda, very much at home, inhaling his cigarette and sipping at citronade, destroyed all of Fleming's hardly acquired equanimity. He wanted to kick the man out of the garden and read the widow a lecture on how to avoid snakes.

"And Harper's the kind that doesn't pack rattles," thought Fleming as he grimly advanced up the steps, Harper lying at ease in the long rattan chair and smiling up at him mockingly.

The widow looked a bit uncertainly from one to the other.

"You men know each other, don't you?" she asked.

"Yes," said Fleming.

"Beyond a doubt," said Harper. "A

bit different from the last place we met, eh, Fleming?"

He managed to suggest an innuendo in the statement, and Fleming felt himself flush as the widow looked at him. The last time he had met Harper Fleming had yanked out of a waterside dump a young cub of a planter's son whom Harper had been trimming at poker with the help of some unsavory friends. And now, by some damnable trick of look and tone, Harper had put the shoe on Fleming's foot.

"Doing fine with your vanilla, they tell me, Fleming," drawled Harper condescendingly. "They can't say you don't know beans now, old man."

He grinned as he noticed Fleming's handshake when he took the glass the widow handed him. It was fun to bait Fleming, Harper thought, a bit dangerous but a lot of fun. He reacted beautifully.

Then the widow interfered. The evidently bad blood between her two guests she attributed partly to jealousy, and therefore it was not entirely unacceptable; but she liked Fleming and did not propose to have any of her callers made uncomfortable.

She liked Harper, too. He both attracted and repulsed her. She figured that any man who did attract her must have some good in him and vaguely wondered who was responsible for the bad, and whether the right sort of woman might not have kept it from materializing or could not now eliminate it. And Harper was decidedly good-looking. Fleming was well-featured enough, and physically he was not very far from perfect; but he was, to use the average feminine vocabulary, not so distinguished looking or so graceful or well-mannered as Billy Harper.

She's had one good-looking scamp, thought Fleming bitterly. "Don't she know enough now to sheer off when she sees another?"

Fifteen minutes Fleming endured

while Harper discussed pearls and the latest fashions he had seen at Suva when the tourists came off the steamer, describing them well enough to draw compliments from the interested widow. Fleming was entirely out of it, sipping a drink that seemed too sour, though it came out of the same jug as that of the others, and resolving to have a private conversation with Harper and tell him to keep clear of the Starkey bungalow — and then realizing that a man in love can not do many things without giving rise to suspicion, slander, and surveillance.

From time to time Harper glanced at him with deliberate malice; and every time the muscles in Fleming's body tautened and his jaws clamped down, all of which seemed to cause Harper exquisite amusement. At last the latter got up.

"I have got to go," he said in a voice that suggested he was literally tearing himself away. "Got to catch the ebb. I'm sailing this afternoon. I shall hope to see you again soon, Mrs. Starkey. Now I'll leave you and Fleming to talk of less frivolous matters."

"You have been a godsend," said the widow with a light laugh as she got up and went with her visitor as far as the gate, whence he departed with a spray of stephanotis in his buttonhole and the air of an accepted gallant.

THE WIDOW came back to the veranda, and Fleming stood to meet her with a slightly conscious air and a heightened color. The knowledge that Fleming was in love with her gave the lady a proprietary feeling and manner, which she used in anticipating any remarks that he might make.

"Captain Harper has been here on business," she said. "I feel that I have done quite a good stroke."

Fleming, who had been choking down many emotions for many minutes, made an ass of himself.

"Then you'd better tell me what it is," he growled, "for I'll bet it's just as crooked as a dog's hind leg."

"My end of it, or Captain Harper's?" she asked with an acid sweetness that should have warned Fleming.

"His."

"I thought men didn't knock each other," she went on.

Fleming got crimson under his tan.

"I'm warning, not knocking," he blurted.

"Have you any proofs that Captain Harper is crooked?" she asked.

Fleming pondered for a minute or two.

"None that I could offer," he said finally.

"Ah!"

She didn't say "I thought so," but the "Ah!" was more illuminating, scorching indeed. Fleming got up to go. It was getting altogether too hot for him. The scent from the garden choked him; the blossoms were too vivid. He itched all over with a pricking sensation.

"Have you got to catch the ebb too?" she asked.

"I have business to attend to," he said.

"Don't let me detain you."

She saw by his hurt face that she had gone farther than she intended. And she had not yet made her point.

"Captain Harper has taken the lease of the island off my hands," she said. "It is very satisfactory. It was only twenty-five pounds a year, but I am very thankful. That was the business he came about."

Here was Fleming's opportunity, an explanation, almost an apology, certainly an opening. But his eyes narrowed. What game was Harper up to now? The island that the late but not lamented Starkey had leased from the government for ten years, and for seven years un-expired rent of which the widow was responsible under the lease, was not good for anything. Starkey had tried to plant coffee and then started a tea plantation, but the soil and Starkey's methods were both poor. He had got out the pearl shell from the shallower spots of the lagoon and found even that of poor quality without a pint of baroques or seeds in the whole lot.

And now Harper was pledging himself to spend one hundred and seventy-five pounds — that is, eight hundred and seventy-five dollars — on a barren islet. Was it for the widow's favor? That, Fleming was positive, would only be bestowed in a manner too honorable for Harper to understand, desire, or — considering other alliances — be able to respond to.

What was he up to? There was a joker somewhere. Harper wasn't spending nearly a thousand dollars for philanthropy or for the mere pleasure of citronade and cigarettes on Helen Starkey's veranda.

"What's the idea?" asked the widow. "Don't you approve?"

"No, I don't," he answered, flatly and foolishly.

"Why not?"

He was dumb.

"You men are all alike," she flung at him. He guessed what she meant. He was jealous, and his jealousy had tinged his judgment., But he was no pincushion, and he considered he had been pricked sufficiently.

"If it's a check he's given you," he

said, "or even bank-notes, I'd advise you to change 'em."

"Thank you. And now you'll have to excuse me. Captain Harper came early, and I haven't even touched my housework. If you'll wait and make yourself comfortable?"

It was the last straw. The housework put aside for Harper, but Fleming could sit around like a house cat waiting to be noticed!

"Thanks," he said. "But I'm busy too; I just dropped in."

She smiled at him as she gave him her cool, slim hand, and he interpreted it as a laugh. He had been idiotic. The widow's house was too far out of the way for any visit not to be purposeful. He strode down the garden, unaccompanied, undecorated with stephanotis. The widow had disappeared inside before he reached the crotons. Fleming went on down the hill with clenched fists, clenched for Harper, aching for a chance to use them. He saw a trim, white whale-boat shoot out from the wharf, the four native boys stroking beautifully, Harper in the stern with the steering-oar, graceful as a gondolier, the boat speeding out to the *Manuwai* — Seabird — Harper's schooner, sweet-lined, seaworthy, and the fastest thing under canvas in the Fijis.

Fleming stood for a minute or two and mopped his forehead, noting the precision of the rowing, the snappy way in which the oars were tossed up at the schooner's side while Harper stepped on deck, the quick attachment to the falls and the up-sway of the tender. When he reached the beach the *Manuwai* had up-anchored and under jib, stay, and mainsail was sliding out on a reaching tack through the reef-channel, held up against wind and current by Harper at the wheel, using perfect judgment. Once more he watched with a swift envy a sweeping return of his love for the open sea and a slanting deck, regrets for his own sold schooner *Tamotu*. Outside the reef Harper's boys raced to sheets and halyards. Up went the foresail, the kite topsails slipped up without a hitch, setting precisely. Splintering the crisp blue seas beneath her forefoot, the *Manuwai* with started sheets seethed westward.

"He's all a sailor, him!" said Fleming, and he mopped his face again and went on to complete preparations for the shipment of his vanilla.

Bᴜᴛ the joy of success had died. Its grave lay up in the widow's garden. He hadn't even told her about his victory. Probably she wouldn't care to hear about it. And he wasn't going to take the chance of getting snubbed.

The widow had dismissed all the native help from the island enterprise when her husband died, paying them their back wages out of what little was salvaged from Phil Starkey's handling of affairs. One man had remained as a sort of caretaker without wages, staying on the island at his own request. This was a Fijian named Tumba, an ancient, with eyes reddened by much drinking of *yanggona* — kava — and memories that led back to times when the week was considered wasted that did not see human flesh served at one meal at least.

Coming out from a merchant's hot and smelly warehouse-office, Fleming saw Tumba, drunk, not with *yanggona*, which paralyzes the limbs, but with trade gin. His red-rimmed eyes were murderous, shifty. He was dressed only in a red *sulu* — kilt — and he swaggered down the sand, his old but still efficient muscles bunching as he swung his arms and moved his shoulders, chanting in Fijian:

"Eh, but I am hungry! I want to eat a man!"

He lacked only a club to look the cannibal. But he had no weapon, and nobody took any notice of him. If he left the beach and annoyed any one, he would be arrested by the member of the native constabulary who stood eying him tolerantly. But the sun and the gin would probably put him to sleep in the shade, and Tumba was allowed the uneven tenor of his way. Fleming recognized him and wondered where he had got the money to buy the gin. Harper must have dismissed him and given him a gift. But Harper had only just acquired the lease. Had he presupposed the widow's acquiescence in the deal?

It was like his infernal impudence, thought Fleming, to do a thing like that. And he had turned off Tumba because the man was too old. Fleming called to the drunkard, "Hi, there, you Tumba, you come along here!"

Tumba stood and stared. His rheumy eyes saw nothing but some vision of memory. Perhaps he really believed what he was chanting, his youth mockingly restored by the gin. Who was this white man who called? Tumba was his own master! He had money yet to spend after this drunk had worn off! *Tchah!*

"Eh, but I am hungry! I want to eat a man!"

Fleming let him go. There was nothing to be got out of him. Tumba might have left the little island of his own accord. There was nothing to keep him there. Fleming forgot him, worrying about some new machinery that seemed

missing but which turned up at last and was shipped on his sloop, crowding both cabin and cockpit.

I T WAS the third morning before he sailed out of the harbor and started for his own holding of Tamotu — named after his schooner appropriately, for *ta motu* can mean "the ship" or "the island." His sloop was called *Lelemotu*, which means "the little ship." It sailed well enough but had no great speed.

Good enough for a planter, thought Fleming, regretful always of his well-found schooner that had once sailed the western archipelagoes. All he wanted now was a vessel big enough to convey a couple of tons of beans and some provisions back and forth. He had only one man with him, a Tanna man from the New Hebrides, a black and ugly-looking savage, but faithful, courageous, indebted to Fleming for his life when the latter had picked him up off the Tanna beach in the face of the arrow-fire of a hill tribe bent upon making *boloko* — human meat — out of Ngiki.

Ngiki swam like a fish and sailed by instinct. He was as good a man aboard, save for navigation, as Fleming himself. Strong as an ox and cheerful, he was the prize of all the Tanna men who helped to plant and train and weed Fleming's vanilla. The fertilizing and the scalding and the sweating in the sun, Fleming attended to himself. It was a little too much, with the necessity of constant overseeing of the men.

He had hoped — Fleming sighed a little and frowned a little as he thought of his aspirations — that he could have got a partner to fertilize the flowers. A light-handed partner, with the deftness for the pinch and the touch with the toothpick that was all the work demanded in the early morning hours of coolness. The widow — but that was over, and Fleming steered the *Lelemotu* between spoke and spoke while Ngiki sprawled out forward in the full blaze of the sun like a lizard, sleek with coconut oil against blistering. He was breaking in a new pipe, his tobacco box of brass stuck into the lobe of his left ear, stretched into a loop by such usage, the right lobe decorated with a small round vanity-mirror of which Ngiki was inordinately proud, using it as much as any haughty beauty of the gentler sex.

East of Ovalau the Fijis break up into scores of islets circling about the Koro Sea. Some are volcanic, most of coral formation. Many are uninhabited, visited only by some wandering schooner, blown out of its course perhaps, looking for fresh water or drinking nuts. Fleming had picked his own leasehold of Tamotu because it had water and a mountain peak that formed its core and mothered two sheltered valleys where the heat was tempered, and that by its trends thwarted the havoc of the occasional hurricanes.

The sloop took it easily, the wind holding steady, sailing on between blue and blue, the cobalt of the sky and the ultramarine of the sea with its indigo shadows. The distant islands and the mainlands showed as humps and juts of deeper blue than the horizon, with here and there a faint gleam of green, opalwise. There was neither fleck of foam nor cloud. The *Lelemotu* slapped along nicely, the water *chuck-chuckling* to the shouldering thrust of her bows and hissing away astern with the delightful suggestion of coolness in the sound of aerated water. Ngiki finished his pipe, knocked out the ashes, cursing softly at the bite of the applewood, and went to sleep like a black cat. Fleming drowsed. He knew every fathom of the way by instinct, every shoaling of the bottom where coral atolls were slowly growing up to the surface, showing as patches of discoloration more or less distinct, according to wind and tide and submersion. The sloop almost knew its own way

home. Fleming, knowing the feel of breeze and current and what the sloop could do, could have guessed his position within a quarter of a mile. He was on a long tack. With luck he would fetch Tamotu without shifting, somewhere about midnight.

NGIKI's flattened nostrils twitched in his sleep as a dog's will twitch. The Tanna-man had the full sense of smell that in most of us has atrophied so that it no more answers the purpose for which it is intended than do the eyes of an astigmatic person. When Ngiki's eyes were closed his ears and nose played sentinel, together with his sense of touch. What disturbed him now was only a hint, the suggestion of something unpleasant, not strong enough to set up the correlation between sensatory nerve and memory cell. It wasn't strong enough to mean anything to him yet. Fleming knew nothing of it at all, though he was still awake.

The sloop was sailing close-hauled on the starboard tack, and the odor was wafted over the port bow. They were heading up to it and at the same time falling off in leeway. But it got stronger. Ngiki sat up and snuffed disgustedly, angry at being awakened. Then the white man got it. Both of them knew instantly what it was.

There are several smells in the South Seas that, once inhaled, are never for-

gotten. The smell of a dead whale to windward, the reek of sugar in the hold, that will permeate even the shell of a hard-boiled egg, the stink of guano and — and this would make a glue factory fragrant by comparison — the stench of rotting-out pearl-shell. It will travel down the wind for miles and salute a vessel leagues away, far out of sight of the offending beach. It gets into the hair, the clothes, tobacco, food, water, everything but an unopened coconut — and that must be swallowed instanter or be tainted. It is thick and it is sticky.

"Wah!"

Ngiki spat over side. Then he looked expectantly along the deck to the cockpit, hoping that Fleming would tack, even if they did get home later. They might crisscross that stinking lane instead of sailing almost straight up it, as they were doing.

"Faugh!"

Fleming's face exhibited disgust fighting with curiosity. He stood up and gazed around him to the blue humps and specks of far and distant land, each of which he knew by name, and approximated their distance.

"No good that smell, *saka* [sir]," said Ngiki. "Too much big fellow stink. Better we make turn back?"

Fleming shook his head.

"You take wheel, Ngiki," he said and dived into the cabin when the Tanna man came aft.

He came out with a chart that he had compiled himself in his trading days and added to from time to time. He cocked his eyes at the angle of the sun, made a brief calculation and chucked the chart down on to the transom cushions.

"All right, Ngiki," he said. "We come about."

The one jib was self-working, on a club-boom. Ngiki took in the mainsheet smartly and hitched it once about the cleat, looking to his master to see if the sail was too taut or too slack. Fleming nodded and Ngiki completed his hitch. For a moment Ngiki was happy. Then he sensed the reason for the tack. They were to head well to windward to offset leeway when they came back once again to close-hauled sailing. For the time they would be only on the edge of the smell, but they would work back into it, nosing along it as a hound on a trail. When Fleming once more gave him the wheel and again went below Ngiki grumbled aloud and to himself.

"What name (why) Falemingi go along that big-fellow smell? My word; it make my belly too much walk about. Spoil smoke."

He eyed Fleming curiously when the latter emerged on deck with a Colt automatic, carefully cleaned and oiled it, filled the clip after one cartridge had been injected into the breech, filled up two extra clips, and tucked them away in his hip pocket.

Ngiki's eyes held anticipation and lust of battle. Through the reek of the rotting shell his mind smelled blood. It was a long time since Falemingi had been in action, a long time since Ngiki, in the too peaceful plantation life, had smelled powder. He did not know whether he would be in on the fighting or not, but the sight of the automatic, a murderous, heavy .44, was as the sight of a shotgun in the Fall to a setter.

Fleming put the pistol away in a holster attached to his belt and sat through the tack with his eyes half-closed, thinking. Some one was rotting pearl on Paruki. Paruki now belonged, under its lease, to Harper. But the lease was exchanged only three days ago, and this shell had taken time to be brought up by the divers and laid on the drying-beaches. Starkey had tried the lagoon with poor results, but Fleming remembered that Starkey, characteristically, had worked only the shallows.

The deeper stretches might have

panned out rich in shell and actual gems. People didn't rot out without some prospects of success. Harper wouldn't. And this must be Harper. If so, he had practically stolen the shell before he saw the widow. If she had refused to let the lease go Harper would have been in the position of a thief. Not that that would have worried Harper overmuch. It was not the first time he had been suspected or accused of crookedness. He would wriggle out of it some way with the pearls if he was given half a chance.

Tumba? Tumba's presence on Ovalau was better explained now. The diving and spreading had started the moment Harper left the island with Tumba aboard. Tumba could not be trusted. He might spill the news at any time. So he was removed before operations began. Fleming did not think there were any natives on Paruki, outside of Harper's crew, who were Malaita boys and not divers. Harper used modern methods for getting his shell, a diving-suit with an oxygen tank, a quick clean-up and away.

That was his style, whether he held a lease and was on the windy side of the law or was pirating a lagoon. It took white men to use a suit. The natives didn't like it. There were probably four or five white men on Paruki, aside from the Solomon Islanders from Malaita.

It was big odds and necessitated careful plans, but Fleming did not hesitate. He was not going to see the widow robbed, and he intended to show up Harper. The memory of that quarter of an hour on the widow's veranda still rankled. He leaned against the weather stays, his big, athletic body pliant to the pitch and toss of the ship. The breeze was freshening a bit, and the sloop was making good time reaching. Fleming's eyes were half closed but Ngiki caught the gray gleam that shone from them, noted the vertical lines between the brows, the bossing jaw muscles, and nodded and winked to himself.

"By and by big fellow trouble he walk along," he murmured happily.

" 'Tend sheets, Ngiki; we're going about!" said Fleming suddenly.

Ngiki jumped and Fleming spun the wheel. Up came the sloop, catching the wind in flattened main and staysail-jib, tossed her bows, and dug into the seas, plowing on to Paruki, into the heart of the stench. Fleming got his binoculars and kept them focused for the first sight of the island peak.

Paruki boasted one cone, sloping abruptly down on one side, its ridges largely barren, denuded of soil and vegetation. Much of the islet was marsh; and the lagoon bit deeply into it, fringed by mangroves. On the northern side there were steep cliffs, part of the lone mount. The water came up close to them and landing was difficult. The cliffs mounted in sheer *palis* — precipices — to the serrated summit of the cone, and then the land pitched down toward the lagoon and the leeward beaches, broad stretches of sand where the shell was rotting. Fleming knew that even if there were men on the lookout by purpose or accident, he could sight the loom of the peak before they caught a glimpse of his sail, unless there was some one on the cone, which was most improbable — and had to be chanced. He intended to effect a landing and make at least a reconnaissance before sunset. Much of the pith of his plan depended upon circumstances.

But something had to be done before the shells were stripped and a cleanup of the pearls effected. And done without warning. Pearls were easy things to hide, hard to identify. A little while and no one could prove the rotting had not taken place within the term of the transferred lease. The fact that Harper had troubled to get the lease at all and to pay for it was to Fleming proof positive that the haul was likely to be so rich that Harper, discovering how the shell was running, resolved to cover himself in case of future trouble. If the news ever leaked out that he had pirated a widow's lease the Government would be after him hot foot. But he knew what he was handling before he put up his eight hundred and seventy-five dollars.

THE PEAK of Paruki swam into view on the lenses of the binoculars like a stain on a microscopic slide. It assumed form, the shape of a double-tooth turned roots up for exhibition purposes. It was right in the wind's eye, and from it poured the cloggy smell. To get to windward of it unseen, Fleming had to slant off on a long leg and fetch up to position on another. The latter would probably have to be broken into several tacks. But there was plenty of time, and the wind blew steady and true. So the sloop leaned from the breeze instead of on it and went scooting off, long before any one on the leeside Paruki could have caught sight of the tiniest fleck of canvas.

It was two hours to sunset when Fleming slipped overboard into the trailing tender and gave Ngiki his last instructions. On a lee shore, with the waves beating on the lava buttresses, Fleming dared not anchor. He took risk enough with his dingy, for the water went licking and spouting up the cliffs and roaring among the boulders and caves in a fashion far from inviting. But he could trust Ngiki to handle the sloop, to sail off and on until he came back

again. And, if anything went wrong, to wing it back to Levuka and present the letter Fleming had written and left in the cabin to the merchant to whom Fleming had sold his vanilla. But not to leave until noon the next day and to keep his eyes and ears wide open for Fleming's coming.

"I may be in a big fellow hurry when I show up," said Fleming, and Ngiki grinned appreciatively.

At the last moment a treacherous undertow combined with a following wave and slammed the dingy down so hard upon a slab of lava that it smashed its bottom strakes and broke its keel. Fleming leaped as it struck and fought through the yeast of sucking water, clinging to a buttress of the cliff until the sea reluctantly subsided and left him free for another rush, a leap across a split and a swift wading, waist-deep, to the gully he had picked out from the sloop as the best chance of ascent.

To a man whose head never dizzied and whose rubber-soled feet never slipped the climb was a little better than possible. Fleming was all in when he got to the top and flung himself panting but safe upon a ledge just below a gap between two of the fanged roots of the peak. The sun was getting low back of him, and the shadow of the cone spread out over Paruki like a violet veil. In the horseshoe lagoon swam Harper's schooner, the *Manuwai,* at anchor. Her canvas was furled, and he could see black figures making her shipshape, shining brasses, and whitening decks. Three or four more natives were spreading out a pile of shell, handling it with five-tined forks, standing to windward for what small protection that would give them from the reek.

Fleming stood up, getting his wind. He saw a weird figure emerge from the lagoon, goggle-eyed, humpbacked beneath the oxygen tank — one of Harper's divers. Harper himself, he fancied, though all the figures were miniature, strolled down to meet the man. Behind the lagoon was the marsh through which a stream ran sluggishly. Back of the marsh the bush, and in the bush a clearing with a tiny bungalow: a wooden-walled, corrugated-iron-roofed house of two rooms with a lean-to at the back of the kitchen. Smoke came out of the roof of the lean-to. Fleming heaved a sigh of relief. The smoke meant that Harper and his companions ate ashore, probably slept there, playing cards during the evenings, smoking and drinking.

He started down, keeping to cover as best he could until he reached the bush, where concealment was easy. He had about fifteen minutes of actual daylight left when he came out of the bush to what had once been a garden of yams, *taro*, cane and corn. With the sinking of the sun darkness would be almost instantaneous, lasting until the stars got their power. There was no moon.

Creeping through the rank growths, Fleming heard a laugh from the house, followed by another and another. There was the clink of glasses, the scent of tobacco stealing out to him as he advanced close to lean-to, the smell of frying meat, and the rattle of pots and pans.

He crouched in the angle between lean-to and house, listening. The outer door opened, and he heard the tread of men on the veranda and their voices

greeting those already in the room. There was a window whose sill he could have peered over by straightening, but he was not yet ready. The newcomers were the diver and Harper.

"Termorrer I lays off," said the diver. "I put in too much time today and the ledge is gittin' deeper. All the best-lookin' shell's comin' up from eighteen fathom. I ain't goin' to git the bends stickin' down too long. Termorrer I lays off, pearls or no pearls. We got all the time in the world, now you've fixed up the lease."

"We can finish up washing shell," suggested Harper. "The place stunk to heaven when I was coming up in the schooner. It's lucky the island's out of the way or some nosy fool would have been rubbering before we got the lease. It came easy though. She fell for the parlor stuff. But it's just as well to clean up."

Fleming appreciated the backhand slap at himself with a grin but Harper's depreciation of the widow sent his hand to the butt of his automatic.

"Pretty soft for you," said a fresh voice. "You playin' the beau to a pritty woman an' then kickin' about the stink of the stuff comin' up — your hide, we live in it. I vote for the clean up. And next time I go pearlin' I pick 'em out while they're alive. The shell can go to blazes when we got a line of pearls like we been findin'. Pickin' through the meat today, I even forgot the stink the way they stacked up. One out of every sixth shell, so help me Jimmy. No seeds. They're old stock — few baroques. Tim got one beauty. I'll bet this lagoon is virgin. Want to see what we got?"

"Let's eat first," suggested Harper.

"An' for God's sake pass the bottle," chimed in the diver. "Stayin' down's dry work. Hurry up the chuck, Fredi," he called out to the man in the lean-to.

It grew darker. The cook in the shed took in the meal, and the men scuffed their chairs about the table, and all fell to with an appetite that Fleming shared but could not relish. The cook was on equal terms with the rest, and that helped. He wanted to have them altogether. Not a Malaitan likely to tackle him in the rear. The native boys were evidently down on the beach or aboard. A lamp was lit. The bottom of the window-sash was up and covered with mosquito-netting. The great leaves of a banana, A-shaped in its length, pendent from the central rib, pressed against and across the netting, admirable screens for Fleming if . . . .

He felt his way through the growth noiselessly, carefully, one hand on the boards of the lean-to, which had a window on the other side, through which he peered. Then he kicked his shin against what he was looking for and picked it up, a wooden packing-box of fairly stout construction. He set this against the wall of the house under the window and stood upon it with his head tucked into the inverted V of the nearest banana banner, waving gently, like its fellows, in the land wind. Its long edges were split here and there and through these tatters, perfectly masked, Fleming looked into the room.

There were four men there besides Harper, and Fleming knew all but one of them. One was Harper's regular mate; another his supercargo. The fourth was a Suva scalawag and the fifth matched him. They were a hard-bitten, reckless lot, hawk-nosed, save for the supercargo, who had had his flattened in a forgotten fight. Harper alone showed any neatness, any attempt at ordinary cleanliness. Two wore beards of ancient growth; two more had not shaved for days. And their faces were inflamed with gross appetites long indulged, as they ate, save for Harper, like a litter of pigs at a trough.

They drank and they boasted and they told rotten stories, and Fleming kept *doggo,* waiting his time.

At last the dishes were shoved to one side and Harper and his mate got up. Harper took down a metal box from a shelf and unlocked it. The mate took a bag of chamois leather from inside his shirt. Harper set the box on the table unopened but the mate poured from the chamois bag on to the wood a pattering rain of pearls, highlighted in iridescent beauty by the lamp, sheeny soft in the shadow.

Fleming puckered his lips in a silent whistle. Surely such pearls had come from a virgin patch. He knew pearls, and there were one or two of the larger of these gems, being handled by grimy, callused fingers, that were worth a cool thousand apiece, traders' prices. Pearls before swine, he thought, as the gleaming globules passed from hand to hand, roughly appraised.

"A good lot," said Harper. "With what there is here in the box, boys, we've got fifty thousand dollars in plain sight. There ought to be twenty thousand more in what's left of the shell on the beach, to say nothing of what we'll bring up. Then there's the shell. Call it a hundred thousand dollars and you're below the mark rather than above it."

"Twenty thou' apiece," said the mate. "And each of us four to give Harper ten per cent of our even shares for swingin' the thing, harpoonin' the widder inter shiftin' the lease, an' the use of the schooner. Not so bad!"

Fleming hunched his shoulders, his body tensing for action. But the stage was not quite set to his liking.

"Fair enough," said another, the scalawag from Suva, known to Fleming as "Bush" Dickson. "Fa-a-ir enough. How about that — Kanaka, Banjo, or Tambo, or whatever his name was? S'pose he squeals that we pulled this thing 'fore we had the right. They're kind of techy down Suva way 'bout the protection of their leases."

"You haven't got rid of the Suva jail

itch yet, Bush," said Harper, and the rest laughed at the pointed jest while Dickson grinned stupidly. "Don't you worry about Tumba. I've fixed it so that Tumba draws a little money each week — only for a week or two, but he don't know that — from Mike Lamed, who runs the Ambergris Hotel and don't mind selling booze to Kanakas. I told Tumba it was a sort of pension from the widow. The point is that he has to go to Larned's to get the cash — it's seven dollars a week and Mike is to give him a dollar a day. Mike is going to see that Tumba keeps drunk into the bargain. That's an easy job so long as he shows Tumba the bottle. After two weeks, if Tumba says anything, they'll think he dreamed it. They won't believe him on dates; a Kanaka's word don't go far anyhow. So don't worry about Tumba."

"Some fox, our skipper, I'll say," said Dickson. "Let's see the rest of them pearls."

Harper assented without demur. It seemed to be a party agreement that the pearls were to be kept in plain sight and inspected upon request of any member of the gang, like the books of a stock corporation. The supercargo scooped up the loose pearls and put them into a small wooden calabash. Harper took another chamois bag from the box, and a small canvas sack.

"Baroques here," he said, tapping the canvas poke.

Then he added the contents of the chamois bag to the pearls in the bowl. The glistening heap pyramided above the rim. Fleming inched his head along the inverted trough of the banana leaf, drawing his gun from the holster. There was just one other thing. . . .

"That the agreement with the widder?" asked the diver, reaching for a paper. "I ain't seen that afore. How's it go?"

Harper took the document and unfolded it under the lamp. He parted his lips for speech but none ever left them.

"Hands up, the bunch of you! Ten hands! Fifty fingers! Up! And high! Up!"

Fleming was lolling in the window, his automatic shifting steadily in an arc that covered all the five.

"Get back into that corner!" he said. "Line up! That's the idea. Good evening, Harper. And keep on trying to touch the roof or you'll be scratching dirt. I mean business, you pack of thieving hounds."

Fleming was ready to shoot if need be, and they knew it. Nothing less would have kept them passive as Fleming set a knee across the sill and eased himself into the room, his gun-barrel never wavering. Their eyes glared like those of suddenly thwarted devils as he slid into his pocket the lease transfer and emptied the calabash of its pearls with one hand into his bandanna handkerchief, which he then placed in his pocket. The gums and teeth of the quintet were drawn back in wolf-snarls as Fleming backed up to the window and eased out on to his box. He had ripped away the rotten netting without a sound before he made his appearance. Once more he lolled across the sill.

"Good night, Harper," he said.

"I'll cut your heart out," said Harper, his words bitter with venom, "if I have to trail you from here to Madagascar.

"Try Levuka first, Harper," said Fleming, smiling. "More likely to find me there — or on Tamotu."

He jumped lightly from his stand, turned, and raced through the dark, deserted garden. Behind him, the room broke into an uproar. From the window came a volley of pistol shots, the bullets tearing through the leaves and stalks as Fleming, head down, broke for the bush. He could hear the five swearing among themselves.

"He's making for the mountain, God damn him!"

"Goin' to circle round to the beach!"

"Where's his Goddamned boat?"

The blundering crash of pursuit sounded in Fleming's rear. Then some one — Harper by the voice — yelled for the Malaitan boys. And then there was silence, save for the noise of Fleming's own going.

But he knew that Harper had done the right thing, had set the Malaitan boys, swift and sure as bloodhounds, on his trail. He came to the edge of the bush, where it broke up into clumps before it faded away on the hard lava of the mountain ridges. Between two of these clumps he darted and instantly a red flare stabbed the dark and a bullet went singing high and to the left.

"That is a Malaitan," Fleming decided. "They're bum shots; that's one blessing. Rifle, at that!"

His guess was proven as the man who had fired at him let out a loud *"Ey-ah-a-ah!"* giving tongue like a dog. And like a fox Fleming went up the cone in the dark, helped by the starlight, but keeping in the shadows wherever cleft or gully offered.

The gap showed above him, a cluster of stars caught in its deep cup. Then the stars were blotted out by the swift, silent passage of a shadowy, silhouetted figure — a native, naked save for a *sulu* cloth, bearing a rifle. The Malaitans, guessing his exit or knowing it the only one, had outstripped him on the trail and cut him off, barring him until the white men caught up.

Fleming's breath was short, his heart pounding and his lungs panting from the burst he had maintained all the way up the steep slopes. The figure had passed, merging into some rock crevice before Fleming could aim and fire.

Back of him sounded a tinkle, the fall of a scrap of weathered obsidian dislodged by a naked foot to a ledge of lava. Fleming was sandwiched. He turned to the sidewall of the cleft, feeling for a niche, hooking his fingers into it and muscling himself up until his rubbered toes caught a hold. He remembered having seen the suggestion of a ledge on this side of the pass when he had come through, and now he was forced to take the desperate chance, also to risk a fall of rock like that which had betrayed the man back of him, who even now was stealing along hoping to catch glimpses or sound or smell of Fleming.

Fleming found his ledge and crabbed along it till the sea-wind blew on his face, turned to the rock. He knew he had reached the mouth of the gap. With infinite care he faced about, fingered for and found a clutch and gazed down. Fifteen feet below him, in the saddle of the pass, his black body merged with the cliff, his head thrust forward, peering, listening, sniffing for the first sign of the fugitive white man, was a Malaitan, still as if hewn out of the solid rock. The glint of starlight on his rifle barrel first betrayed him. Inch by inch Fleming stooped and then literally swooped down upon the man, lighting on him in the perilous footing of the pass, landing between the man's shoulders and smiting with the heavy automatic. The end of the muzzle jarred against the savage's tough, thick skull behind the ear and he passed out of any control of sense or muscle.

Below, Fleming saw the sloop coming up on an inshore tack. Apparently Ngiki had heard the sound of firing. The vessel was little more than a shadow, save for the streaks of sea-fire that made up her wake. Down the steep declivity Fleming slid and leaped, expecting every moment to find himself targeted. But he was close to the bottom before a gun was fired, and that at random, for he could not be well seen from above. But presently he would be a shining mark as he swam off to the sloop. To say nothing of the sharks. A bullet thudded and flattened on the rock ledge at his feet as he ran out from the cliff face, shouting to Ngiki, thankful that the tide was at flood because of the depth it would give him for the dive, and took a header into the heart of a high comber streaked with phosphor.

Bullets spattered about him as his head came clear and he struck out hand-overhand for the sloop. Ngiki called to him:

"Look out for s'ark! Rope at stern."

He saw the line trailing and made for it as the sloop lunged past. The flashes were coming from the cliff fast as he rolled when he caught the rope and began to haul himself in. Ngiki had to watch the wheel in those waters. But the aim from above was poor. Seemingly the white men had not come up or had gone back. He felt pretty certain that the shots that had come so close were white marksmanship.

Suddenly Fleming saw Ngiki appear above the taffrail, the wheel abandoned, reaching for the line and hauling.

"S'ark, *saka*, s'ark!" he gasped. "Hurry!"

Fleming hoisted himself from the water, thankful for the flat counter that gave him a temporary foothold, as Ngiki leaned far over and caught him in the hollow of one knee. Fleming managed to surmount the rail and the two men went rolling together to the wheel, where Fleming jumped to his feet and controlled the spokes just as a *williwaw* flurried down through the gap in the cone and almost set the sloop aback.

"Look!" said Ngiki.

A bullet skitted through the mainsail and dug itself into the deck close to Fleming, but he stared where Ngiki pointed while the sloop came up into the wind again. The high dorsal of a shark, trailing bluish-green streamers as it went, passed on its patrol. Fleming shivered a little as he headed out, Ngiki paying out the sheet. To have escaped the rifles on the cliffs only to have dived into the maw of a shark was not a pleasant thing to think of.

But they were not out of it yet. A mile from land Ngiki touched Fleming's elbow and pointed aft. Under the stars stole a shadowy shape that showed two tiny eyes, one green, one crimson. It was Harper's schooner, that could sail three knots where the sloop sailed two, coming up fast. She was plain in the night-glasses, apart from her side-lights, surely lit out of mockery, for there was little need of navigation regulations in these lonely waters of the Koro Sea. With the wind aft, Harper's schooner could make twelve knots easily; Fleming was doing well if he logged eight. The schooner would be alongside in fifteen minutes. Long before that they would commence firing with their rifles and Fleming had nothing aboard of heavier caliber and longer range than his automatic. Ngiki had no weapon save knife or belaying pin. The odds would be four or five to one.

It was impossible to shake them off. On board the schooner they could see

the sloop through their glasses under the tropical starlight far too clearly for Fleming to make any attempt at a split tack. The wind was brisk, inclined to blow hard, and the seas were snappy and crisp with foam. Fleming dragged a balloon jib out of the forepeak and set it, sparring it out to port with a boat hook. He swayed out the main boom to starboard and prevented it with a line forward. The *Lelemotu* squatted like a duck and scudded her fastest. Somehow the schooner did not seem to gain as she ought. Fleming fancied she was foul. But the chase couldn't last long. Little by little, the red and the green lights sneaked up and spits of fire showed at the schooner's bows where they were wasting lead.

Fleming gave the wheel to Ngiki and lit the cabin lamp, digging among his charts. He found what he wanted and then turned the pages of an astronomical almanac. Coming on deck, he found that the schooner was overhauling them slowly but surely. He had brought up a lantern which he bent on to his flag halyards with marlin and hoisted, running it on the halyards to the starboard spreader and down again as if in defiance. The next time they fired from the schooner Fleming shot off his automatic three times, trusting it might be seen, though it could not be heard up-wind. Ngiki stared at him curiously but said nothing. He had learned long ago not to interfere with his white chief in emergencies. If Falemingi wanted to show exactly where they were, that was his business. Besides, he might be signaling. But he ventured a remark when Fleming came aft, leaving the lantern half-mast high:

"They got one-two reef along that schooner."

The schooner was close enough now for Fleming to see, with the night-glasses that Ngiki's savage eyes did not need, that the gaffs of both fore and main were low. Evidently the natives, when they furled, had not taken out the reef last used; and so far Harper did not bother to shake it. He very well knew the wide expanse that Fleming would have to cross before he made a landfall. With something of the cat-and-mouse attitude he deferred his certain victory and regain of the pearls. As for Ngiki and himself, Fleming never doubted what would be their probable ending if they were overhauled. Killed — at long or short distance — and sunk with the sloop! The five white men on the schooner would have committed a dozen murders apiece for the twenty thousand dollars that was their anticipated share, half of which was now in Fleming's possession.

"If he doesn't shake out those reefs in half an hour," said Fleming more to himself than Ngiki, "we've got him. Sea's rising nicely. I'm going to fix up some dynamite with short throwing fuses, Ngiki. They can't sink us by rifle-fire and if we can keep alive until they board us well scratch 'em a bit."

Ngiki nodded. He didn't think much of their chances. He knew nothing of Fleming's mission, only that their pursuers were in deadly earnest. But he puffed away at his pipe complacently, conserving for the final rally.

Twenty minutes went by with waves mounting and the wind beginning to howl through the rigging. The main boom of the sloop began to skim the crests and Fleming took it up with the topping lift, shifting his peak and throat halyards. A mishap would be fatal. The schooner was less than half a mile away and every now and then a missile would go **whup** through the canvas. Under starlight, in such a sea, at such a distance, close work was not possible. Only a lucky — or unlucky — chance could score a hit. The sound of the shots came down the wind.

Fleming studied his stars as he hum-

ored the sloop, head-heavy of canvas, inclined to swerve like a shying horse as she swept down the valley of the seas or struggled up the opposing slopes. Every yard might count, and he got the best out of her.

"They shake out reef," announced Ngiki.

Harper, tired of fooling, had issued the order at last before it was too late to risk it, for all signs and the barometer clearly indicated now that there was going to be a gale. But Fleming only chuckled.

"I think, Ngiki, I'll bet five to one on it, that they're going to be too late. Take the wheel. I'm going for'ard."

Ngiki, uncomprehending, watched him go into the bows with the night-glasses. Imperturbable, the native did not flinch when the bullets began to buzz like bees above his head or land with a **chuck** in the taffrail and the head of the companionway. Once he turned his head as a shout came from the schooner, a taunting order to come into the wind. A sniping bullet hit the bowl of his pipe and tore it from his teeth. Ngiki snarled and rubbed his aching jaw with one hand. Then Fleming came aft again, a grin on his face.

"Five minutes more, Ngiki, and we shall see what we shall see. They're coming up fast, but —" He staggered back. A bullet had clipped him in the left forearm. He slapped his hand over the

wound and the blood came through the sleeve of his coat.

"No bones broken, I fancy," he muttered between set teeth. "Well, it's going to be cheap at that, if —"

The schooner was little more than two hundred yards away and coming on like a cup-winner. Her sails, out wing-and-wing, caught the faint star-shine on the rounded curves of the canvas. She seemed to soar as she lifted over the top of a wave, to come seething down its slope in a smother of spray that was thick with phosphorescence. Shot after shot came from her bows. Fleming shook his sound fist at her.

"I'll pack a rifle aboard after this," he said. "Planter or not, I'll take no chances. Wait till you get a little closer. Wait!"

But the automatic was no good for anything over fifty yards. Each wave saw the distance a little diminished. The schooner appeared bent upon running down the sloop, so true did she keep in its course, now actually entering the tail of its wake.

The color of the water alongside changed. It had been deepest blue, almost black, streaked with sea-fire. Now it became suddenly greener and every pint of it was aflame with phosphor. Also there was twice as much foam. The seas were yeasty with it and they seemed to run more tempestuously.

A megaphoned roar came from the schooner. "Heave to, Fleming, or I'll sink you!"

Fleming jumped for his own megaphone and yelled back against the wind.

"Come on and try it! Come on!"

The sloop suddenly swung off its course, threatening to jibe as Fleming's warning shout and hasty hand to the spokes showed Ngiki the danger of losing the mast. Ngiki was staring aft.

"Look, *saka*, look. By Goddamighty, she go ashore!"

Right in their course the schooner

reared as if mounting on a giant sea. But her bowsprit remained pointing skyward; her sails shivered, and then the foremast snapped and the canvas wrinkled and bellied in a confusion of stays and halyards. She tilted slowly to one side and began to slew round with the waves breaking over her.

"She's fairly on," said Fleming. "Harper hasn't charted these seas as I have. She draws sixteen foot to our ten and she's on fair and fast. He'll be there this time tomorrow unless he tries for land in his whaleboats. We'll stick around a bit and see. Better get a watch-tackle on that mainsheet against the time we tack, Ngiki; I've only got one arm."

It was hard work to get in the balloon jib but Ngiki accomplished it and flattened the mainsail. The sloop shot off on a reaching tack and back again, saved by reason of her lesser draft and Fleming's soundings of the island-to-be, whose coral builders were still well below the surface. Fleming had led the schooner deliberately into the trap and stranded her.

As they came close they saw her hard on the reef, the wreck of her foremast dragging overside and pounding at her hull, spume flying over her. And, rowing hard against head-seas and headwind on a painful progress, two whale-boats made slow laborious work of it/bearing Harper and his discomfited comrades.

"IT is a good thing," Fleming said later to Helen Starkey, "that I've made a success of the vanilla proposition. Otherwise, now that these pearls have turned up, they might be saying that I wanted to marry you for your money."

The widow gasped a little.

"You're not very complimentary," she said.

"I never am, somehow, when I mean to be," said Fleming.

"You haven't said you did, you know," she said.

"Did what?"

"Wanted to marry me. Why?"

Fleming turned fiery red and fussed with the bandage of his wounded arm, but he got it out at last.

"Because I love you."

"If you had said that a long time ago." she said, "it would have saved a lot of time and trouble."

"But," she added the next time she spoke, which was after a considerable period during which Fleming silently lamented the luck that had deprived him of the use of one arm at a time when he most needed two, "if you had, I wouldn't have got my pearls."

Fleming had lost the connection and looked at her lovingly but blankly.

"If I had what?" he asked.

"Nothing," she answered smilingly.

"Instead of which," declared Fleming, using his one arm to the best advantage, "I have everything."

THE MID-WATCH TRAGEDY

by VINCENT STARRETT

Jimmie Lavender was on his vacation when he stepped aboard one of the big Atlantic liners, but even the vacations of famous detectives may turn up murder, robbery, and sudden death.

THE military-looking gentleman produced a thin, expensive watch from his waistcoat pocket, and put it away again.

"The bar," said he sagely, "will be open in half an hour."

I acquiesced with a smile. He flicked the end of his cigarette overboard, and idly watched its descent until a wave took it. Then, as if the action had removed a weight from his mind, he turned briskly and continued. "Do you play bridge, Mr. Gilruth?"

"No," I said thankfully, "I don't."

Where the devil, I wondered, had he got my name? We had been hardly an hour at sea. He was excessively friendly — much as, I understood, were the professional gamblers against whom the company had thoughtfully warned its passengers.

"My wife will be disappointed," said he. "You and your friend are about the only eligibles she and her sister have

discovered, to date. I can play — but I won't."

I resented his easy assumptions. My acquaintance with Jimmie Lavender had not been without its practical value, and I had learned to distrust plausible strangers.

"That, I believe, is my friend's situation, also," I replied stiffly. "However, he must answer for himself."

"Of course," said he with a courteous nod. "My respects to him, please. His reputation is well-known to me. My name is Rittenhouse," he added, handing me his card. "And now I must run along and see what has become of my women."

He turned away, and I watched him for a moment as he threaded the crowded deck before I, too, turned and went in search of Lavender. It was Lavender's vacation, I mused, and I was in a sense his nurse — at any rate, his companion — and I did not intend that he should be bothered, if I could prevent. Not that Lavender was ill, but certainly he was tired; and even if the plausible Mr. Rittenhouse were not a professional gambler, bridge was no game for a man who needed rest.

I circled the promenade deck in my search, and at length climbed to the boat deck, just in time to see Lavender appear at the top of the aft companionway, closely followed by a deck steward dragging a couple of chairs. The detective indicated a spot amidships, somewhat sheltered, and balanced on either side by a giant air funnel.

"Dump 'em down here," he ordered. "Hullo, Gilly! This looks like as good a place as any. A quiet spot on the aft boat deck is always to be preferred to the chatter and publicity of the promenade. I'm sick of crowds!"

"See anybody you know?" I asked casually.

"Nary a soul," said he, "and don't want to. I've seen the purser, however, and the dining-room steward. We're to sit at the purser's table — all men. It's rough on you, Gilly, but I haven't enough small talk to be good company for the women."

"There are two of them looking for you," I said grimly, and told him of my meeting with Rittenhouse, at whose card until that moment I had not troubled to look. It revealed that the military-looking man's name was Joseph, and that he was a Major, retired, in the United States Marine Corps.

Lavender snatched the card, as if to verify my assertions, then chuckled delightedly.

"By George!" he cried. "It's Rit!"

"You know him, then?" I asked, somewhat taken aback.

"Know him! Why we've hunted *men* together! He served two terms as police commissioner of Los Angeles, where I met him. A better man never held office.

And you thought he was a crook!" He chuckled again with great happiness. "Where is he?"

"Looking for his wife and her sister, I believe."

"I must hunt him up. I hope you weren't rude, Gilly! Anybody else of interest on board?"

"I've looked over the passenger list," I replied airily. "There's a British lord — Denbigh, I think; a Sir John Rutherford; Betty Cosgrave, the screen actress; an Italian baroness whose name I forget, and the Rev. Henry Murchison of Cedar Rapids, Iowa."

"Good!" laughed Lavender. "You have them pat. The baroness, I fancy, is the dark woman who looked me over carefully as I came on board. She was standing at the rail, and I thought she looked as if she knew me, or believed she did. She looked Italian, anyway, and she was romantic enough looking to be a baroness. I thought for a moment that she was going to speak to me, but if she was she thought better of it."

"Confound it, Jimmie," I said, "I hope you're not going to be bothered by baronesses or Majors, or Majors' wives, on this trip; or Majors' wives' sisters, either. Your nerves are all shot to pieces."

"And you are an idiot," was the amused reply. "However, I'll promise not to play bridge."

"It would be just our luck to blunder onto trouble of some sort," I went on morosely. "Jimmie, if anybody robs the ship's safe, you are not to interfere. Let the Major run down the thief, since he's such a good man."

He laughed again. "All right," said he, "I'll go and see him about it now." And off he went, to hunt up his erstwhile crony, the retired Major and manhunter, whom, I suspect, he discovered in the smoking-room (which was also the drinking-room), for the bar had been open for several minutes.

And that is the way it all started, the memorable voyage of the trans-Atlantic liner, *Dianthus*, which added laurels to the reputation of my friend Lavender, and began his vacation in a manner — from Lavender's point of view — highly satisfying and successful.

Actually, it was the evening of the second day at sea that the first whisper of the trouble I had predicted reached our ears. My sardonic prophecy, however, was not accurate in its detail. The ship's safe — if it carried one — remained unmolested.

The day had been warm enough, but the evening called for wraps. The promenade deck was a scene of some activity, what with the hustling stewards and the eternally tramping Britons, who toiled around the oval like athletes training on a track. An Englishman is never happy unless he is walking or sitting before his fireplace; and the ship had no fireplaces. The boat deck, however, was comparatively deserted; and Lavender and I, wrapped in our rugs, looked out into the windy darkness and smoked contentedly. Our nearest companions were a spooning couple some yards away, half hidden by funnels, and wrapped in blankets and their own emotions. Major Rittenhouse, a likable fellow, as I had rapidly discovered, had surrendered at discretion, and was playing the amiable martyr in the card room.

An occasional steward drifted past, and once the second officer of the ship stopped for a word and a cigarette, but for the most part we were left to ourselves.

"Indeed," said I, "I believe we have the choice of locations, Lavender." And at that instant the Italian baroness hove into view.

Her name, we had discovered, was Borsolini — the Baroness Borsolini. She came forward uncertainly, wavered in passing, passed on, and in a few moments came back. She was quite alone, and obviously she wished to speak to us. On the third trip she had made up her mind, and came swiftly to our side.

"You are Mr. Lavender?" she murmured. "I must speak with you. May I sit down?"

"Of course," said my friend, and rose to his feet to assist her. "Something is worrying you, I fear."

"You are right," said the baroness. "I am very much afraid."

Her English was perfect. Her manner was pretty and appealing.

"Something has frightened you?" asked Lavender encouragingly.

She bent forward and studied his face closely in the darkness.

"You are a good man," she said at length. "I can tell. I think you are a poet."

Lavender squirmed and feebly gesticulated. Before he could deny the amazing charge, she had hurried on.

"Yes, I am afraid. Last night — after I had retired — someone was in my cabin!"

"A thief?"

The words came eagerly from the detective's lips. In his interest, he forgot her preposterous notion about his profession.

"I think so. But nothing was taken away. He did not find what he sought."

Lavender's interest deepened. "What did he seek?" he asked.

"My jewels," said the baroness. "What else?"

"They are valuable then?"

"They are very valuable, my friend. They are valuable because it would cost a fortune to replace them; but they are priceless because they are my family jewels. I speak of replacing them, but believe me, they could not be replaced."

My friend's cap came off to the breeze. "Tell me how you know there was someone in your cabin," he said.

"I awoke suddenly — I don't know why I awoke. I suppose I felt someone there. There were little sounds in the room — soft, brushing sounds — and breathing. Light, so light, I could scarcely catch it. It was only for an instant, then the man was gone. I must have made some little sound myself that alarmed him. As he went, I almost saw him — you understand? He seemed to glide through the door, which he had to open to escape. He made no sound, and what I saw was just black against gray as the door opened. I only half saw him — the other half I *felt*. You understand?"

"Yes," said Lavender, "I understand perfectly.

But how can you be sure it was a man? Probably it *was* — but are you sure?"

"I think so — that is all. It is my feeling that tells me it was a man. I cannot explain — but if it had been a woman, I think I should have known."

Lavender nodded. "No doubt you are right," he said. "Whom have you told of this, Baroness?"

"I have told no one but yourselves. You will advise me whom I should tell?"

"You had better tell Mr. Crown, the purser. He will, if he thinks best, tell the captain, I suppose, or whoever handles investigations of this sort. At any rate, Mr. Crown is the man to whom the first report should be made. I am sure he will do whatever is necessary. Probably he will have his own way of getting at the man who did this. I would see the purser at once, Baroness, if I were you."

She rose promptly. "Thank you. I am sure your advice is good. I shall go to Mr. Crown at once. You are very good."

"Meanwhile," said Lavender, "we shall, of course, say nothing. Good night, Baroness, and I hope you will not be disturbed again."

We rose with her, and watched her as she tripped away to the companionway. With a wave of her hand, she descended the steps and vanished. Lavender shoved me down into my chair.

"Stay here, Gilly," he said. "I'll be back shortly."

A moment later he, too, had disappeared in the direction of the lower deck.

Well, it had come! My unthinking prophecy had borne fruit, and Lavender was already involved. Where would it end? I lay back in my deck chair and earnestly consigned the baroness and her family jewels to perdition. It occurred to me that it had been nothing less than criminal for her to come on board our ship with the infernal things. She could just as well have waited for the *Maltania*! And Lavender might then have been allowed to have his vacation in peace.

In ten minutes, the subject of my paternal flutterings was back.

"She went, all right," said he laconically.

"I should hope she would," I retorted. "Did you think she wouldn't?"

"I wanted to be sure, Gilly," answered Lavender kindly. "I'm wondering why she didn't go to the purser first; why she singled me out for her attention; why she didn't put her blessed jewels in the purser's charge when she came on board — it's the thing to do. I'm also wondering how she knows *me*. For I'm convinced that she does know me, in spite of her assertion that I was singled out because I look like a 'good man.' I am more than ever convinced that she recognized me when I came on board. She wanted to speak to me then, although she had no attempted jewel robbery to report yesterday. Really, it's all very interesting."

"Yes," I admitted, "it is. Do you think there will be another attempt, Jimmie?"

"I wouldn't be surprised," said he thoughtfully. "In fact, I would almost bet on it."

II

IN THE dining saloon, the next morning, the company had perceptibly thinned out, for a stiff breeze and a choppy sea had sprung up in the night. At the purser's table, however, we sat six strong, as we had begun the voyage. Crown, the purser, pink complexioned and almost ridiculously fat, beamed good nature upon his charges, from his seat at the head of the table. He was in jovial spirits.

"If there were a prize offered for the table that showed no desertions," said he with a chuckle, "I think we should win."

Beverley of Toronto, who sat at my left, growled humorously. "There are several days ahead of us," he significantly observed. "I, for one, do not intend to crow."

Lavender, who had been the last one to sit down, was looking around the room. The Major's wife, thinking him to be looking in her direction, raised her brows and smiled; and he caught the gesture, and smiled and nodded back. He spoke to the purser, beside whom he sat.

"Two of the notables have not materialized," he remarked casually. "The baroness and the clergyman are missing."

The purser looked startled.

"Yes," he answered, "I noticed that. Murchison is ill, I hear; but I don't understand the baroness' absence. She looked to me like a sailor."

He seemed worried for a moment, and looked back at Lavender as if longing to confide in him; but the presence of the others at the table prevented. Lavender himself, having given the officer the hint he intended, devoted himself to his breakfast. From time to time, however, during the progress of the meal, he glanced toward the baroness' seat at a neighboring table, as if hoping to see that it had been occupied during the moments of his inattention. But the breakfast hour passed away and the object of his solicitude did not appear. The purser, too, continued to be worried, although he kept up a lively flow of conversation.

Outside the saloon door, the detective and the ship's officer paused while the passengers dispersed.

"She may be ill, of course," said the purser, at length. It was almost humorously obvious that he would have been relieved to hear that the baroness was very ill indeed.

"Of course," agreed Lavender, "but we had better find out. She told you, I suppose, that she came to me first?"

"Yes," said the purser, "one of my assistants tried to look after her, but she insisted on seeing me. I'm glad she was so cautious about it. Usually, a woman gets excited, tells everybody her difficulties, and then in loud tones demands to see the captain. As a result, the trouble — whatever it is — is all over the ship in no time, and everybody is nervous. I suppose I'm a fool, Mr. Lavender, but somehow I'm nervous now, myself. I hope there's no further trouble."

"What did you do, last night?"

"Spoke to the night watchman. He's supposed to have had an eye on her cabin all night. Of course, he couldn't watch it every minute, and do the rest of his work, too; but he was ordered to notice it particularly every time he passed, and to hang around a bit each time. I fancy he did it; he's a good man."

"And the baroness herself?"

"Refused, in spite of all my persuasion, to place her jewels in charge of my office. Of course, in the circumstances, if anything does happen to them, it's her own lookout. Just the same; that sort of thing, if it gets out, gives a ship a black eye, so to speak."

"Well," said Lavender, "we'd better have a look at her cabin. Nobody seems to be interested in our movements. Come on, Gilly!" He started up the stairs to the cabin deck to have a look at her cabin. Nobody seemed to be interested in our movements. "Who is her stewardess, Purser?"

"Mrs. King, a nice old soul. I spoke to her, too, but all I said was that the baroness was nervous, and to do what she could for her. We'll see Mrs. King at once."

He sighed and rolled heavily away, and we followed closely at his heels, down the corridors of the lurching vessel to the stewardesses' sitting room. Mrs. King, however, had nothing to tell us.

"She didn't call," said the woman, "and I didn't go near her."

"She wasn't down to breakfast this morning," explained the purser, "and we thought perhaps she was ill. You haven't been to her cabin yet, this morning?"

"No, sir," replied Mrs. King, "having had the lady's own orders not to wake her if she didn't choose to get up."

"I see. Well, you must go to her now, and see if she needs you. She may be ill, or she may just have missed the breakfast gong and be sleeping. Give her my compliments, and say that I was inquiring for her."

The woman seemed reluctant, and hung back for a moment; then she moved slowly off to the door of the cabin numbered B–12, where she paused uncertainly.

"All right," said the purser impatiently, "knock, and then go in!"

Mrs. King timidly knocked, and again stopped as if in apprehension.

"What's the matter?" asked Lavender, in his friendliest tones, seeing that the woman was frightened.

The ship lurched heavily, lay over for a long moment, and came up again. We all braced our legs and clung to the nearest woodwork.

"She doesn't — answer," said the matron faintly.

"Open the door!" ordered the purser.

Thus adjured, Mrs. King turned the handle, and with a terrific effort put her head inside the door. In an instant the head was withdrawn. The woman's face was pale and scared. The purser looked angry. Lavender, however, knew what had happened. With a quick frown, he pushed past the motionless woman and entered the little cabin, the purser and I at his heels. We filled the place.

There was no particular disorder. The port stood half open, as it had stood through the night, to allow ventilation. On the upholstered wall bench stood the baroness' bags. Her trunk half projected from beneath the bunk. The curtains blew gently with a soft, swishing sound.

Even in the bunk itself there was small disorder. Yet beneath the white coverings, with tossed hair and distorted features, the Baroness Borsolini lay dead.

For an instant, we all stood in silence. Then, from the corridor without, sounded the frightened whimper of Mrs. King, the stewardess. Lavender beckoned her inside, and she docilely obeyed.

"Stay here until we have finished," he quietly ordered.

"Good God!" said Crown, the purser, in awed dismay. Then he continued to stare, without speech, at the bed.

Lavender bent over the silent figure of the woman who, only the night before, had whispered her trouble to him.

"Strangled," he murmured softly. "Killed without a sound."

"Good God!" said the purser again.

Once more the stewardess' scared whimper sounded.

"Don't, please," said my friend, gently. To me, he said, "Gilly, can you say how long she has been dead?"

Anticipating the question, I had been examining the body, although without touching it. Now I stepped forward for a closer examination.

"Six or seven hours, at least," I said at length. "The ship's doctor — Brown — will tell you better than I."

"We'd better have him in," said Lavender, "although you are probably right. Excuse me, Mr. Crown," he added. "I don't mean to usurp your position in this matter."

The purser shuddered. "Go ahead," he said. "I'll be glad to do whatever you suggest."

"Then get the doctor here, quietly, and ask Rittenhouse if he cares to come down. What else there is to do, you will know better than I — that is, I suppose you will have to report to the captain, or something of the sort. You'd better take Mrs. King out of this, too, Crown. I would like to talk to her a little later, though."

He looked keenly at the frightened, shaking woman, but his touch on her arm as he uttered his last words was gentle. I knew that he was wondering about her hesitation before opening the door. I, too, had been wondering. Was it merely a woman's uncanny prescience, or something more significant?

When the purser and the matron had gone away, he turned to me.

"A queer, unhappy case, Gilly," he quietly remarked. "Do you sense it? The beginning, if I am not mistaken, of something very curious indeed."

Without further words, he turned from the bed and began a swift search of the cabin. His nimble fingers flew as he worked, and under his touch the possessions of the murdered baroness came to view and disappeared again with skillful method. Apparently he found nothing to guide him.

When he had finished, he said, "The question is, of course: did he, or she, or they — whichever may have been the case — find what they were looking for?"

"The jewels are gone?" I asked. "You don't find them?"

"They are not here," he replied, "unless they are very cleverly hidden. The second question we are bound to consider, Gilly, is: *were* there any jewels?" That startled me. He answered my surprised glance.

"We have no proof that she ever had any jewels. She was vague enough about them, when she spoke to us — vague about their value — and she refused to deposit them with the purser, which was her proper course. We have only her word for it that she possessed the jewels, and that she carried them with her. None the less," he added firmly, "she may have had them, and they may have been stolen. Certainly she was not murdered as a matter of whim."

"I think you suspect something that you are not mentioning, Jimmie," I remarked, with another glance at the dead woman.

He followed the glance. "Yes," he replied, "you are right. I believe this all began somewhere on shore. Almost the most important thing to be done, is to establish the identity of this woman."

"You doubt that she is —?"

"The Baroness Borsolini? Well, yes and no. She may have been just what she claimed to be, and yet nobody in particular. 'Baroness,' in Italy, means nothing of importance. The last Italian baron I knew was floor-walker in a Chicago department store. And, of course, she may not have been a baroness at all. My doubt of the poor woman, I will admit, goes back to the fact that she seemed to know me. However, if we are fortunate, we shall know all about her before long."

Again I looked a question.

"Last night," said he, "I sent a wireless, in code, to Inspector Gallery, in New York. I was curious about the baroness and her tale, and suspecting further trouble, I tried to anticipate some of our difficulties."

"You anticipated — this?"

"No," he flared quickly. "Not this, by Heaven! If I had, Gilly, I'd have stood guard myself all night long. I anticipated another attempt on the jewels," he added in lower tones. "Another attempt on whatever it is this woman had that her murderer wanted. We must have a talk with that night watchman, too, before long. I wonder who occupied the cabin across the way?"

"We can soon discover that," said I; and at that moment the purser came back with the doctor.

Brown, a fussy little man with a beard the color of his name, had heard the story from the purser, and was prepared for what he saw. He conducted a swift and skillful examination that proved his ability, and verified my statement as to the time the woman had been dead.

"Let us assume seven hours, then," said Lavender. "That would fix the murder at about two in the morning — possibly a little earlier, possibly a little later. Where the devil would the watchman have been at that hour? No doubt he had just passed on, for certainly the murderer would have been watching for him. By the way, Crown, who occupies B–14?"

The baroness' cabin was at the corner of an intersecting passage, and its entrance was off the smaller corridor. B–14 occupied the corresponding position across the passage, and was the opposite cabin to which Lavender had referred.

"I'll find out for you," answered the purser; but the doctor replied to the question.

"A clergyman," he said. "Murchison, of some place in Iowa. He's ill. He had me in, last night."

"Last night?" echoed my friend.

"Yes," said the doctor, "and it can't have been very long before — before this happened! About one o'clock, I think. It's not nice to think that this may even have been going on, while I was just across the way."

"How is he?"

"Oh, he's sick enough, but it's the usual thing. It was new to him, though, and I suppose he thought he was going to die. The poor chap is pretty low."

"He may have heard something, if he was awake," suggested Lavender. "Can he be questioned?"

"Oh, yes, but I doubt if he heard anything but his own groans. Somebody's with him now. I heard talking as I came by."

"I told Major Rittenhouse," volunteered the purser. "He said he'd be right down. He ought to have been here by this time."

"We'd better go to my stateroom," said Lavender. "There's nothing further to be learned here, I think. I shall want to talk with the night watchman, Purser, when I can get to him. I suppose he's asleep now. Doctor Brown, would you care to speak to your patient across the way? Ask him if he heard anything in the night, you know; and press the point. Any trifle may be important."

The door opened and the tall figure of Major Rittenhouse entered softly. He closed the door quietly behind him.

"I heard the last question," he remarked, then glanced at the bed. For just an instant, his eyes rested on the dead woman, then without emotion he continued. "I have already questioned Mr. Murchison, Lavender. It occurred to me as a good idea to look up the nearest neighbor. In a case like this, time is of considerable importance. Murchison was awake most of the night, and had the doctor in, once. About four o'clock he got up and staggered around his room a bit, then opened his door. He saw someone leaving this cabin, and supposed the baroness to be ill, too, for he thought no more about it."

"Four o'clock!" cried Lavender. "And if he thought the baroness was ill, he must have seen —"

"Mrs. King!" gasped the purser, with new horror in his voice.

"I don't know her name, and neither did Murchison," said Rittenhouse; "but the woman he saw was one of the stewardesses."

III

Rain fell heavily throughout the afternoon, filling the smoking-rooms and lounges of the floating hotel with animated conversation; but in Lavender's stateroom, as the great liner shouldered through the squall, a grimmer conversation went forward, unknown to the hundreds of our fellow passengers. It was feared that, soon enough, the ill tidings of death would spread through the ship, and throw a blight over the happy voyagers. Meanwhile, the task of apprehending the murderer of the unfortunate baroness had to move swiftly. It is probable that no shipboard mystery ever occurred more fortuitously; that is to say, with two more admirable detectives than Lavender and Rittenhouse actually on board to handle the investigation; but it is equally probable that no more mysterious affair ever engaged the talents of either investigator. We were a little world of our own, isolated from the rest of civilization by hundreds of miles of salt water; our inhabitants were comparatively few in number, and there was no opportunity whatever of escape. Somewhere in our midst actually moved and ate and slept a man or a woman guilty of

a hideous crime of violence; yet not a single clue apparently existed to the identity of that individual, unless Murchison's testimony had supplied it.

Mrs. King, the stewardess, was reluctant to an extraordinary degree, when for the second time she was questioned about her murdered charge. At first, she denied point-blank any knowledge of the events of the night, but then, as Lavender continued to probe, she burst into a storm of hysterical weeping. Confronted with the purport of the clergyman's information, she made a statement that only added mystery to the case.

"I did go in there at four o'clock," she said tearfully, addressing the purser, "and, so help me God, Mr. Crown, she was already dead!"

The purser's astonished glance went round the cabin and settled on my friend; but Lavender only nodded.

"That is what you should have told us at once," he said. "You were afraid of compromising yourself, but you only compromised yourself more deeply by keeping silent. You see, Rit," he continued, turning to the Major, "the time element remains unconfused. The murder occurred at about two o'clock, as the body indicated. Now, Mrs. King, let us have no more evasions and no more denials. If you stick to the truth, no harm will come to you that you don't deserve. Tell us exactly why you went to the baroness' cabin at four o'clock in the morning."

"She — she called me!" whispered the woman, in a voice so low that we caught the words only with difficulty.

"That, of course, is nonsense," said Lavender, severely; but Major Rittenhouse had caught a glimpse of the truth.

"You mean that the call board showed a call from her room," he interrupted. "But you didn't hear the bell ring, did you?"

The woman shook her head.

"She was probably asleep, Jimmie,"

continued the Major. "She didn't hear the bell, but when she awoke, some hours after it had rung, the board showed the baroness' number up. She answered — and found the body!"

"Is that what happened?" demanded Lavender of the woman.

Again Mrs. King responded with a gesture of the head, this time affirmative. The purser was angry.

"You are the night stewardess," he cried. "You have no right to be asleep."

"Nevertheless," said Lavender, "she was asleep. It doesn't help matters now to scold her. What happened is this: the murderer entered the cabin about two o'clock, and the baroness woke — possibly she had not been asleep. She heard the intruder, and sat up. Before she could scream, his hands were at her throat. There was a struggle, sharp but brief, and somehow the victim managed to reach and touch the call button. The ringing of the bell in the passage alarmed the murderer and he fled. Mrs. King was asleep and did not get the call. Two hours later, she awoke, saw that a call had come from the baroness' cabin, and responded. Murchison, across the way, opened his door and saw her leaving the room. A pity he didn't open his door at two o'clock!"

Rittenhouse nodded and took up the quiz. "You saw nothing in the room when you entered?" he asked. "Nothing that would give you an idea as to who did this thing?"

"No," answered the woman faintly.

"Was there a light in the room?"

She shook her head.

"Then how did you know the baroness was dead?"

"I — I turned on the light."

"Why did you turn on the light?"

"She had called me," answered the woman, somewhat defiantly. "I spoke when I went in, and she didn't answer. I thought maybe she had got up and gone out — I thought maybe she was ill. So I turned on the light, and then I saw — I saw her!"

Rittenhouse nodded again.

"And then you turned out the light, and went away?" Lavender finished. "Why didn't you tell somebody what had happened?"

"I was afraid," said Mrs. King simply. "I was afraid they would think I had done it."

"Hm-m!" said Lavender. He looked at the Major, who shrugged his shoulders.

"I guess that's all, Purser," said Lavender, at length. "Let's have the night watchman in."

But John Dover, the night watchman, an ex-sergeant of the British army, could tell us nothing. His story was straightforward enough.

"Yes, sir," said he frankly. "Hi passed that room many times, sir. There was no trouble that Hi could see, sir, hat any time. Hif there 'ad been, Hi'd 've looked into it. There was no light in the room, sir, hat any time."

This, after an hour's questioning, was still his story.

"It's probably quite true, too," observed Lavender, when the man had been cautioned to keep his mouth shut and had been dismissed. "The murderer wouldn't be fool enough to attract the watchman. Well, Rit, where are we?"

"Just about where we began, Jimmie, I should say," answered the Major.

"You believe the stewardess' story?" asked the purser dubiously.

"There's no earthly reason to disbelieve it, as yet," responded Lavender. "She *could* have done it, I suppose, but so could a dozen others. Extraordinary as her statement is, it has many of the earmarks of truth. I believe she did exactly what eight out of ten women would have done in the circumstances. We can't leave her out of our calculations, of course, but certainly we must allow her to believe that we accept her story *in toto*. In fact, I do accept it."

It was not long after these developments that tidings of the death of the Baroness Borsolini were all over the ship. Exactly how the news was started, nobody knew, for everybody with direct knowledge had been sworn to secrecy. It is a difficult thing, however, to hush up as serious a matter as murder, particularly on shipboard; and no doubt the leak could have been traced to the night watchman or Mrs. King, or the clergyman or the ship's doctor, or possibly even to the Major's wife or her sister. It is not the sort of knowledge one human being can possess without telling to another.

The purser, Crown, was deeply annoyed, for he was worried about the good name of the ship; but Lavender only grunted and said it could not be helped. As a matter of strict accuracy, it was the very revelation of the murder that brought us one of our strongest and strangest clues. It brought to Lavender's stateroom, the Hon. Arthur Russell, of Beddington, Herts., England, son of that Lord Denbigh whose name I had discovered on the ship's passenger list.

All over the ship the rumor of tragedy flew, once it had started, and the passengers gathered in groups to discuss the fearsome occurrence. In the smoking rooms, the male passengers bragged and told each other what *they* would do to apprehend the murderer, and in the lounges the women twittered and hissed like the gaudy birds of passage that they were. Many were frankly alarmed at the thought that the assassin was still at large, walking among them. They stated their fears audibly, and the purser was stormed by brigades of them, seeking information and assurances of safety.

"We may all be murdered in our beds," said they, in effect, so vehemently and in such numbers that Crown probably wished in his heart that many of them would be.

"Idiots!" said Lavender to me in pri-

vacy after the harassed purser had told him what was going on. "They are, if anything, safer than before. The murder of the baroness was not a result of bloodlust, nor the beginning of wholesale assassination. The selected victim has been killed, and for the murderer the episode is over. Quite the last thing he would do, unless he is crazy, is kill someone else. What he wants to do now is keep himself a secret, not to advertise himself by further crime. People are funny, Gilly; they don't think. Most murderers are really very safe men to be near, after they have committed their murder. They have it out of their system; their hate or their vengeance has been satisfied; the one who stood in their path has been removed, and in all probability they will never again commit that crime. The way to stop murder — philosophically speaking — is not to lock up or kill murderers, but to prevent the accomplishment of crime, or even the desire to kill, by scientific, educational methods. This, however," he added, with a smile and a shrug, "is not a doctrine that I often preach, and never in public. It would land me in the insane asylum!"

I was inclined to agree with his last assertion; but Lavender is a queer fellow, and his philosophy, as he states it, is very plausible. I merely smiled politely, and at his suggestion rang the bell and asked that our tardy luncheon be sent to the stateroom.

As it happened, the Hon. Arthur Russell came in with the tray — that is, he was hard on the heels of the waiter who bore it, and he apologized profusely for interrupting. He was a mannerly young Briton, handsome and likable, and we asked him to sit down and have a cup of tea.

I supposed him to be spokesman for his father, or for some group of the passengers, but his mission, it developed, was quite a different one. He was not seeking information; he had it to impart.

"I say, Mr. Lavender," he began, "is it all true, this that I hear? That the Baroness Borsolini is dead?"

"Yes," replied my friend, "quite true. She was found dead in her berth, this morning."

"And that she was" — he boggled over the word 'murdered,' and substituted another one — "that she was killed?"

"Yes," said Lavender. "There is not a doubt in the world that she was murdered, Mr. Russell."

"Good Lord!" said the boy. He drew a long breath. "That's what everybody is saying. I couldn't believe it!"

"Why?"

"Because — well, I couldn't, that's all! It seemed too horrible. Why, only last night, sir, she was with me on deck — full of life — and happy — why, I may have been the last person to see her alive!" he finished.

"The individual who killed her was the last person to see her alive," said Lavender coolly.

"Of course!" cried the boy. "I didn't think of that. Say, that's clever!"

Lavender smiled a little, not displeased by the boy's quick admiration.

"I think perhaps you have something to tell us, Mr. Russell," continued my friend. "Don't hesitate, if you have. Any information is very welcome."

The Hon. Arthur Russell gulped his tea, suddenly and convulsively, then put it aside.

"Well, I have!" said he. "Not much — but I've got her address!"

"Her address?"

"Yes, sir. She gave it to me last night.

You see, we had struck up an acquaintance, and we liked each other. We sat out on deck and talked, pretty late. I told her about my school life, and she told me a lot about America; and when we were parting, I said I'd like to write to her. So she gave me her address. Wrote it on a piece of paper and gave it to me. Here it is!"

With something of the air of a conjurer, he produced the paper. His youthful face was alight with the excitement of his news, which he believed to be of the highest importance. He could have been no more than twenty, while the baroness had been all of thirty-five, although pretty enough. Apparently, the boy had been greatly smitten. It was rather amusing, and rather pitiful.

As he spoke, he handed Lavender the scrap of paper that he had taken from his pocket.

"That's it," he concluded. " 'Florence, Italy. The Hotel Caravan.' That's her writing, sir!"

Lavender rose to his feet and carried the paper to the light. The boy too rose, and followed him. The interest of both was profound, although for the life of me I could see no reason for excitement in the discovery of the dead woman's address.

"Interesting," said my friend, at length. "Very interesting indeed! And, if I'm not mistaken, very important, too. I'm really very much obliged to you, Mr. Russell."

"I'm glad if it's a help," said the boy, flushing. His eyes sparkled. "I'd like to think that I had —" Suddenly he broke off, and his eyes bulged. "Why," he cried, "you're looking at the wrong side!"

"No," said Lavender, with a little smile, "this is the right side. I saw the other side too, and it's interesting also — particularly as there *is no* Hotel Caravan in Florence, that I ever heard of. But it is the reverse that interests me most. You say that she took this paper out of her bag?"

"I didn't say so," answered the boy accurately, "but as a matter of fact, she did. Tore it off a large piece, and wrote on it. That's her handwriting!"

He was still stupefied by Lavender's curious action, and still certain that in a veritable specimen of the baroness's handwriting he had furnished us with a sensational clue. But Lavender continued to study the reverse of the fragment. At length, he handed it to me.

"What do you make of it, Gilly?" he asked.

I looked, and saw nothing but a fragment of what apparently had been a printed form of some kind, for there were upon it several words in small print, and a perforated upper edge. The words were quite meaningless, removed from their context. Above the small print, however, was the one word 'line' in larger type.

"A ship's form of some kind?" I hazarded. "Torn from a book of similar forms?"

"Exactly," agreed Lavender. "The word 'Line,' of course, is the last word of 'Rodgers Line.' The rest, at the moment, means nothing. If we had the whole form, it might be very illuminating."

There was a tap on the door, and a moment later Major Rittenhouse entered the stateroom.

"Jimmie," said the newcomer, "there's a message coming in for you, upstairs. One of the wireless boys just told me, and asked me to let you know. What've you got? Something new?"

"Yes," said Lavender. "What do you think of it, Rit?"

Rittenhouse turned the paper over in his fingers, and at the baroness' written name and address, he blinked.

"We are indebted to Mr. Russell for it," explained Lavender, and repeated the young Briton's story. "But what do you make of the other side, Rit?"

After some cogitation, the Major made of it exactly what I had made.

"Well," said Lavender, with a sigh, "I may be wrong; but I thought I saw more than that." His eyes narrowed. "I'll tell you what, Rit," he added suddenly, "take it to your wife, or her sister, and ask either one what it is. I'll gamble that one of them will tell you."

The Major appeared surprised.

"Are you joking, Lavender?" His tone was a bit indignant.

"Not a bit of it. I'm intensely serious. Will you do it?"

"Yes," said Rittenhouse. "I'll do anything you say, Jimmie; but I'm damned if I know what my wife has to do with this thing!"

"Meanwhile," continued Lavender, "let's see what New York has to report on the Baroness Borsolini. I've a feeling that another revelation is at hand."

"May I come?" asked Arthur Russell eagerly.

"If you like," smiled Lavender, "but I'll be right back. Better stay here, all of you. We don't want to parade about the ship in groups, and start a new set of rumors."

He hurried away, and we sat back in our seats and impatiently awaited his return. In a few minutes he was back, with a small square of paper folded in his palm.

"Another interesting document," he observed. "This is Inspector Gallery's reply to my request for information concerning the baroness. It is in code, but I have translated it. Bear in mind, Rit, that he didn't know when he wired that the baroness was dead."

He began to read the message.

"Baroness Borsolini probably Kitty Desmond, well-known adventuress and international character. If she has a small mole at left corner of mouth it is —"

"She has!" interrupted Arthur Russell, in high excitement.

"Yes," said Lavender, "she has." He continued to read: *"— it is almost cerain. Jewels probably famous Schuyler jewels, worth half million, stolen here two months ago. Have cabled Scotland Yard to meet you at Quarantine Gallery."*

IV

At the purser's table that evening, the murder of the Baroness Borsolini was the sole topic of conversation. We still sat six. Besides Lavender and I and the purser, there were Beverley of Toronto, Dudgeon of New York, and Isaacson of St. Louis. The latter three were acquainted with all the rumors, and they questioned Lavender and the purser diligently. That Lavender was a famous detective, and had been placed in charge of the case, was a piece of news that had circulated with the rest of the reports. Our fellow passengers at table felt themselves very fortunate indeed, to be so fortuitously placed with reference to the fountainheads of information, and I fancy they were vastly envied by passengers at the other tables. Throughout the meal, heads were turned constantly in our direction.

The rotund Crown, who, by virtue of his office, had been harassed even more than had Lavender, was inclined to be reticent and a bit short. Lavender merely smiled coldly, and replied with scrupulous accuracy to all questions leveled at him. The facts, he admitted without reserve, but he declined to indulge in speculation.

"It is obviously a case of a falling out of crooks," he concluded. "I have received a wireless message from New York, which positively identifies the baroness as a well-known and, if you like the term, a high class crook. The stolen jewels, if they have been stolen — and apparently they have been — are said to have originally disappeared in New York, some two months ago. I have no doubt that the baroness was on her way to Europe with them, and that the division of spoils was to take place there.

Possibly she was to sell them. Her accomplices in the original theft, I should imagine, are for the most part on the way to Europe on other vessels. One, however, it would seem — or, any rate, somebody who knows the truth about the jewels — is on board this vessel. There is no cause for alarm. The decent passengers are quite safe."

"She would have had to smuggle them in, wouldn't she?" asked Beverley of Toronto. The remark was more of a statement than a question.

"Yes," replied Lavender, "but that plan was probably worked out to the last comma. Smuggling offers no great difficulties to a clever person."

At the close of the meal, we were surrounded by interested questioners; but not even the wiles of Betty Cosgrave, the screen star, could shake Lavender's reserve. We heartlessly left the purser to answer all interviewers, and hurried on deck. On the way up, we passed the captain, a pleasant-faced Englishman somewhat past middle life. He had something on his mind.

"Er — Mr. Lavender," he observed, "Mr. Crown has been keeping me informed, of course, of this exraordinary business. Nasty — very nasty indeed! Sinister! Mr. Crown, of course, acts for me and for the company. I have no wish to interfere with what is in better hands than my own; but you will understand that I am deeply affected by it all. May I ask whether you anticipate a — a successful conclusion?"

"Entirely successful, Captain Rogers," replied Lavender seriously. "It is the sort of case the very simplicity of which makes it difficult; but I believe it is yielding to treatment. I believe, quite honestly, that before long I shall be able to present you with the murderer of the Baroness Borsolini, and to turn over the stolen jewels."

"Thank you," said the captain with a nod. "I have every confidence in you. And in Major Rittenhouse, too. Crown tells me you are both quite famous men in your field. I am sorry I could not have you at my table. If I can be of service, please command me."

We finished our journey to the boat deck, without further interruption, and found our long-unused deck chairs awaiting us. The night had cleared, but a cold breeze was blowing over the sea, and we wrapped ourselves in rugs to our chins.

"You seem pretty confident of success, Jimmie," I ventured, when our pipes were going strongly, and the moment seemed propitious.

"I am confident," said he. "It is beyond credence that this fellow can escape. I am working privately on an idea of my own that, I confess, may not work out; but it looks promising. Frankly, Gilly, it has to do with that fragment of paper that the baroness gave young Russell; but that is all I dare say about it, at present. And I will ask you to keep that much a secret. What I want, of course, is the other piece of the paper — the larger piece."

"Did Mrs. Rittenhouse identify it?" I asked curiously.

"She did," replied my friend, almost grimly. "She identified it in a moment, because both she and her sister have papers exactly like it. Rit is working with me in this, and I may hear from him at any minute. He is less of a figure than I, in this thing, and can snoop about with less attention."

We sat in silence for a few moments, listening to the throb of the ship's great engines, and the rush of water beyond the white line of the rail. Then I spoke again. "Gallery was a bit previous, wasn't he, Jimmie, in cabling Scotland Yard to help you?"

"No, it was all right," replied my friend, with a little smile. "Don't be jealous, Gilly. I know exactly why Gallery did that. He thought that I might, at the

last moment, feel some embarrassment in using the wireless; that is, that I might find myself in a position where I could not use it without betraying my suspicions, whatever they might be, to the person suspected. He anticipates that my use of the ship's wireless, if my actions are being watched — and, rest assured, they are being watched — may alarm the murderer. It was a piece of clear thinking on Gallery's part, a resourceful man's safeguard against chance or probability."

I nodded, and again we sat without speech, until a step sounded along the boards, and the tall figure of the Major hove in view. Rittenhouse seated himself without a word beyond a greeting, and for a few moments we all smoked in silence.

"Murchison is still ill," he said, "but he's coming around. I've seen him again. He has nothing to add to his first statement. He saw no one but the stewardess last night; he is willing to swear to that. I've had another whirl at Dover, the watchman, too. He now remembers seeing the doctor leave Murchison's cabin. The incident made no impression on him, and he didn't think of it before; it was just a part of routine to him, to see Brown in attendance somewhere or other. All in all, Jimmie, there is no escaping your conclusion, and I am prepared to accept it."

"Yes," replied Lavender, "it's pretty certain; but the fellow must be made to betray himself. We haven't enough to go on, as it is. It's dangerously near being guesswork. You asked Crown about the baroness's papers?"

"I did. He has them in safekeeping. Not a thing in them, he says, that gives us a clue."

Lavender smiled. "There wouldn't be," he rejoined laconically. "Anyway, I've been through them twice, myself."

"However, I told him of the fragment of paper Russell gave you," continued Rittenhouse. "It startled him."

"When are you going to tell *me*?" I demanded, at this juncture. "Where do I come in, Jimmie? Can I do nothing?"

Lavender turned to me very seriously.

"The fact is, Gilly," he said, "you will be a much better witness in all that is to follow, if you know nothing for a while. You can do one thing, though; you can keep an eye on me! I mean it. The fat is in the fire, if I'm not mistaken, and from now on, I shall be a marked man. I shall go calmly about my business, as if all were well, and it is up to you and Rit to see that I don't get a knife in my back, or something equally unpleasant. Rit and I know the murderer. The question is: does he know that we know? I don't think he suspects Rit; but he may suspect me. And the more innocent you appear, Gilly, the better it will be all around. But keep your eyes open."

"All right, Jimmie," I replied obediently. But I was horrified by the turn the case was taking, and for a long time I sat and thought deeply, while the two curious fellows who were with me actually sat and talked about baseball.

Who, by any chance, could have committed the crime? Who had the opportunity? I faced the problem squarely, and admitted that there were plenty of persons who could have done it. In addition to the great numbers of obscure passengers, first and second class, who had not even been named in the inquiry, there were undoubtedly half a dozen principals who might very well be definite suspects. The second class outfit, I was inclined to disregard, for a second class passenger surely would have been noticed by one of the stewards, if he trespassed on holy ground. And yet, as I came to think of it, was there so much difference between a first and a second class passenger? Actually, I was forced to admit, there was none, so far as appearance was concerned. Of the principal figures, however, five at least, as I now numbered them, stood forth clearly as possibilities. All had been, or could have been, near the scene of the murder at the time it occurred. And with something of a thrill, I realized that I must add young Russell to the list. I did not for a moment suspect him, but for that matter I hardly suspected any of the others.

And Lavender was in actual, active danger of one of them! Clearly, there was only one thing for me to do, and that was to watch everybody. I resolved to watch the entire ship, from the captain on down, not excluding Rittenhouse himself. Since I was to be Lavender's guardian, by Heaven, I would suspect everybody!

In this frame of mind, I went to bed and dreamed a mad, fantastic dream in which the captain of the liner, which curiously had become a pirate ship, stole into Lavender's stateroom and stabbed him with a fragment of paper, while the Baroness Borsolini joined hands with Rittenhouse and danced around them. Waking with a start, I sat up and listened. Finally, I knocked three times on the wall of my cabin, and listened again. After a pause, there came back to me Lavender's reply, in similar code. And after this performance, I turned over and managed to get to sleep.

THE morning of the fourth day broke clear and fair and cold. I went at once to Lavender's room, to find him already up and gone. He did not appear until breakfast, and I had no opportunity to ask him where he had been; but it oc-

curred to me that he was not playing fair. If I was to guard him against assassination, he ought at least to keep me posted as to his movements. So I thought.

BREAKFAST passed with the usual chatter about the uppermost subject in everybody's mind, and at a table not far removed from ours sat Murchison, the Iowa clergyman, eating his first meal in the saloon. He looked pale and thin, but happy to be on earth and able to eat. Later, I saw him in conversation with the purser, and still later with the captain. Was he, then, the heart of the mystery, and were the coils beginning to tighten?

Lavender too had a brief talk with the captain, after which they vanished in company, while Rittenhouse and the purser talked in low tones at the door of the latter's office. Obviously, something was afoot, and I felt strangely out in the cold. Then Mrs. Rittenhouse, and her sister, Miss Renshaw, corralled me, and for an hour I was forced to sing the praises of my friend Lavender to their admiring accompaniment.

After this, however, the suppressed excitement seemed to loosen up, and for an entire day the routine of ship life went quietly forward with only casual mention of the crime. Some gayety was even apparent in the lounges and in the smoking rooms, and I reflected sardonically on the adaptability and the callousness of human nature. The fifth day would be the last on board, for the sixth morning would bring us into port. It was this knowledge, I suppose, that cheered the passengers, although the Lord knew that

the voyage had been anything but boresome.

When I asked Lavender what progress had been made, he answered merely that he was "waiting."

ON the fifth morning, I suddenly remembered that this was the anniversary of my birth — not a particularly significant occasion, Heaven knows, but at least a subject for trivial conversation. Lavender, however, greeted the tidings with singular enthusiasm, and promptly ordered a splendid dinner for the evening; Rittenhouse ordered wine during the afternoon, to drink my health, and Mrs. Rittenhouse and her sister embarrassed me immensely by presenting me with ridiculous speeches, with tiny bottles of perfume and of post-shaving lotion, purchased of the ship's barber. The dinner went off with gusto, with everybody ordering champagne and making idiotic addresses, to which I lamely responded.

My humble birthday, indeed, was made an occasion for strained nerves to relax and for worried men to forget their problems. To cap the climax, when I went to my cabin in the evening, there was a gorgeously wrapped and tied box of cigars and cigarettes, with the captain's card attached to it, and a huge box of candies, with the purser's compliments similarly presented. I felt excessively guilty about these latter gifts, feeling as I did that they were intended to show appreciation of Lavender's services. Lavender, however, only laughed and was pleased that my birthday should have passed off so well.

"Any occasion is good for a celebration, at sea," he observed.

Late in the afternoon, we had dropped anchor in the outer harbor of Cherbourg, while a tender took off our passengers for Paris. Then, with a fresh breeze, we had headed for England and the end of the voyage. I had noted that, during the transfer of passengers for France, Lavender stood at the gangplank stretched between the steamers, and carefully observed every person who went aboard the tender. For a time, I had looked for fireworks, but apparently there was no call for his interference.

We sat late that night, upon the deck, the three of us, and for a time the purser made a quartette. It was with reluctance that Crown took his departure.

"We dock in the morning," he said, as he prepared to go. "I've a nasty report to make to the company, Mr. Lavender. You haven't anything to tell me that will make it easier?"

"The report will be full and complete," replied my friend. "The murderer will be apprehended at quarantine, by Scotland Yard officials, and the jewels will be turned over at that time."

Crown was startled and amazed.

"You don't mean to say that — that you've got your man!"

"Not yet," said Lavender, "but I shall certainly get him. Crown, he is one of the officers of this ship."

The purser's jaw dropped; his fat cheeks sagged. His eyes searched the eyes of Lavender.

"My God!" he said. "I'm almost afraid to ask you — who he is!"

Suddenly he got to his feet. "Will you come to my cabin?" he asked. "This is no place to discuss what you have to tell me."

Lavender nodded his head and stood up. They moved off together in the direction of the forward deck.

"Ready, Gilruth!" said the Major, sharply, and I saw that his face was hard and set, his limbs braced. "After them quickly."

The sudden intelligence seared my brain like a hot iron, and then I went cold. But Rittenhouse was already on his way, and mechanically I followed him.

We were none too soon. Lavender

and the purser had barely disappeared beyond the cheek of the wireless cabin, when the huge criminal fell upon his companion. There was a shout, and then a scuffling of feet and the sound of blows. The next instant, Rittenhouse and I were on the scene.

In the deep shadow of the piled lifeboats, a desperate struggle was in progress, with the rail and the water dangerously close. Even as we reached them, the wrestlers pitched toward the edge; the great bulk of the purser was forcing the slimmer figure of Lavender back over the rail. I heard the cold rush of the water, and the heaving breathing of the combatants. The wind snatched away my cap, and tingling spray beat upon my face.

Then Rittenhouse was upon the purser like a wolf, and with cleared wits I was beside him, aiding.

The powerful Crown fought like a maniac, but the odds were now against him, and slowly we wore him down. Haggard and disheveled, he struggled to the last. At length, Rittenhouse tripped him and brought him down with a thud that seemed to shake the deck. Kneeling on the great heaving chest of the beaten man, the Major forced the purser's wrists together, while Lavender snapped on bracelets of steel. As the struggle ended, Captain Rogers and his first officer ran up out of the shadows.

"Mr. Crown, Mr. Crown," panted the captain, "what is the meaning of this?"

But as the purser could only glare and foam, Lavender, slightly breathless, replied for him.

"It means, sir," said he, "that Mr. Crown has just been frustrated in an attempt to throw me overboard. Major Rittenhouse and Mr. Gilruth prevented him. As I explained to you, our actual evidence was slight, and it became necessary to force Mr. Crown to incriminate himself. The attempted murder of James E. Lavender will do for the present charge. Later it will be changed to something more serious."

The first officer was incredulous.

"Do you mean," he began, "that Mr. Crown had anything to do with —?"

"I believe the murder of the Baroness Borsolini to have been accidental," answered Lavender. "None the less, it was Mr. Crown who committed the crime."

Suddenly the fat face of the prostrate man wrinkled like that of a child, and the great frame began to heave. Then sobs of anguish broke from the lips, and incredible tears rolled down the massive cheeks.

"I didn't mean to kill her," sobbed the purser. "I swear to God, Captain, it was an accident! I never meant to kill her. So help me God, it was an accident!"

V

WITH the purser safely locked in his room, under heavy guard, Lavender, in the captain's cabin, repeated the tale as chronologically it should be told.

"The Baroness Borsolini," said he, "was really Kitty Desmond, a well-known adventuress. Crown has made a full confession to me and to Rittenhouse. Miss Desmond was made the repository of the stolen Schuyler jewels, and sent to England with them, where they were to be sold, I imagine, and the money divided. She recognized me when I came on board, and wondered if I were on her trail. It worried her, and she made the bold play of coming to me with a cock-and-bull story of attempted theft, in order to find out what I knew and, if I knew nothing, to gain my sympathies. I am convinced that there was no attempt on her room, the first night.

"Crown, however, recognized *her*. She had been a frequent voyager on the Atlantic, and many men knew her. She had been pointed out to Crown, a year ago, on another ship. He knew only that she was a police character, and probably

up to no good. When I sent her to him, to test her story, she was obliged to carry the thing through, and tell him the same story she had told me. She trusted Crown's office, as she had every right to do, and actually deposited the jewels there, and received the usual receipt.

"But the temptation was too great for Crown. He was desperately hard up — deeply in debt — back home in England. It looked to him like a sure thing. He would keep the jewels himself, steal the receipt which had been issued to Kitty Desmond, and defy her to say anything. He was, of course, in a position to fix the records in his own office, and being a matter of routine no one else likely to remember the issuing of that particular receipt. There could be no appeal for the woman; her story would be laughed at, if she reported it, for her reputation was against her. Probably she would accept the inevitable and make no outcry.

"Crown's slip occurred when, on the second night, he stole the receipt which had been given her. She woke up, and to keep her from screaming, he choked her. His reputation depended upon his silencing her, at least until he could talk to her. If he had not killed her, he would have offered her — when she caught him in the act of theft — a share of the profits. Unfortunately, she died under his hands; he is stronger than he suspects. He got the receipt, however, and fled. No one saw him; he had timed everything very well.

"As it happened, in giving young Russell a false address, the night before, the Baroness — so to call her — had torn off a fragment of the receipt, the only piece of paper that came to hand in the darkness. Whether she knew what it was, or not, we shall never know. Perhaps she did, for she tore off only a small piece; not enough to spoil the receipt. But there was enough of the print on the reverse of the written address, for me to guess what the entire paper must have been. If then, she had deposited something with the purser's office, the purser had lied when he told me she had not. In the circumstances, the logical conclusion was that she had deposited the jewels.

"Crown is a bold man, and he played his part well, once he was forced to it. But in the end, I let him know, through Rittenhouse, the importance I attached to a certain fragment of paper. As he had the rest of the paper himself, he knew very well what it was that I had, and what I probably suspected. He tried to bluff it through, even tonight, for he wasn't positive that I *knew,* and he had destroyed the rest of the receipt. Nevertheless, he was badly frightened, and he had already resolved to get rid of the jewels, and try to clear his skirts.

"As for me, my case was purely circumstantial, and would have been difficult to prove in law; I had to force Crown to incriminate himself. I told him point-blank, just before he sprang upon me, that he would be arrested, told him where the jewels were, and asked him what he intended to do about it. You know the rest."

"And a wonderful beginning of your vacation it has been!" I said bitterly, looking at his lacerated hands.

"Don't be silly," said Lavender. "I never enjoyed myself more in my life. This has been just what I needed. And I'm sure the sea air, as a background, has been very beneficial to my nerves."

"But where are the jewels?" asked the captain suddenly.

"I asked Gilruth to bring them with him," replied Lavender with a smile. "As a last resort, Crown tried to get rid of them, as I said, and so he palmed them off on Gilly. The birthday gave him his chance. The jewels are at the bottom of the box of candy, which was the purser's gift to my friend."

Whereupon, I emptied the box onto the table; and the chorus of exclamations that followed were Lavender's reward for his efforts, and the final proof of the truth of his deductions, even though later the suicide of Albert Crown made legal proof unnecessary, and made unnecessary the prosecution of that unfortunate man. ⊕

THE REMITTANCE-WOMAN

by Achmed Abdullah

"I SAY, old bean!" Marie Campbell addressed a long, rather limp youth with a pleasantly innocuous face.

"Wha-at, old thing?" he asked languidly.

"Feel energetic?"

"Quite."

"Good! I'll shoot you a game of cowboy pool before lunch."

"Stakes?"

"You bet," said Marie Campbell. "The drinks and a fifty-spot."

As Tom Van Zandt rose to follow her into the billiard-room of the country club at the Maine resort, a cough she knew well came from the farther door and caused her to turn

"Yes, father dear?" — with a slightly martyred air.

"I want a few words with you, Marie."

"Now?"

"Immediately!"

She walked up to him.

"What is the trouble?" she asked.

"I was in the next room. I heard what you've been saying to that young jackanapes of a Tom Van Zandt."

"And what did I say you could possibly take exception to?" Marie's voice rose.

"Oh, calling Tom 'old bean!'" He pronounced the words as if they hurt him. "And him calling you 'old thing.'"

"Dad, that sort of talk happens to be the fad just now in our gang —"

"Gang?"

"Set — if you prefer. Why, Muriel Brewster always calls her father 'darling old turnip.'"

"I don't care what she calls him! I don't care what anybody calls — oh — anybody," he finished weakly.

"What's all the fuss about, then?"

"Your lolling around here with Tom —"

"Nothing much wrong with him except his brain and the color of his socks, dad —"

"And," her father interrupted, "asking him to shoot you a game of cowboy pool — and betting him — what was it?"

"Oh — the drinks and a fifty-spot."

"The drinks and a fifty-spot!" echoed Anthony Campbell, with a groan of almost physical pain. "The drinks and a — it's your language I'm kicking about, and your whole darned conduct. 'Cowboy pool!'" he quoted, with an accent of personal injury. "'Fifty-spot! Old bean!' It isn't becoming a girl. And," — crescendo — "that isn't all!"

"No?"

Her voice was as cold as ice. She

was fond of her father, and he of her, in a curiously impersonal manner. But both were impatient and headstrong. Never at odds in vital questions, they clashed frequently on small, negligible side issues. For a number of years — Mrs. Anthony Campbell had died in giving birth to Marie, and there was a challenging silence whenever the girl mentioned her mother — father and daughter had lived in the uncomfortable relations existing between two intimately connected persons who realize that the atmosphere about them is surcharged with innumerable little explosive atoms.

"Darn it all!" her father exclaimed. "You've lost all your feminine sweetness and restraint. You talk like a man, behave like a man, smoke like a man, and," — he wound up accusingly, furiously, yet somehow triumphantly — "you make debts like a man! Here!" And he produced a thick sheaf of varicolored papers.

"Bills?" she inquired, bored.

"Yes." He tossed them on the table.

"Must I look at them all? Now?"

"No. I've made a little compilation of them for your benefit, young lady." He took a typewritten sheet from his pocket. "Here!"

She picked it up and glanced at the items, which totaled up to a respectable sum.

"Surely you can afford to pay it, can't you, dad?"

"Of course. That isn't the question."

"What is?"

"The sort of stuff you spend my money on. For instance, I don't mind this seven hundred dollars for frocks and frills and all that. Nor this — Madame — oh — Hickama-doodle's bill for a dozen hats. But — look at this — and this — and that!"

She did.

"Polo-mallets, one hundred and seventy-five dollars. English hunting-saddle, ninety-five. Yes?" She looked up questioningly.

"Go on. There!" He pointed at another detailed row of items. "Walking sticks! Sporting-rifle! Hunting-crop! Cigarettes! Poker chips! And — breeches! By God — *breeches!*"

"But," she rejoined mildly, "you told me only the other day that I could buy myself a new outfit —"

"A woman's! Not a man's! Breeches! Cigarettes! Poker chips!"

"What are you going to do about it, dad?"

"I'm going to give you your choice. Do you want to be a girl, and behave like one, or be treated like a man?"

"You mean that, dad?"

"Absolutely!"

"All right," she said. "In the future you may treat me as if I were a man."

"In everything?"

"Rather."

He looked at her, slightly incredulous.

"You realize what you are choosing?"

"Quite, dad."

"You are willing to take the same chance I took when I was a young chap?"

"Yes."

"Marie," he said, "I accept your choice. You will start your new career at once. Tomorrow we go back to

town. I'll give you a check there. I'll make it a thousand —"

"Why a thousand?" she drawled.

"To start you in life."

"Did you say you'd give me the same chance you had when you went out into the world?"

"Yes. Well?" — as he saw her smile,

"Dad," she said slowly, "last year I went to Scotland — and saw grandfather. He told me things about you — when you were a young man."

"Oh!" Mr. Anthony Campbell was getting embarrassed.

"He told me something about how agreeably surprised he had been when you finally made good."

"What has all that to do with —"

"Wait! He told me how irresponsible you had been for years after leaving college — how at last, in desperation, he asked you to leave Scotland for Scotland's good. In fact, you came over to America as a remittance-man, didn't you?"

"I did. But — I *did* make good."

"Never mind that. I'm speaking about your chance in life — your first start. Grandfather gave you a thousand dollars every three months on condition that you'd keep away from the Old Country. True, isn't it?"

"Yes," he admitted in a low voice.

His THOUGHTS roamed back down the vista of the gray, dead years — his impetuous youth, two terms at Oxford, expulsion on a number of charges of which drinking was the mildest. Scrapes, right and left. His father had sent him to America, and he had become a remittance-man. A thousand dollars every quarter, and it had never lasted more than a month — whisky, cards, dice, women, horses.

And step by step, he had drifted down the ladder until one day, suddenly, something like a colored ball of glass had shivered to pieces in his brain, had shown himself to himself in the naked, pitiless light of self-understanding.

That was in the Northwest, not far from the Washington–British Columbia boundary-line. He was completely broke. But that day the little red wilderness gods had piped to him, and he had followed their call, across the boundary-line into British Columbia, north, up along the Michel Creek — to find what he might. He had trekked on foot, finding occasional work in mines and lumber camps. Then one day, clearing the snow from the ground to make a fire, he had found a little crumbly, black powder — coal!

He had been too poor to buy dynamite. And so Jack Henderson, the Crow's Nest Pass storekeeper, who was nearly as poor as himself, grubstaked him for all he could. He had worked with pick and shovel all that winter into the summer. But he had found his first true vein, and today Campbell & Henderson — the same Jack Henderson of the Crow's Nest Pass store — were the biggest coal operators in the Northwest, solidly rich, with offices and town houses in New York and country places in Maine and on Long Island.

Since then his life had been a steady routine of work and success. He had interrupted it only once, a little over twenty-two years ago, when he had gone on a trip round the world, and had spent over a year in China, whence he had returned, white-haired, rather bitter, with a little baby girl in his arms. Yes — he had curtly told Jack Henderson and his other friends — he had married in China. And — yes — his wife had died in childbirth.

Today the beginnings of his fortune seemed very far away; very far away, almost unreal, seemed the days when he had been a remittance-man.

But he was an honest man.

"YES," HE SAID to his daughter; "once I was a remittance-man, and my father sent me a thousand dollars every three months."

"Very well," she went on coolly. "You promised me the same chance you had. Only — make it fifteen hundred a quarter instead of a thousand."

"Fifteen hundred? Why —"

"Higher cost of living," she explained.

"All right," he gave in finally. "Fifteen hundred a quarter." He looked at her narrowly, to see if she were bluffing. "Of course on the same conditions which my father —"

"Yes," she interrupted. "I'll get my remittances just as long as I stay away from America —"

"Any time you want to come back — and behave like a girl —"

"I know. But I'm really tickled to get away. Always been crazy to go to China."

"China?" He looked up, startled.

"Yes, dad. I was born there, wasn't I? What other reason could there be — except perhaps inherited *Wanderlust?*"

"Yes — yes." An expression of suspicion left his face.

"Well — there you are! I shall start this week. About my remittances, where to send them and all that, I suppose you'll want me to talk to your secretary."

"Marie!" came his half-choked appeal, his pride giving way a little to his love.

He held out a nervous hand and she took it in both hers. But her voice was one of finality.

"It's quite settled, dad."

"Very well." He lit a cigar. "By the way — remember that little Chinese vase you had ever since you were a baby?"

"You mean that brittle thing with the two funny, wriggly gold dragons?"

"That's the one. Take it along. And," — he coughed, evidently searching for words — "don't show it to people — and don't talk about it — unless," — he hesitated — "unless you absolutely have to."

"But — what —"

"I am a Scot." He gave a forced laugh. "And so you must forgive my Scottish superstitions. But — is it a promise?"

"About the vase?"

"Yes."

"All right, dad. I promise."

ALL THIS had happened over six months before, and now Marie Campbell was in her hotel at Canton, at the edge of the Shameen, the Foreign Concession, with a view, in the distance, of White Cloud Mountain. She wondered what she should do. Of course she could cable to her father, and the reply would be immediate and generous.

But it was not alone her inherited pride which prevented her from doing so. It was also that, somehow, even in these few months, China had got beneath her skin in a strange way.

For, in her non-thinking moments, there was always about her a curious impression that she belonged here. Yet — what was there for her to do?

Two weeks before, her quarterly check had come. She had spent every cent of it in the gorgeous silk and jade shops near the Gate of Eternal Purity. And here was Liu Po-Yat, the Manchu chambermaid, with a note from Monsieur Paul Pailloux, the hotel manager, asking Miss Campbell to settle her bill before ten o'clock the next morning, or —

"Or?"

She turned to Liu Po-Yat, who looked down at her from her great height, her handsome face inscrutable beneath the glory of her raven-black hair.

Then, suddenly, the Manchu woman smiled.

"Miss Campbell," she said in perfect English, "I see no necessity for the 'or.'"

"Don't you?"

Marie Campbell was surprised that Liu Po-Yat, who, ever since she had come to the Great Eastern Hotel to live, had not opened her mouth except to answer in gliding Mongol monosyllables to the few Chinese words — enough to ask for fresh towels and ice-water — Marie had managed to pick up, was able to speak English — fluent, careful English, not the pidgin of the river coolies.

"No," Liu Po-Yat replied to her question. "You see — there is Mr. Moses d'Acosta —"

"Look here —"

"Mr. d'Acosta is waiting for you downstairs in the *salon*," Liu Po-Yat finished imperturbably.

Mr. MOSES d'Acosta had seen the light of day fifty years earlier in Constantinople in a crooked, dim street a stone's throw from the Yedi Koulé Ka-

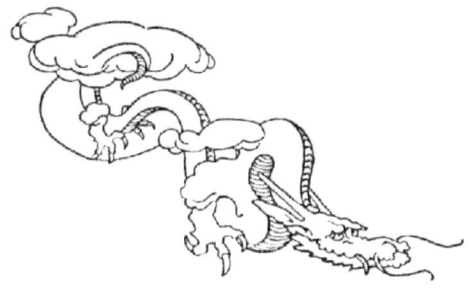

poussi, the Gate of the Seven Towers. He spoke Turkish as fluently as he spoke Arabic and French and English and German and the Levantine *lingua franca*. But his native tongue was an archaic Spanish, which he used, even in preference to Hebrew, when he chanted his prayers to Jahveh, the God of Abraham and of Jacob. For he was a "Spaniol," a descendant of one of those noble Spanish-Jewish families who were driven from their native land when the last of the Moorish caliphs went down under the straight swords of Castile and Leon, and who migrated, some to Morocco and Tunis, others to Turkey.

Today he was one of the richest men in the Levant, with interests that reached from Peking to London. He was a typical Jew in so far as he was both a doer and a dreamer: the rarest, most irresistible of combinations, and that — this according to Mademoiselle Claire Droz, a Parisian *chanteuse* whose light feet for years had trod the rickety boards of occasional theatres catering to European exiles in Oriental lands — he swayed habitually emotional incoherencies into intellectual coherences.

MARIE HAD met him first a week before in a mazed bazaar near the Temple of the Five Hundred Lohans and, the same night, in the hotel lobby. She had noticed him immediately. Nobody could help noticing him — very tall, broad, dark, with black, inscrutable eyes, the nose an enormous, predatory beak, the chin flagging and combative. He had bowed to her deeply, and she had inclined her head curtly in return.

Then, only two days ago, she had met him again, as she came from a Chinese shop where, with utter recklessness, she had spent a hundred dollars, the tail-end of her quarterly remittance, for an exquisite vase of Ning-yan porcelain.

The shop being in the slums of Canton, a rabble of Gilyak Tatars, former soldiers, discharged since the Chinese revolution and holding the "foreign devils" responsible for the downfall of the Manchu dynasty, had followed her and were pelting her with mud when Moses d'Acosta swung round the corner, dispersed the mob at the point of his revolver, and seen her home to the hotel, where he, too, lived.

On the way there he had talked to her — at first about impersonal matters, then suddenly he had made a remark which had surprised her.

"Good ship — the *Empress of Malaysia*."

"Oh, you know that —"

"That you took the C.P.R. liner to Hong Kong — and then came up here on the British Navigation ship? Of course."

"How do you know?"

"Curiosity is my middle name, I suppose." And, suddenly, disconcertingly, "Why did you decide all at once to come to China?"

"Oh — I —" She had found herself uneasy and nonplused, and when, back at the hotel, he had asked her to dine with him that very night, she had been conscious of her desire to accept, although her lips, almost mechanically, had formed the glib white lie: "Thank you, but I'd rather not — headache, you know."

"Very well, Miss Campbell," he had replied. "Some other time." And he had repeated questioningly, "Some other time," and had added, almost in a whisper, "Our tastes are the same, you know."

"In what?"

"In Chinese porcelain, don't you think?"

He had not even waited for her answer, but had walked away and, looking after him, she had seen him step up to and exchange greetings with an elderly, enormously stout Manchu dressed in brocaded silk.

"Sun Yu-Wen, the famous Pekingese banker," the desk clerk had told her in answer to her question.

"MR. D'ACOSTA is waiting for you downstairs," repeated Liu Po-Yat. "He has expressed to me his hope that you will approve of the dinner which he took the liberty of ordering."

"Dinner — you said that he ordered —" Marie was thoroughly roused.

"Gray molossol caviar as first course," went on the Manchu woman. "He had noticed in the dining room that you are fond of it."

"I never had any caviar since I came here."

"No? Perhaps, then, on board ship,"

"He wasn't there."

"Somebody may have told him," said the Manchu woman. "Anyway, it will be served tonight. He gets his own caviar direct from Astrakhan — through the courtesy of Prince Pavel Kokoshkine."

Suddenly, unreasoningly, the situation struck Marie as startlingly amusing.

"Liu," she asked, "far be it from me to butt into your private affairs. But — *what* do you know about molossol caviar? *How* do you know? And *who* taught you to express your views in such ripping English, old dear?"

The Manchu woman looked at Marie for a long time, silently, doubtingly. Then she seemed to make up her mind.

"My father," she said — and she said it as a New Yorker might mention that his people were Knickerbockers, not boastingly, but as a simple statement of fact — "was the hereditary captain-general of the Seventh Manchu Banner Corps. He was a cousin-in-blood to the Son of Heaven, a *nurhachi* — an iron-capped prince. For years he was Chinese minister for the old Buddha, the dowager empress, in different European capitals. I was educated abroad. I am —" Again she spoke unboastingly "— an aristocrat."

"Oh, you are? And today you are —" She indicated the other's neat uniform.

"Today," came the rejoinder, "I am still an aristocrat, still a cousin to the Son of Heaven."

"But the Son of Heaven has been deposed and imprisoned."

"Indeed?"

Marie laughed.

"Not a very sound believer in the Chinese republic, in lusty young Democracy, are you?" she asked.

"Are *you*?"

"What have I to do with China? I am an American."

"Oh, yes," — the other gave a gliding smile — "I almost forgot."

Marie smiled back. She liked the other better and better.

"Of course," she said, "being a woman and an American, I am curious. Tell me — why didn't you ask me to mind my own business?"

"Because I trust you."

"Why do you trust me, a stranger?"

"Perhaps I do not consider you altogether a stranger."

"Flattering, old dear!"

"And perhaps," continued the other, "it is just a woman's whim."

" 'Sisters under the skin,' eh? All right. Let's stick together. But — Which reminds me — *why* Moses d'Acosta?"

"He has money," coolly replied Liu Po-Yat.

But the other was not deceived.

"Now you're giving me an Oriental half-truth. Of course he has the tin. But there are also other reasons why you want me to dine with him."

"Perhaps," smiled Liu Po-Yat.

"That's right." Marie laughed. "Pull the Buddha stuff! No way of persuading you to tell me the real truth?"

"Some other time."

"Very well. The main question is: Would you dine with him if you were me?"

"If I had to." Liu Po-Yat pointed to the manager's dunning note.

"I guess you're right. But — what'll I do with him? I feel a bit like the fox-terrier who runs after the motorcar. What'll he do with it after he catches up with it?"

"Remember that you are a woman — and clever — and beautiful," the Manchu woman replied. She turned to the telephone, "Shall I tell the desk clerk?"

"No; go down yourself and speak to Mr. d'Acosta. Bring him up with you in half an hour. No, thanks!" — to the other's offer. "Far be it from me to ask a cousin of the Son of Heaven to help me with my gown. Anyway, I'm going to wear my rose charmeuse, and it's a self-hooker. Wait." — as the Manchu was about to open the door. "Tell him that I prefer my champagne rather sweet — Russian style."

"Do you?" asked Liu Po-Yat. "So does the Prince Pavel Kokoshkine. You will get on very well with him."

"Is the prince going to be at dinner tonight?"

"No. The prince would like to dine with you tomorrow night."

"Wh-what?"

"If it is agreeable to you, Prince Kokoshkine would be honored. He will call for you tomorrow night at seven."

LIU PO-YAT had shuffled out of the room before Marie could find words to do justice to her stupefaction. Two dinner invitations, from two strangers! And she was enough of a woman of the world to realize that both invitations were the result of her financial embarrassment, that somehow Moses d'Acosta as well as Prince Kokoshkine must have found out about it.

"Can't be helped," she thought, as she chose a necklace of mutton-fat jade, looked at her other jewels, considering if she should pawn them.

"Not yet," she decided.

She rummaged in her jewel-box; then, when her fingers encountered the little Chinese vase which her father, explaining his wish by a reference to his Scottish superstitions, had asked her to take along, she hesitated. She liked it. It was no bigger than a thumb-nail, but absolutely perfect in shape and color, green, with two gold dragons as handles, and painted on the inside with figures so small that one would need a magnifying glass to make them out. She picked it up now; then, obeying a curious instinct, slipped it in the fold of her girdle.

She surveyed herself in the mirror, smiled back at her reflection in the glass.

"You'll have to play salamander tonight," she addressed herself. "And — tomorrow night —" She wondered. She had never seen the Russian, but knew about him, as did all Canton — Prince Pavel Kokoshkine — a figure both romantic and pathetic!

HE WAS a Russian aristocrat of the old regime, who had fought through the war as a captain of Cossacks. Like many of his class, he had found himself unprepared for the brutal sweep of the revolution. He did not know what to do. The basis of his life was smashed. So he left Russia and, embittered, like many others of his race and caste, turned his eyes eastward, to Mongolia, China — the yellow lands whence, centuries earlier, certain of his Tatar ancestors had come. China, caught in the backwash of its own revolutionary troubles, with the Manchus intriguing in the north, the Japanese in Shantung, and ultraradical elements in the south, was more than ready to avail itself of his military knowledge, though in his own country he had been identified with reactionary politics. Today he was a major-general in the Chinese Republican army, stationed in Canton, with headquarters not far from the Nan-Hai prison and in command over the Southern Shen-chi Ying, or "Augustly Divine Mechanism Army," as the Chinese call their foreign-drilled field forces. He seldom set foot in the Shameen, the European quarter, avoided all intercourse with Europeans and Americans as much as he could, and lived in the manner of a mandarin — and he had asked Marie to dine with him tomorrow night!

SHE WAS perturbed as she thought of it, and felt rather relieved when the door opened and Liu Po-Yat announced Mr. Moses d'Acosta.

"Good-evening," he said.

"Good-evening, Mr. d'Acosta."

He was completely sure of himself, neither brazen nor malapert in the way he bent over her hand nor was he embarrassingly apologetic for his unconventional invitation. Suddenly, he walked over to the center-table, picked up the hotel bill and tore it negligently across and across.

"That's all right," he said, in answer to Marie's expostulation. "It was just a silly mistake on the part of Monsieur Pailloux."

"But —"

"What have I to do with it? Why, I own the hotel." He bowed. "You will be my guest, Miss Campbell."

"But —"

"My dear young lady, there are no obligations. I've been often the guest of —" He coughed, was silent.

"Whose guest?"

"Well, shall we call him your uncle? Or shall we call him Mr. Mavropoulos? Or shall we go straight back into ancient history and call him — ah — what is the old Tatar title he loved so? — the Ssu Yueh, eh, Miss Campbell?"

Marie recoiled before the avalanche of meaningless words. Yet, looking at the man's cold eyes, she knew that meaning there was in them, grave, ominous.

"But — what —"

Almost instinctively, she choked the questions that crowded to her lips as she happened to catch the Manchu woman's eyes, with a sharp message of warning in their depths.

"Quite so," she went on lamely. "Shall we go downstairs?"

"Just a moment, please!"

He crossed the room in a leisurely manner. In the farther corner stood an inlaid and lacquered rosewood table that supported the many Chinese curios on which she had squandered her quarter's remittance during her strolls through the bazaars — bronze and jade, but mostly porcelain. He picked up and examined a few of the pieces.

"Charming!" he said, as he held up a tiny vase of crackled ruby and green. He looked at her narrowly. "Pardon me —"

"Yes, Mr. d'Acosta?"

"Have you, by any chance, a specimen of Tchou-fou-yao porcelain?"

There was something in the innocent-enough question which filled her with uneasiness, caused her to look, as if for support, at the Manchu woman who stood there silent and rigid. She could have sworn that d'Acosta had intercepted the look, that a slight tremor of rage, quickly suppressed, was running through him. The Manchu woman coughed. Something dramatic was in the atmosphere, something almost sinister — and Marie gave a little shudder.

"Why," she replied, and she had to control herself to keep from stammering, "I am not an expert when it comes to Chinese art, I just like these things — hardly know their names —"

"Of course you don't!" said Mr. d'Acosta, with a gliding wink in his eyes that gave the lie to her words. "Shall we go down to dinner before the Chinese cook gives way to his racial leanings and puts rats' tails into our caviar?"

He said this with a laugh. But again Marie Campbell was conscious of a tragic undercurrent.

SHE LEFT the room and walked quickly downstairs to the crimson-and-gold dining room, the man by her side, both talking vaguely about the weather.

The last she saw, as she half turned on the threshold of her room, was the

Manchu woman staring after her, an inscrutable message in her eyes.

The scene in the dining room was typical of the snobbish, self-centered foreign colony in the Shameen. The place might have been a Broadway cabaret, a restaurant in the Chicago Loop, a London supper club, or a shimmering, glistening dance place of the Parisian boulevards. Marie saw, felt. The scene depressed her, and she was grateful to Moses d'Acosta, who, helping her to caviar and champagne, said, with quick, almost feminine intuition:

"Don't you mind them. I know how you feel about China."

"Do you?"

"Of course. And these people do not matter. China is like a huge lump of rubber. You can make an impression on it by pressing hard. But take your fingers away — and the rubber will jump straight back into place. There will not even be a mark left. And these people here — with their jewels and their low-cut dresses and their millions — they'll die some day — and China will live."

"Why, I've been told that you are a multimillionaire yourself — and your interests in China —"

"Quite right. I am rich. But I am an idealist, a constructive idealist. I am a good friend of China. I wish I could make you see it. Then perhaps you would help me, instead of trying to —"

"What?"

"Play 'possum — that's what you call it in America, eh? Never mind. We'll talk about it some other time."

She was about to tell him that, honestly, she did not know what he was driving at.

"Mr. d'Acosta," she began, "I assure you —"

"Never mind, Miss Campbell," he repeated.

A little later he referred again to her apocryphal uncle.

"Mr. Mavropoulos used to like this place. It amused him."

"Mr. Mavropoulos?"

"Call him the Ssu Yueh; call him by his Tatar title, if you prefer. I don't think the republic will mind."

He accompanied his remarks with a low laugh, as if to warn her that she wouldn't tell the truth, and that he knew she wouldn't.

"I hope you are enjoying this little party," he said. "I owe it to your uncle's memory to be nice to you."

"I don't call that a compliment," she replied, and, the next moment, his words echoing in her mind, she caught at something in their meaning — when he had mentioned her apocryphal uncle's "memory." The little mischievous imp in her heart caused her now to probe more deeply into the mystery she felt gathering about her, to throw out a slightly grieved:

"Did you say my uncle's *memory?* Is he —" She paused, wondering how far she dare go.

"Yes," d'Acosta replied; "he is dead. They got him. He always knew they would. And you hadn't really heard that he died?"

"No," she replied, truthfully enough, tremendously thrilled, curious what would come next.

"And yet you left America — came here —"

"On an impulse." Again she spoke the truth.

"Strange coincidence!" He stared at her, his fingers nervously curled round the stem of his champagne glass. "Then, I take it, you haven't seen the papers recently. The *North China Gazette* had quite an article — sensational — but only so to the initiated. Here you are!" He drew from his pocket a newspaper clipping. "Outsiders wouldn't be able to make head or tail of it. It's put in the form of a literary curiosity, a translation of some ancient bit of Chinese mysticism — I suppose you have the cipher —"

"I'll read it afterward," she replied, cramming the clipping into her purse.

"Very well." And, to her disappointment, he led the conversation back to impersonalities, to interrupt himself, with the same disconcerting suddenness and to ask her again the curiously innocent, curiously disturbing question he had put to her in her room.

"Tell me, Miss Campbell; have you not really a specimen of Tchou-fou-yao porcelain?"

"But," — she was becoming embarrassed at the tremendous earnestness that throbbed in his accents — "Mr. d'Acosta —"

"Tchou-fou-yao," he insisted. "The porcelain of emperors! A tiny vase no bigger than a thumb-nail, with two gold dragons snarling over its lizard-green surface, an orifice belled like the cup of a flower, and painted on the inside with infinitesimal figures."

Marie's hand stole to her girdle. She felt the little vase there, said to herself that it seemed to tally with the one of which d'Acosta was speaking. She felt sorry for the man. Should she tell him? Should she show him the vase? Then she remembered her father's strange warning the day they had parted: "Don't show it to people, and don't talk about it unless you absolutely have to." She gave a little shudder of apprehension. What was this mystery into which she felt herself drawn as if into a whirlpool? This stranger knew about it, the Manchu maid, and also her father. What was there back of it all? Why had her father never spoken to her about it? Then she recalled her own feelings during the last few months; how, subconsciously, it had seemed to her that China mattered more to her than she knew and that — yes; the realization came like a shock — that she mattered to China.

She felt disturbed, nervous, but decided to hedge for time. She would talk to the Manchu maid, beg her to explain. She would cable and write to her father. In the meantime, she would fence with d'Acosta.

"Why," she said, "you talk like a typical collector — the frantic sort, you know, who holds his friends' Wedgwood teacups upside down and then pronounces them to be forgeries!"

But her humor was forced, and he brushed it aside with an impatient gesture.

"Don't play with me," he said, "Can't I make you see? Can't I make you understand?" He was tremendously in earnest, and for a moment Marie felt like confessing that she had been playing with him. But, somehow, she again recalled her father's warning. "But — Miss Campbell — please — won't you —" He slurred, stopped.

Again the little mischievous imp rose in her heart and whispered to her to fathom this mystery.

"Mr. d'Acosta," she said ingenuously, "why don't you tell me the truth?"

"Eh?" He looked up sharply.

"I mean, rather, why don't you put *all* your cards on the table?"

"All my cards? But — you know them all."

"Do I?" she countered.

"You know you do! Don't you — won't you understand? It is not a question with me of dollars and cents. No, no!"

She felt nonplused. Then she decided to aim another shot into the blue, recalling certain conversations between her father and his partner, Jack Henderson, when they were searching for the usual explanation through which too rich people like to excuse their greed to themselves.

"Power," she said serenely. "It's power you're after, Mr. d'Acosta!"

"No. Power — why — that's an old tale to me. I am bored with power. What I want is something big, basic! And if you have any of your uncle's blood, you would —"

"Here's my mysterious uncle again!" thought Marie, and the next moment Mr. d'Acosta features were blotted into a reddish-purple smudge as a great shadow fell across the table.

Marie, looking up, beheld the Peking banker, Sun Yu-Wen, whom, a few days earlier, she had watched in such animated conversation with her host. His immense body was dressed in a rather extravagantly Peking style — a long robe of orange-colored, satin-lined grenadine silk embroidered with black bats, and on his round cap a button of transparent red, the emblem of a mandarin of the first class, worn in calm defiance of the fact that the republic had forbidden the wearing of imperial insignia.

"Ah — good-evening!" His words were soft; his fat, ivory-yellow, pas-sionless face was suffused with a patient kindliness. Yet, for all this kindliness, he gave Marie the impression of something impersonal, very ancient, very tired, even, in a passive way, unhuman.

Mr. d'Acosta had risen and bowed. The other had returned the salutation, Chinese fashion, with his hands clasped over his huge chest. Both looked at each other tensely, observantly. To Marie, it was like a scene out of a play — a moment of tremendous suspense, of waiting — for what? "Enemies," — the melodramatic thought came to her — "bitter enemies!" Yet the smiles on keen Semitic and bland Mongol faces were not sneers. It was a smile from the heart, of genuine mutual liking.

Still, as she heard the gliding Manchu words which presently the Chinaman addressed to d'Acosta, although she could not make out the meaning of a single syllable, she sensed in them a certain minatory undercurrent, and saw it confirmed by the look of almost alarmed inquiry that came into the Levantine's eyes. He replied in Manchu, in tones that were clear, high-pitched, but somehow marred and tainted.

Then, on another buzzing, purring word from the Pekingese, d'Acosta shrugged his shoulders, spread his lean hands with a gesture as if submitting to the inevitable, and turned to her.

"Miss Campbell," he said, "allow me to present Mandarin Sun Yu-Wen."

"Charmed," she replied. Her uneasy fear came and went in waves.

Sun Yu-Wen lowered his obese bulk a little gingerly into the frail Louis-Quinze chair. He smiled at d'Acosta.

"I suppose," he said in English, "it is all settled."

"No, I told you — nothing is settled," the Levantine replied, with the suspicion of a snarl.

"Oh, is that so?"

Sun Yu-Wen turned to Marie, and again the fear of this secret dramatic combat of unknown forces into which she felt herself drawn against her will rose in her soul. She was on the point of blurting out the truth — that she knew nothing, that she had simply followed a hoydenish, adventurous impulse, that she was sorry — when, as from a great distance, she heard Sun Yu-Wen's voice, soft, insistent.

"Ah — then there is still hope for me?"

"Listen — I —" She could not go on. Her confession choked her. She looked pitifully at Sun Yu-Wen.

"Never mind," he said. "Presently you will decide. Presently you will follow your whim or, perhaps, your conviction and play — ah — Fate to a very great issue." He turned to d'Acosta.

"My friend," he continued, "it is strange indeed how back of everything there is the soft hand of woman, how the fate of the many millions hangs always and always from a woman's jeweled earrings — in China — in Europe — belike in the moon. A woman, willful and stubborn as only a woman can be — or a cat! What does it say in the classics? *'Po-nien-jou-chi i-tien-jou-ki'* — 'Stubborn as a rock, hard as ancient lacquer.'"

Again he addressed Marie.

"An appropriate quotation, don't you think?" he asked. "Perhaps — although you do not speak the language of your native land —" and Marie looked up, startled, when she understood that the fact of China being her birthplace was known to the mandarin "— you are familiar with our literature, at least in translation. Perhaps," — he lowered his voice —

"you even take an interest in such rubbish as a brittle bit of Tchou-fou-yao porcelain."

Marie could not restrain herself any longer. With a choked mumble of apology, she rose and almost ran from the dining room.

HER FIRST impulse was to go to her room. But she reflected that perhaps one or both of the men would follow her. Finally she thought of an upstairs parlor, reserved for the use of women guests. She went to it quickly. It was empty except for a soft-footed Mongol maid. She sat down and lit a cigarette, and it was not long before calmer reflection came to her and with it, typically, her American sense of humor and her inherited Scots common sense of building up and investigating logically, constructively, fearlessly. She walked over to the writing desk, found pencil and cable-blanks, and scribbled rapidly:

Anthony Campbell,
Broad Street, New York, U. S. A.
Cable immediately, care Grand Hotel, particulars about vase; also let me know about Uncle Mavropoulos.

She stopped, considered if she should ask for money; then decided she would not. She knew her father would order her to return by the next steamer, and she was not yet ready. She was still a remittance-woman, and here was China, mysterious, fascinating, beckoning. Here was adventure! She called to the maid:

"Take this down to the desk. Have them charge it up."

When the maid had left, Marie remembered d'Acosta's allusion to the article in the *North China Gazette* in regard to the death of her mythical uncle, who seemed to have gone under a variety of names. She took the clipping from her purse and looked at it. It was entitled:

Translation
of an Ancient Example
of Tatar-Chinese Mysticism

and read:

Omniscient Gautama! Far-seeing, all seeing Tathagata!

How multiform the consolation of Thy Word! How marvelous Thy Understanding! Was this, then, also one of the myriad illusions painted before Thy eyes by Mara in the black, black night when the earth rocked like a chariot of war in the shock of battle?

"My word!" She put down the clipping. "Just about as clear as pea soup!"

She was still puzzled when, a few minutes later, the maid returned.

"Send off the cable?" asked Marie.

"Yes, missy."

"Thanks! By the way, you couldn't find out if those two gentlemen I dined with are still in the hotel?"

"Yes, missy. They drove off in carriage five, ten minute back."

"Thank you again."

She crossed over to the telephone, gave the desk clerk strict instructions that she was at home to nobody, and took the elevator up to her room, deciding on the way that now was the time to "pump" the Manchu maid.

SHE REACHED her room, switched on the electric light, and went toward her bedroom. There, suddenly, she shrieked as she stared straight ahead.

For there, on the bedroom threshold, she saw Liu Po-Yat stretched out in a darkening pool of blood.

Marie rushed over to the woman.

Liu Po-Yat was bleeding to death from a dozen knife-wounds. She had almost reached a state of coma. Marie gathered all her courage. She knelt down and lifted up the maid's bleeding head.

The freezing lips tried to speak. A gurgle came from the contracting throat. Finally a few incoherent words peaked out.

"*Chuen to yan —*" And again, "*Chuen to yan —* "

"Please!" implored Marie "Speak English — oh, please —"

"*Chuen to yan,*" repeated the other. "*Chuen to yan.*" — as if trying to give a message.

"*Chuen to yan?*" echoed Marie.

"Yes! Remember! Tell him —"

"Who?"

"Your — friend."

"Tell me! Who is the friend you mean? D'Acosta?" Liu Po-Yat shook her head negatively, "The mandarin?"

"No —" the dying woman gurgled out the words "— not friends — those — like other will be —" Suddenly she revived a little. She lifted her right hand in a supreme spasm of energy;

then, even as her body was stiffening, she pointed into the bedroom.

Marie rose, crossed the threshold. She found her jewel-box upset, its contents strewn over the table itself, a few scattered on the floor.

Her hand went to her girdle. The little Tchou-fou-yao vase — that is what the murderers had been looking for!

No piece of jewelry was missing.

Who was the assassin? Moses d'Acosta? Sun Yu-Wen? But the next moment she dismissed the suspicion. For she had dined with them, and the Chinese maid in the parlor had seen them drive off. And the dying woman had not mentioned either of them, but had spoken repeatedly, insistingly of *"Chuen to yan"* — whatever the Mongol monosyllables meant.

"Who, then, did it?" she asked herself. "And what is this vase? What is its sinister significance?"

She took it out, looked at it, examined the lizard-green surface, the tiny painting on the inside.

What was its meaning, its secret? And what had she to do with it? Or, perhaps, came the next thought, her mother, who had died in giving her birth, here in China, where her father had married her, whence he had returned white-haired and rather bitter and taciturn — her mother, whom her father never mentioned, or her grandfather?

But murder had been committed, and she realized that she must notify the hotel management.

SHE WENT downstairs and entered the private office of Monsieur Paul Pailloux, the manager, a pudgy Parisian exile who carried his black beard ahead of him like a battering-ram and who bowed before her with opulent superciliousness.

"Ah — Miss Campbell!" he said. "That bill — it was a mistake —"

"It isn't about the bill."

"No? Then — what can I do for you?"

"You can send for the police,"

"Police? Ah — your delicious American sense of humor —"

Marie's father would have been shocked if he could have heard her slangy reply.

"Cut it out! There's nothing humorous in murder!"

"Murder? Ah — *nom de Dieu!* Murder?"

"Exactly." And she told him.

Her immediate reaction after she had finished telling Monsieur Pailloux was one of surprise — at the other's lack of surprise.

"Are you sure, Miss Campbell?" he asked,

"What do you mean — am I sure? Didn't I see her? Didn't she talk to me before she died?"

"What did she say?"

"Just a few words."

"What exactly, Miss Campbell?" insisted the Frenchman.

It was partly her revolt at the man's cold-blooded curiosity, partly obedience to a peculiar impulse telling her that Liu Po-Yat's dying words had not been meant for everybody's ears which caused her to reply evasively:

"I couldn't make out. I was naturally excited."

"Of course," he said soothingly.

"Let's go up to my room."

"No," he said in a kindly manner. "Such a harrowing experience — I shan't permit you —" He walked to the door. "I shall go upstairs myself and investigate. Rest here until I return." He left the office, closing the door.

It was a small room, hardly big enough to hold a roll-top desk, three chairs, and, wedged in between desk and wall, a little safe with its door swinging open.

MARIE WAITED, ten minutes, twenty, twenty-five. Finally, impatient, she stepped out, but as she was about to turn toward the elevator, the house detective, a half-caste with a flat, brutish face, stopped her.

"Please wait in there," he said. "Monsieur Pailloux just sent for me. And he wants no scandal, no excitement — you understand, don't you?"

She went back into the office and sat down. She was in a conflicting state of mind. She felt deeply moved at the Manchu woman's tragic death. She also felt conscious of a personal loss, rather more selfish. For Liu Po-Yat had evidently been familiar with the coiling of the mysterious forces which were sucking Marie into their whirlpool, had doubtless only been waiting for a propitious moment to take the American girl into her confidence. And now she was dead; Marie felt very lonely and young and homesick.

Time and again her thoughts returned to the little vase. Twice she took it from the fold of her girdle, looked at it. She had taken it out for the third time when, outside the door, she heard footsteps, voices, and she tried to slip the vase back. But her nail caught in the thin fabric; a seam ripped. She realized that she could not return the vase to its hiding-place, and, dimly sensing that she did not want whoever entered to find the thing in her hand, she looked round for a place in which to conceal it — the safe! It was open. Rapidly she stepped up to it and pushed the vase into the farthest corner among a lot of papers.

SHE HAD already straightened up when the door opened and Pailloux and the house detective entered.

"Well?" asked Marie. "What did you find out?"

Pailloux smiled.

"We found that you were mistaken. No murder has been committed."

"But — Liu Po-Yat — I saw her —"

"Doubtless a hallucination, Miss Campbell. Mr. De Smett and I —" pointing at the detective "— went to your rooms, and —" he spread eloquent hands "— we found nothing."

"N-nothing?" Marie stammered.

"A hallucination." Pailloux smiled. "Perhaps — pardon — a little too much champagne?"

"Too much champagne — my eye!" cried Marie. "You are crazy, both of you!"

"Are we?" asked the detective. He turned to the manager. "Perhaps Miss Campbell would prefer to see with her own eyes?"

"I'll say I do!" affirmed Marie.

"Very well."

And, followed by De Smett, Pailloux led the way to her suite.

"Look!" he said, as they entered,

Marie looked, looked again, doubting, for a moment, her sanity. No body was there, no blood spots, no signs of struggle, of murder. She went into her bedroom and glanced at the dressing-table. The jewel-box was in its old place, unopened.

No doubt, she said to herself, the manager himself, with the help of the detective and most likely other employees, had utilized the half-hour she spent in the office to remove the body and all traces of the tragedy and straighten the rooms. They had done it for a reason. What was it?

Very quickly, and as rationally as she could, she gathered her straying thoughts. By tomorrow her father would have replied to her cable. That would give her some sort of clue to the mystery. Until then she would have to make the best of a bad situation. So she smiled at the two men.

"Gentlemen," she said, "I apologize. I must have had a drop too much champagne. Shocking, don't you think?"

Pailloux coughed.

"Miss Campbell," he began, "I would — I regret — but —"

"What? Come through!"

"You are —"

"Under arrest!" The detective completed the other's sentence and took a step in the girl's direction. She stood her ground.

"Why," she said, "this time it's you who must have had a drop too much to drink! Arrest me — me — you said?"

"Yes."

"But I thought you said no murder has been committed?"

"There hasn't," said the detective.

"What's my crime, then?"

"Crime?" Pailloux shrugged distressed shoulders. "Hardly a crime — at least —"

"At least?"

"If you prefer to make immediate restitution, Miss Campbell —"

"Restitution of what, may I inquire?"

"Of a little Chinese vase. A bit of Tchou-fou-yao porcelain," smiled the manager, "Come, Miss Campbell! You are accused of — pardon — not stealing it — no, no —"

"Nothing as crude as that, eh?"

"Of course not! But perhaps you saw the little vase, liked it too much, eh?"

"You'd better give it back," growled the detective.

"Oh!" She drew in her breath. Here was the vase again. She had hidden it in the safe. Doubtless it was this tiny piece of porcelain which the murderer had come to steal, which the Manchu woman had protected with her life, not knowing that her mistress had taken it along. D'Acosta wanted the vase. So did Sun Yu-Wen. And her father — She remembered his words.

"Monsieur Pailloux," she said, "I do not know what you are talking about."

"Miss Campbell," now implored the man, "I beg of you — you put me into a very awkward situation —"

"Not half so awkward as the situation you are putting me in!"

"I am helpless. The person who accuses you —"

"Who is that person?"

"You will be told at the police station — in jail!" cried the detective roughly.

"Oh — jail, is it?"

"Please," said Pailloux, "do not force me to go that far. Give up the vase —"

"I haven't got it!"

"But —"

"The police station — right-o!" she continued. "Heavens — what would the New York society editors say if they knew?"

"Miss Campbell," cried the manager, "you are frivolous!"

"And you talk exactly like my father!"

"You will be searched at the station — and if they find the vase —"

"Miss Campbell," cut in the detec-

tive, "I want to warn you that everything you say —"

"Will be used against me?" She laughed, "How gorgeously like home, sweet home! America — ah — that reminds me — I want you to notify the American consul at once, Monsieur Pailloux."

"Can't be done!" De Smett interrupted quickly.

"Is *going* to be done!" said the girl. She turned to the manager. "I'll come along without a fuss if you telephone the American consul right now, in my presence, or let me ring him up myself. If you refuse —"

"Well," asked the detective, "what would happen? Going to hit me over the wrist with the fringe of your shawl?"

"Don't forget — we are bound to pass through the hotel lobby. And I give you warning. I went to Vassar, misspent two years there — so the dean told me. But I was cheerleader at our basketball matches. And, when it comes to shouting, why — to quote my favorite black-face Broadway comedian — you haven't heard nothing yet."

The two men looked at each other silently, questioningly.

"Do I win?" asked the girl.

"You do!" growled the detective.

"Good! I'll ring up the consul."

"Let me do it," said the manager.

"All right, my dear Gaston!" laughed the girl. "Politeness first in a Frenchman — eh? — even when he is as crooked as a bull-pup's tail!"

The manager winced, was going to say something, thought better of it, and unhooked the telephone receiver while Marie stood over him, telling him word for word what to say:

"Hello? Mr. Coburn? Pailloux talking. A young American girl has been arrested . . . A Miss Campbell. . . Theft. She wants you to come to the jail . . . In an hour? All right!" He slammed the receiver back.

FIVE MINUTES later, the girl, sitting between the two men, was driving through the Shameen, out of it, and into the native quarter.

In ten minutes the carriage stopped in front of a tall, imposing structure, with, above its broad entrance way, an ornate Chinese sign in scarlet and. gold flanked by a smaller one which read, in English:

SOUTHERN CHINESE REPUBLIC
Headquarters of Canton
Metropolitan Police

"Here we are," said Pailloux. "And — Miss Campbell — I give you one more chance — if you want to give up the vase —"

" 'Lay on, Macduff!' " she quoted frivolously. And, with a laugh, she preceded the two men into the building.

In the room she entered were half a dozen desks along the walls, behind which sat pompous Cantonese captains of police as well as a few Europeans, attended by orderlies, and, at the farther end, on a platform, a red-faced Englishman was presiding, flanked by two Tatars in black gowns and strange head-dresses. Afterward Marie found out that it was a police headquarters and court of law combined and that, presided over by the red-faced Englishman, and in deference to the turbulent times with revolution and counter-revolution rife on every side, justice was being given here day and night.

But Marie's joy at the thought that here people spoke English and that a

number of the officials were Europeans was short-lived. For while Pailloux and De Smett had stepped forward to register their complaint, a friendly Liverpool sailor who, as he explained to her, had come here as a witness to help a Chinese pal out of trouble, told her in answer to her question that, ever since the establishment of the Southern republic, all the European riffraff of the treaty ports had found service under the republican administration.

"Rotten bloody swine they are — if ye'll pardon my language," said the sailor. "By the way, lydy, wot are *you* doin' 'ere, if I may arsk?"

"I've been arrested."

"But it's the Chinky police station! Yer gotta be judged by the European courts."

"Oh!" Here was news for Marie.

But when she was asked to step in front of the red-faced Englishman, who was the presiding judge and whom Pailloux addressed as "Mr. Winchester," and when she told him that he had no right to try her here, the man only laughed.

"Don't talk to me of rights!" he said. "Might — that's what counts here —"

"Wait till the American consul comes."

"All right," he said; "I'll wait. In the meantime — I do not want to be too severe. I'll dismiss the complaint if you give up the vase."

"I haven't got it."

"Stubborn young baggage, aren't you?"

He spoke in Chinese to one of the orderlies. The latter left, and returned a few seconds later with two elderly, capable-looking Chinese women. The judge spoke to them, then turned to Marie.

"They're going to search you," he said. "Go — and don't make a fuss,"

MARIE WAS furious, but submitted without a word. She was led into another room. The searching was thorough, but, of course, the two women found nothing and told the judge so when they had returned to the courtroom.

The judge turned a hectic purple.

"Miss Campbell," he said, "I warn you most solemnly. You are in a dangerous situation. Tell me — now — immediately. Here," — quickly thrusting out pencil and paper — "don't tell me; write it down." He dropped his voice to a whisper. "What did you do with the vase?"

"I refuse to answer. You have no right to —"

"Right be blowed! Might — that's what counts; didn't I tell you? Going to own up?"

"No!" Her eyes gleamed. "And I —"

The judge interrupted her.

"Remove the prisoner!" he shouted, and a Chinese orderly rushed up.

"Remove the prisoner — nothing!" she cried, now thoroughly roused, "I don't know what your laws are here, and I don't care! But —" and suddenly all her great, latent nationalism blazed up into white-hot heat — "I am an American, I insist on *my* rights! And — first of all — I want to know what the charges against me are."

The judge had regained his composure. "A female Saul among the Prophets?" he inquired with irony.

If at that moment she could have cleared up the whole thing, she would not have done so; for it was beginning to become a question of principle with her, national principle as well as personal.

"I insist on my rights," she said. "What are the charges against me? And who preferred them? I tell you again I am an American!"

"Very interesting, I am sure," commented the judge, with a wink in the direction of Pailloux. "But what I say goes." He tinned to the orderly. "Remove the prisoner!"

Marie again faced the judge. This time she was speaking very quietly.

"You are an Englishman?"

"What about it?"

"Do you call this British fair play? And you," — turning to Pailloux — "you call yourself a Frenchman! Bah!" She snapped her fingers derisively. "You are renegades — both of you!"

The two men colored. The hotel manager looked at the other man with a helpless expression; he whispered to him. The judge gave a lopsided smile.

"Very well, Miss Campbell," he said; "I shall tell you since you are so insistent. You are under arrest because you are accused of having purloined a certain vase —"

"I know!" she cut in impatiently. "I want you to tell me who —"

"You are, furthermore, under arrest," continued the judge, "for a much graver reason."

"What?"

"You are suspected of being an enemy of the Southern Chinese Republic, of having conspired with the republic's foes to bring about its downfall."

Momentarily the girl was frightened. But almost immediately she regained her composure.

"I beg your pardon," she said courteously. "But, once more — have I the right to know who preferred these charges against me?"

"Well — just to oblige you — I shall tell you. The charges are brought against you by three people. They are myself, as presiding judge and chief of the Southern Chinese intelligence service, Monsieur Pailloux, and —" he leaned across his desk "— by the Chuen to yan of the Temple of the Protecting Deities."

He stopped, staring at her closely, evidently eager to see what impression the information had made on her. Marie was silent for a few moments. Two thoughts were in her mind. One had to do with the words: *Chuen to yan.* They were the same words which the Manchu woman had used just before she died, when Marie had asked her who had attacked her. What did the words signify? Well, she would ask Mr. Coburn, the American consul; he would be here within the hour. Her other thought dealt with the temple of which Winchester had spoken. She knew it. It was the temple of Canton's guardian saints, though foreigners preferred calling it the "Temple of Horrors." On either side of the entrance gate and farther up the walls were life-sized wood and stone figures that represented people undergoing the tortures inflicted in the ten kingdoms of the Buddhistic hell. There were some being bored through the middle, sawn between two boards, precipitated upon turned-up swords, boiled in oil, or crushed by the slow descent of a red-hot bronze bell. The Temple of Horrors! The Tchou-fou-yao porcelain! And what had she to do with it all? What —

She would own up that it all meant nothing to her — nothing, that she had put the little vase in the hotel safe, that she was just a headstrong, adventurous American girl who had had her fill of adventures and thrills and wanted to go home by the next steamer to the sane life, the safe and sure. She turned to the judge.

Then again, suddenly, she felt a riot of strange sensations surging in her soul and heart. Again she had an impression of half-forgotten things, a gauze-veiled memory of something she had lived through.

All right; there was the American consul; there was her father at the other end of the cable; there was, lastly, the "friend" to whom the dying Manchu woman had referred. Not Moses d'Acosta or Mandarin Sun Yu-Wen. A third! Perhaps — she wondered — Prince Pavel Kokoshkine, the Russian exile in the service of the Southern Chinese Republic, who had invited her to dine with him the next evening!

"Well?" asked Mr. Winchester. "What is the answer?"

"The answer is that I'll go to jail," replied Marie Campbell.

"By Jove!" exclaimed the judge, with something like admiration in his accents, "I must admit that at least when it comes to nerve, you are a Simon-pure American!"

"You'll find out more about that when the consul gets here."

"Doubtless! Doubtless!" He smiled.

He turned again to the orderly, with quick instructions in Chinese. The orderly spoke to Marie.

"Coming, missy?" he asked.

"Right-o, old dear!" said the girl, and followed him.

THE PRISON CELL turned out to be not a prison cell at all but a fair-sized and comfortable-enough room with two large iron-grilled windows, a door that was open, a couch, and a few rocking chairs which spoke eloquently and nostalgically of Grand Rapids, Michigan, U.S.A. She touched their golden-oak wood tenderly.

"If anybody had ever told me, in the days when I went in for early-Colonial furniture, that Grand Rapids would make me feel sentimental, I would have called him a liar!" she said out loud, very much to the surprise of an East Indian who was hovering round the door, evidently the jailer.

He was a brown-laced, agate-eyed *baboo*, very fat and oily, and clad in white gauze, which, considering his fantastic bodily contours, gave him a grotesque appearance.

Twice she talked to him. But each time he shook his head.

"Against regulation number fifteen, paragraph three, to talk to prisoners suspected of political crimes. Yes-s-s, *memsahib!*"

Marie laughed.

"How I adore being addressed as 'memsahib'! Really — it thrills me so! It makes me feel no end Kipling!"

But it made no impression on the man. He continued to stare at her silently with that passionless gaze of the Indo-Aryan to whom eternities are only a vulgar matter of a yawn and a stretch, and to whom excitement and interest in worldly subjects are merely the ungentlemanly and unintelligible pastimes of crude Western barbarians. Minutes moved on in a sullen, maddening procession.

ONLY ONCE was the silence interrupted, savagely, by a scream, then an outburst of elaborate quarter-deck profanity. She was walking up and down at the time. When she heard the noise, she stopped near the door and looked out, while the *baboo*, who had turned to see whence the row came, had his back to her. Across the corridor, not very far away, she saw another room with the door open, and inside, being cross-examined by two bullying Chinese officials, the Liverpool sailor who had befriended her in the courtroom.

"You will stay here until you confess to whom you delivered the guns," said one of the officials.

Again the sailor broke into wholehearted profanity, winding up with:

"Just yer wyte till I gets out o' 'ere, yer plurry, rotten chink yer! I'll —" he choked with rage "— aw — the things wot I'm goin' to do to yer — wot ho — it'll be a bleedin' shyme! Just wyte!"

"Bravo!" cried Marie. "Hello there, companion in misery! Three cheers!"

But immediately the door to the sailor's room was shut from the inside, while the *baboo* turned to her.

"*Memsahib*," he implored, "it is against the regulations —"

"All right, Booker T.!" interrupted the girl. "Don't get excited."

She sat down. A dozen thoughts whirled in her brain. If she could only decipher the clipping from the *North China Gazette* which Mr. d'Acosta had given to her! She opened her purse, looked at it. It was useless. And all the time the *baboo* stared at her, without uttering a single word and with an air of worldly detachment which finally got on her nerves.

"Look here, you piece of coffee-éclair fraud!" she cried at last, thoroughly annoyed. "Say something, or I'll throw this chair at you!"

The *baboo* stared at her,

"*Memsahib*," he replied, with the precise and unhuman deliberation of a phonograph, "speaking in my strictly official capacity, I beg to point out to you that it is against the law of the Southern Chinese Republic to throw chairs or other hard substances at the heads of members of the judiciary. Please, *memsahib*, be so kind as not to throw the chair!"

Marie burst into laughter.

"Booker T.," she said irreverently, "you get the prize! I herewith endow you with the brown-velvet derby hat and the India-rubber doughnut! As a George Ade, you are a perfect dumbbell!"

After which decidedly slangy and unladylike remarks she decided that she was tired. She closed her eyes, falling into easy sleep. It did not seem more than ten minutes when she was called by the *baboo's* falsetto voice.

"Be pleased to awaken, *memsahib*. The American consul has arrived."

She sat up straight.

"The American consul!" she cried. "Show him to me, my lad!"

BUT WHEN, shortly afterward, Mr. Tecumseh Coburn, a tall young man with a high nose, a Virginian drawl and a super-Virginian manner, came in, bowed to her, and waved the *baboo* outside with a courtly but dragooning gesture and sat down across from her, her joy was destined to be short-lived.

"Miss Campbell," he said, "I am afraid you are in a very awkward situation."

"Right-o! That's where you come in."

"I — but —"

"Don't I — I mean my father — pay most exorbitant taxes? Didn't I — again I mean my father — vote for the party which put you into your consular swivel chair?"

"That's exactly it!" said Mr. Coburn. *"Did* your father vote?"

"I believe that he —"

"Or could he have voted if he had wanted to, Miss Campbell?"

"I don't understand,"

"When I heard that they brought you here instead of to the consular court in the Shameen, I became very indignant. I went straight to the Chinese civilian governor and I registered a kick. But that bland Mongol assured me by all his household divinities and proved it to me — yes; proved it to me, for he had cabled to Washington for the official information — that your father never became naturalized, that therefore you had no right to appeal to the American consul."

"Mr. Coburn," maintained the girl stoutly, "I am an American — every bit of me!"

"Yes," he said; "you are. In feeling and —" he smiled " — in looks. In pluck. In resourcefulness. But — nationally — legally — I am so sorry —"

"All right," she replied. "The British consul, then."

"I thought of that. I talked to him. And —" He coughed, was silent.

"Yes?"

"We went back to the Chinese governor together. Mr. Winchester, the judge of this court, was already there."

"What happened?"

"The Chinese authorities produced proof that you are a Chinese subject."

"With the name of Campbell?" she mocked. "I know that I was born in China, but —"

"They proved that, according to an old law not yet abolished by the republic and reaching far back to the days of Tatar dominion, the children of Tatars and kindred Central-Asian races, on both the father's and the mother's side, are Chinese subjects."

"My father is Scotch!"

"What about your mother? Perhaps she — Certainly you ought to know —"

"I ought to know!" cried the girl. "Oh, yes — you are quite right — I ought to know. But —"

She was silent, staring straight ahead of her; she felt utterly alone as suddenly through the mists of her apprehension floated down the full realization of the fact that her father had never taken her into his confidence as to her mother, who and what she had been. Mystery, intrigue, tragedy were on every side of her. Her father must have sensed something of the sort, or he wouldn't have made that allusion to the little Chinese vase. Why, then, had he let her go without telling her the full tale? Her glance crossed the man's, and he took her right hand in his.

"I wish I could help you more," he said. "But — don't you see? I am the American consul, and this is a political case of a foreign government against one of its own subjects. There is diplomatic etiquette — my consular oath. In fact, before the Chinese officials allowed me to see you alone, I had to assure them that —"

"I understand, Mr. Coburn."

"Don't give up the ship, though! I don't know exactly why you are here in this predicament. But I was given to understand by the Chinese officials and by Judge Winchester that you can get out of it simply enough by telling them something — I don't know what — which they seem keen on knowing. It must be political, or they wouldn't be so excited, so upset —"

"Are they really? I am glad of it."

"Why, Miss Campbell?"

"Vindictiveness, revenge! That's the Scots of me! I don't like Mr. Winchester or Pailloux or all the rest."

"Never mind that. Tell them what they want to know and they'll release you at once. They are even willing to pay your passage home. What do you say?"

"I say, 'No!' "

"But — listen —"

"I am grateful to you, Mr. Coburn. But —" She hesitated. She thought of the murdered Manchu woman, of Pailloux's and De Smett's flagrant duplicity, of Winchester's pompous brutality. She was indignant at these people's lack of fair play, and she made up her mind that she would hurt them, even if it were dangerous for herself. They were after the vase for some grave and vital reason. She would not tell them where she had hidden it, or would they dream of searching Pailloux's private safe for it, "Mr. Coburn," she continued, "all this is something to me."

"What?"

"A matter of principle."

"Principle?"

"You are a Virginian, aren't you?"

"I plead guilty, m'lady,"

"And, as a Virginian, aren't there certain principles you respect — deep down in your heart — even though the rest of the world may deem them foolish and quixotic and self-hurting?"

"I reckon that's right."

"Very well. I am the same way. And one of my principles is that I will not quit under fire."

"Bravo!" he cried. "I adore your delicious folly. If I weren't a married man —"

"I am sorry you are," she smiled, "but so glad for the sake of your wife." She was serious again. "Listen —"

"Yes?"

Should she tell him about the murdered Manchu woman? The next moment she decided that she would not. The consul, too, would say that it must have been a case of too much champagne. But she told Mr. Coburn she had cabled her father.

"Oh!" he said, "You cabled?"

"Yes." And, as he looked at her, shaking his head, "What is the matter?"

"I told you martial law has been proclaimed. All cables pass through the censor's hands."

"Oh! You think that my cable —"

"Was most likely never ticked off at all."

"Mr. Coburn," she said, "won't you —"

"Please!" he interrupted. "I know what you want me to do, but I can't. If I send a cable to your father in my private capacity, the censor will stop it, just as he stopped yours. As to my official capacity, I explained to you —"

"Yes. Your oath of office — and the very ticklish political situation, and —" bitterly "— it seems that I am not an American citizen — legally. Oh, it isn't fair!"

"I am so sorry. I do wish there was something I could do to help you —"

"You can. I want to know something about Mr. Moses d'Acosta and Mandarin Sun Yu-Wen. Do you know them?"

"Who doesn't?"

"Are they influential in Canton?"

"Yes — and no. The local officials do not like them, in fact, hate them, would like to see them dead and buried —"

"Then," asked Marie, "seeing how unscrupulous these Southern Chinese officials are, why don't they cause them to disappear?"

"That's where the rub comes in. D'Acosta and Sun Yu-Wen are *too* rich, *too* influential. If anything happened to them — why — heaven alone knows what might come of it. You see, where two are concerned, the Southern republic is really between the devil and the deep blue sea."

"Good enough! What do you know about Prince Pavel Kokoshkine?"

"What all the world knows — that he is a Russian — an aristocrat — a gentleman — and a former officer in the czar's army. He puzzles me. He is an imperialist — an aristocrat — and yet here he is in the service of these Southern radicals. It's beyond me."

"Where does he live?"

"On the other side of the river, not far from Nan-Hai prison, on the corner of the street of the Leaning Plum Tree."

"Thank you."

The consul rose to go, but Marie put her hand on his arm.

"One second," she begged. "There is a British sailor across the landing. He is in trouble, too."

"Oh? — Tommy Higginson?"

"You know him?"

The consul laughed.

"We all do in Canton. In trouble — and serves him right. It seems that he has been doing a little private gun-running, and so he has put himself outside the consular jurisdiction and protection. It looks black for him."

"You can't help him out, can you?"

"Neither I nor my British colleague."

"But," said Marie, "is there a reason in the world why you can't give him — let's say — a few cigarettes, just for the sake of humanity?"

"I reckon I can."

"And — is there any reason why you can't give him some of *my* cigarettes? Finally, is there any reason why, being a Virginia gentleman, you can't turn your back on a lady for a few minutes when she asks you nicely — and although you are the consul, and under consular oath?"

He looked at her significantly; then he laughed.

"Very well," he said, and turned his face to the wall

She opened her handbag and took out a package of Bostanioglo cigarettes she had bought that morning. Rapidly she scribbled a few words on the inside of the box, closed it again and handed it to the consul.

"Here you are," she said. "Give it to Mr. Higginson. Tell him the cigarettes are from me. Tell him they are good cigarettes, that they were made in dear old London. Tell him, furthermore, that the advertisement on the inside cover of the box may make him think of home. You understand?"

The consul smiled. "I think I heard the scratch of a pencil."

"Forget it, please!"

"I will Good-night, Miss Campbell!"

"Good-night, Mr. Coburn! And thanks!"

The consul left and, a few seconds later, the *baboo* returned.

"Booker T.," Marie said, "I am going to take a little nap — on that chair there. So would you mind remaining outside?"

"*Memsahib,* I regret very much, but it is against —"

"I get you, old dear! On the other hand, consider my feminine prejudices and inhibitions. Consider your own sense of delicacy —"

"But —"

"Don't be a little chocolate-éclair-colored jackass! See — I'll curl up on that rocking-chair — and," — suiting the action to her words — "I'll put it right near the door. You can stay just beyond the threshold, where you can look at me any time you want to. I am tired, very tired, but I know I couldn't sleep if you stay here in the room. Aren't you armed with that big revolver of yours?"

"But —"

"Please!"

She gave him a brilliant smile, and — thought Marie — at last he showed certain signs of strictly male humanity. He bowed.

"Yes-s-s, *memsahib,*" he replied, and he took his place beyond the threshold while she sat on the chair near the door, imitating a moment later the deep breathing of an exhausted sleeper, but watching carefully from beneath lowered eyelids and listening to whatever might happen on the landing.

There was a silence — swathing, leaden, and unbroken, except occasionally by the creaking noise of a sentinel outside grounding his rifle or the click-clank-click of a metal scabbard-tip being dragged against the stone pavement as the officers of the night watch went on their rounds.

MARIE GLANCED across her shoulder at the iron-grilled windows. It was still night, heavy, deep violet, with a froth of stars tossed over the crest of the heavens.

She looked at her wrist-watch. Two o'clock in the morning, she could tell, by the rays of the single electric bulb on the landing. She felt despair creeping over her soul, and, pluckily, she decided to fight it back. So she began to marshal her thoughts as logically and constructively as she could. By this time she had completely dismissed any idea of coming to terms with Judge Winchester and Pailloux and whatever political party and influence they represented. These men were intriguing, unscrupulous, thoroughly evil. But what about Moses d'Acosta, the masterful, idealistic Turkish Jew, and about Mandarin Sun Yu-Wen? How did they come into the focus of this dark-coiling adventure? It seemed that they were both dangerous enemies of the Southern radicals — thus, logically, both working for the same end. Too, they seemed to have genuine liking and sympathy for each other. Yet, she remembered, there had been that undercurrent between them as if, somehow, they were opposed one against the other; and both had been anxious about that little Chinese vase which had been the real root of her troubles — which had begun with an overdue hotel bill and had wound up with her here in a political prison. Then there was Prince Pavel Kokoshkine's enigmatic figure, and the *Chuen to yan* of the Temple of Horrors, whom the murdered Manchu woman had mentioned with her dying breath. What did *"Chuen to yan"* mean? Why hadn't she thought of asking the American consul? She was quite angry with herself.

Try as she might, she was not able to fit the pieces of the puzzle into a reasonable whole. There was a missing link, and it consisted in her own relation to this mystery — her own and her mother's. So once more her thoughts returned to the latter. She must have been a Chinese subject, Tatar or Central Asian, but whatever her race and blood, she must have been important during life, even from beyond death.

Marie speculated and wondered. What and who were her mother's people? There was that uncle of hers, dead, murdered — Who, what had he been? How had he been connected with it all? Quite clearly she recalled d'Acosta's words:

"Shall we call him your uncle? Or shall we call him Mr. Mavropoulos? Or shall we go straight back into ancient history and call him — ah — what is the old Tatar title he loved so? The Ssu Yueh?"

Mavropoulos! It sounded to her like a Greek name. How could she be connected with it?

"My word!" she thought. "What a mess!"

She stretched her cramped limbs a little and yawned. But the next moment she imitated again a sleeper's deep breathing as she heard Judge Winchester's pinchbeck Lancashire accents in the corridor:

"All right, Pailloux. We shall see what the man wants."

The door being open at a convenient angle and the *baboo's* back not obstructing her vision, she saw the two men coming along the corridor, saw

them, through a minutely raised eyelid, stop at the door of her room and peer in.

"By Jove!" whispered Winchester. "Fast asleep! Has nerve that girl!"

Then they crossed and entered the room where Higginson was imprisoned.

She heard the judge's first words: "You asked for me?"

"Yes, yer 'Onor," replied the sailor.

"I suppose you have decided to make a clean breast of it, my man."

"Well, yer 'Onor, I got some valuable information for yer. For a price —"

"Name it!"

"I want yer to release me."

"I'll see what can be done. First, the information. About the gun-running, eh?"

"To 'ell with them blanked guns!" came the reply in the picaresque diction of the London docks. "It's something different — and a bleedin' sight more important, cully!"

"Oh!" countered the judge. "For instance —"

Marie sucked in her breath. It was now evident to her that the sailor had read and understood the message which she had scribbled on the inside of the cigarette-box.

"Yes, yer 'Onor!" said the man. "It's about a vase wit' a funny nyme — 'eathenish and chinky —"

"Sssh!" interrupted Winchester.

"Sssh!" echoed Pailloux.

They stepped into the sailor's room and closed the door from the inside, and again there was silence, while Marie waited, excited, expectant. The message she had written on the inside cover of the box had of necessity been short. But she relied on the sailor's shrewd cockney sense to supply the missing links, all the more that she had learned from the consul that the man was in real danger and would grasp at the proverbial straw to save his neck. She glanced in the direction of the window. She did not want morning to come before she had her chance. It was still dark enough outside, with just the faintest sign of morning blazing its purple message. Ten minutes she waited, fifteen, twenty, and the purple morning light increased in vividness; it took on a slight tinge of gold and deep red.

"Dear God, help me!" prayers of her childhood, long forgotten, rose to her lips.

SHE WAITED another five minutes, and then the door of the sailor's room opened and, from beneath lowered eyelids, she saw Winchester and Pailloux on the threshold, and between them Higginson, who was gesticulating for dear life.

"Stroike me pink," he exclaimed, "if I ain't tellin' yer Gawd's truth!"

"I do not believe you," said Pailloux.

"Listen!" continued Higginson. "Call me a sanguinary organ-grinder's ring-tailed monkey if I'm lyin' to yer two gents! I tell yer I seen that 'ere vase —"

"Nom d'un nom d'un nom!" interrupted the hotel manager. "Do not name it! Call it 'the thing!' We told you before that it is dangerous to mention it by name, that nobody, except the judge and me and perhaps three or four important Chinese officials, know of the thing's existence."

"Wot ho! Wot bloody ho!" cried the sailor triumphantly, while Marie blessed his ready mother-wit. "If nobody except yerselves and mebbe 'arf a dozen toffs knows about this 'ere bloomin' — now — thing, then 'ow,

in the nyme of me sainted grandaunt Priscilla, can *I* know about this 'ere syme — now — thing, eh? Don't yer see that I'm givin' it to yer straight?"

"Logical!" suddenly exclaimed the Frenchman. "Absolutely logical!"

"Now ye're talkin', Mister Whiskerando!" said the sailor. "It's the truth, don't yer see?"

"By Jupiter!" admitted Winchester. "I am beginning to believe it myself!"

"Truthful 'Arry — that's wot me mytes calls me aboard ship!" cut in Mr. Higginson in a splendid outburst of seafaring imagination.

Winchester took Pailloux to one side and whispered to him earnestly. Then he approached the sailor once more.

"My man," he said, "we have decided that you are speaking the truth. You could not possibly know about the existence of the — ah — thing unless — well — unless you knew. And you described the thing correctly. You know its name. Very well. We shall give you the chance you ask for."

"All I wants is ten minutes alone with the lydy," said the sailor. "I'll myke 'er 'fess up, or me nyme ain't Truthful 'Arry 'Igginson, gents' I knows wot to say to 'er! I —" again his imagination surged up riotously and magnificently — "I knows a few things about 'er that'd myke yer 'air turn gray. Let me tell you, gents —"

"Some other time. We are in a hurry to put our hands on the thing."

"Right-o! Ten minutes with 'er, mebbe fifteen. Alone. That's all I aisk."

"Alone?" objected Monsieur Pailloux. "But —"

"I got to talk to her gentle-like first. She won't spill unless I gets 'er confidence first — and we got to be alone for that."

"Still, I don't see —" said the Frenchman.

"We'll leave the *baboo* in the room. Oh, yes," — as Higginson was about to expostulate — "got to be done!" He called to the *baboo*. "Hey, there, Hurree Chuckerjee!"

The latter approached and salaamed.

"Yes, *sahib?*"

"Armed, aren't you?"

"Yes, *sahib.*"

"Mr. Higginson is going to talk to Miss Campbell for a few minutes, and you'll stay in the room with them."

"But — yer 'Onor —" interjected the sailor.

"You can talk to her in a whisper, Higginson. And it's up to you to watch, Hurree Chuckerjee — understand?"

"Listen is obey, *sahib!*"

"It's all right," Winchester said to Pailloux. "The windows of the room are barred with iron, and there are sentinels in the street."

"Very well," said Higginson. "I'll talk to 'er. And then, if I'm right and I myke the lydy 'fess up, all ye've got to do is look for the — now — thing after she owns up — and, gents, she'll own up soon enough! And then, after ye've found it, yell squash that there gun-runnin' indictment against me and let me go back to me ship — and wot ho for the briny and Liverpool and the barmaids of the Old Crocodile!"

"Agreed!" said Mr. Winchester.

A MINUTE later, Marie Campbell simulated surprise and indignation when the *baboo* took her by the arm, calling, "Ho, *memsahib!*" and when immediately afterward Winchester, flanked by Higginson and the Frenchman, walked up to her and

told her, with a thin laugh, that he wanted "this person, Mr. Higginson, able-bodied seaman," to have a few minutes' private conversation with her.

"I don't know Mr. — oh —" she cried, "whatever his name!"

"Aw — lydy," cut in the sailor, with every appearance of hurt feelings, "don't yer remember Truthful 'Arry?" He appealed to the judge. "That's gratitude, yer 'Onor! After it was me who 'elped 'er to —"

Marie cut in rapidly, afraid the sailor's imagination might defeat its own ends.

"I don't know you," she repeated.

"Don't you?" smiled the judge.

"But, Miss Campbell," exclaimed Higginson, winking a watery blue eye at her, "don't yer recall as 'ow yer told me *only* larst week —"

"I don't remember a thing!"

"You will remember — presently," said Judge Winchester. He turned to the sailor.

"Higginson," he said, "come straight to my private office when you are through with Miss Campbell. Know where it is, don't you?" He smiled disagreeably.

"Yes, yer 'Onor. It's the third door beyond the turning of the corridor, ain't it?"

"*Mon Dieu*, no!" exclaimed the Frenchman.

"Indeed, no!" echoed Mr. Winchester. "It's the fourth door. Be careful! I shall instruct the guards to let you pass."

"Thanks, yer 'Onor," said the sailor, pulling at his forelock. The two men walked away, while Hurree Chuckerjee and Higginson stepped fully into the room, closing the door, the former remaining near the threshold all the while playing nervously with the butt of

his revolver while the latter walked up to Marie.

"Now, lydy," he said in a loud voice, "I 'ad a long talk with the judge, and I promised 'im I would myke yer 'fess up. Now — come through!"

"I don't know you!"

"Aw, 'ow yer 'urts my feelings!"

"Leave me alone!"

"Look a-'ere!" Higginson sat down close to Marie and dropped his voice to a whisper. "Wot ho, but ye're a bloomin' good actress!"

"Am I not?" Marie whispered back.

"Right-o! I got yer note, lydy — and now — wot are we goin' to do with it — as the monkey sed when 'e 'ad grabbed the red-'ot poker?"

So they conversed in low, tense accents for several minutes, while Mr. Hurree Chuckerjee looked on, wild-eyed, staring, all the nerves in his cowardly *baboo* body writhing as he saw the powerful play of the back muscles beneath the sailor's thin shirt. He touched the sacred wool thread of his caste that circled his obese waist, and he prayed silently but fervently to an assortment of his favorite Hindu deities. For he knew these rough seafaring sahibs, and he did not trust them — no — not at all. Which proved that he had more than a little common sense as well as, evidently, more than a little experience on docks and waterfronts in the days before he left Calcutta for a life of adventure in yellow China.

But, alter all, it appeared that Mr. Hurree Chuckerjee's fears had been groundless. For just at that moment Higginson turned away from the girl and walked up to him, a sunny smile in his watery blue eyes and a laugh on his lips.

"Mister 'Indu," he said, "it's done!"

"Yes-s-s, *sahib?*"

"Right-o! The little lydy 'as decided to jolly well spill the truth. 'Aven't you, Miss Campbell?"

"Oh, yes," she said demurely. "And now for me interview with the judge," the sailor went on as he crossed to the threshold.

"The third door, eh, Mr. 'Indu?"

"No!" cried the latter, waving pudgy, excited hands. "The fourth! The judge warned you most especially, Higginson *sahib!*"

"That's so," admitted the able-bodied seaman. "Forgetful 'Arry — that's wot me shipmates calls me, when they don't call me Truthful 'Arry."

"You must not make a mistake about the door!" implored the *baboo.*

"I 'opes as I won't. Wot's behind that other door, Cully, that ye're all so bloody well frightened about it?"

"Nothing, *sahib.*"

"Right o! Secret diplomacy — wot?"

"You must be careful," repeated the *baboo.* "Perhaps I had better come with you part of the way — until you meet the guards."

"I do think you 'ad better. Although," — the sailor hesitated — "are you allowed to leave this 'ere lydy alone?"

"It is against regulation fifteen, paragraph eight. But, *sahib,* the windows are barred and I shall lock the door. For the first time in my life I shall therefore not adhere strictly to the printed regulations."

"Yer *are* a broad-minded josser!"

came the hearty reply "Let's go!" And Higginson put his left arm through the *baboo*'s right with a friendly smile, and then, the very next moment, before the latter knew what was occurring and how, it seemed to him that an entire firmament filled with a million blight stars was bursting somewhere in the back cells of his brain while a terrible pain shot knife-like through his eyes.

What had really happened was that Higginson had suddenly reverted to the shirtsleeves diplomacy and tactics of the quarterdeck. With great rapidity he had drawn his left arm from the *baboo's* right, had turned with catlike agility, had thrust his left hand into the *baboo's* eye, his right into his throat, and the man went down as though he had been struck by a high-power bullet.

"Quick! We ain't got much time!"

HIGGINSON turned to the girl, and, with her help, inside of a few seconds they gagged the *baboo* securely with the sailor's handkerchief and the girl's gloves. Working feverishly, they tore the waist-shawl from the unconscious man and, with that and the sailor's coat and belt, tied him hand and foot. Then the sailor helped himself to the *baboo's* revolver and motioned to Marie to follow him.

"If we meet the guards, it'll be all right. The judge told them to let me pass — and that goes for you, too. We only 'ave one chance."

"You mean — that third door beyond the turning they all seem so scared about?"

"Right-o!" — as his hand turned the knob. " 'Ere we go, all aboard for Blackpool! Step out plucky and unconcerned-like."

"I will."

They left the room, quickly closing the door behind them, and a few steps farther down the corridor they met one of the guards, a big, red-faced Tatar in full uniform and heavily armed. Higginson walked up to him casually.

"Did the judge tell you —"

"All light. Top-side plenty good!" came the reply in pidgin-English, and the Tatar soldier kept on his way, unsuspectingly turning his back while the sailor whispered rapidly to the girl:

"Sorry I ain't got no time to fool with Queensberry rules. I got to treat 'im as I did 'is nibs back in yer room. Can't afford to have 'im prowlin' round —"

Again, with tremendous agility, he turned. Up flashed his right hand which held the revolver, the steel butt hitting the Tatar on the lower part of the brain. The man went down without a sound.

"Got to shyke a leg!" said Higginson to Marie, the light of battle in his blue eyes. "Ain't got no time to tie and gag 'im. Still — that sleepin' powder I administered to 'is bean will keep 'im in the arms of Murphy for a jolly good while."

"You are such a sweet and peaceful soul, Mr. Higginson!" smiled the girl.

"I am!" maintained the sailor stoutly. "Peaceful 'Arry — that's wot me pals calls me. I'm a bleedin' lamb until some blighter steps on me toes —" He interrupted himself, pointed. "Look! 'Ere's the turning!" They made it at a run, hand in hand. There was no other guard about. "Now, then —" as they stopped in front of the third door.

"Shall we —" breathed Marie, wondering what lay beyond the threshold.

"We bloomin' well got to!" replied the sailor. "It's our only chance, lydy." He touched the door rather gingerly. "Mebbe I was a fool doin' wot yer arsked me in that there note yer wrote on the cigarette-box! Well — never mind. I likes the color of yer eyes. Come; step into me parlor." The door opened easily enough. He peered in "Gawd — ain't it dark? Well — can't be 'elped. In we pops!"

They crossed the threshold. Groping with his fingers, he found that the door had an automatic latch on the inside. He snapped it shut, then turned away from the door, Marie at his side, both feeling warily with their feet.

"Stairs!" she whispered, her heart beating like a trip-hammer.

"Right-o!"

They groped their way down the stairs slowly, carefully, perhaps a couple of dozen steps, worn slippery and hollow as by the tread of hundreds of naked feet, down, straight down. There was not even the faintest ray of light, and the air was heavy, terribly oppressive, stagnant. But they held on their course, carefully setting foot before foot, hands stretched out at right angles from their bodies to give warning of unfamiliar objects, and finally they landed dead against a wall.

"Wot now?" asked Higginson.

"Let's see."

Presently, by groping tentatively here and there, they discovered that they had debouched on a narrow landing which stretched right and left. Which way should they go, they wondered. They had to turn somewhere, and so they chose the left, for no particular reason. But often since Marie speculated what would have happened to them and how the whole adventure would have ended had they gone the other way.

Still they kept on, the sailor in front, Marie following, until suddenly there was a dull noise, Higginson let out an oath.

"Gawd! That hurts!"

It appeared that he had struck his forehead a terrific bump against a low beam that barred the way. He leaned down and investigated.

"There's space beyond. Careful, lydy!"

Bending down, they stepped under the beam and, by feeling, found that they were in a small cubicle, less than five feet in height and no bigger than six or seven feet square. The road seemed to end there. They crouched low, wondering what next to do.

"I'm goin' to strike a match," whispered the sailor.

"You think you'd better?"

"Ain't nothing else to do. Got to."

Up flared the match with a brutal lemon flare, and they looked about quickly. There was no door — nothing, except —

"Look!" said Marie, and pointed at the low ceiling where, square in the center, a curved metal handle was protruding. The match flickered out. "What now?" asked Marie.

"Got to try the 'andle, lydy," said Higginson, with British stoicism.

A jerk and twist — and suddenly half the ceiling slid to one side, into a well-oiled groove, sending down a flood of haggard light.

"Come on!" said the sailor, and he lifted the girl through the hole in the ceiling and followed after.

THE ROOM in which they found themselves was empty. It was lit by the dull-red, scanty glow which came from an open-work silver brazier swinging on delicate jeweled chains from the vaulted ceiling. A tiny window was set high on a wall, and a door led. away from the left. On the wall opposite, another window, lower than the first and larger in size, was boarded by heavy wooden planks painted with bright and intricate designs of snarling golden dragons in a tossing sea of crimson and black. Higginson studied the first window speculatively.

"Too 'igh up," he decided, "even for an able-bodied seaman, and too small to crawl through — chiefly you in your evenin' dress, lydy — why, it'd rip to shreds!"

"Let's investigate the other window."

AFTER A FEW minutes' examination they found a small crack in the boarding and, since the sailor's knife had been confiscated in prison, they used woman's favorite weapon, a hairpin, until they had enlarged the crack sufficiently to look through. At first, they saw nothing except a mass of varicolored incense smoke. But presently Marie's eyes grew used to it. She stared — and let out a scream, which she quickly suppressed.

"Wot's wrong?" asked Higginson.

"Nothing much — only, I think, by escaping from the prison, we rather jumped from the frying-pan, into the fire. Look!" She pointed through the thin crack. "It's the Temple of Horrors!"

"'Orrors is bloomin' well right," admitted Higginson as, emerging from the swirls of incense smoke, he saw looming up ghastly images of people being killed by slow Chinese tortures; as presently, even as they watched, a farther door opened into the temple and, with a savage thumping of drums, a clash of cymbals and a shrilling of reed pipes, a procession of masked Chinese priests entered, led by a giant high priest who was naked to the waist.

They were followed by a dozen torch-bearers, their flaming torches lighting up the interior with many colors. Then came a procession of soldiers. They were officers, judging from the embroidered, insignia on their tunics, and they bore swords and pistols and daggers which, as if asking for divine blessing, they deposited at the feet of the idols, while, at the same moment, a chant arose, rather a long-drawn wail, in Chinese monosyllables. The high priest turned. He faced the crowd. He lifted his hands in an annular, straight up-and-down motion, commanding silence, which dropped like a pall. Then he bowed three times before a great statue of the Buddha. Another priest handed him a human skull on gold chains that was filled with burning embers. He blew upon them till they shot forth tongues of vermilion light. He bowed again, and like a herald, roared out a single Tatar word:

"*Kieng-sse!*"

"*Kieng-sse!*" The crowd took up the word in a mad, whirling chorus, and the sailor clutched Marie's arm.

"I knows that word!" he whispered raucously. "I've picked up a bit of Mongol lingo 'ere and there. A sacrifice — that's wot the word means! That sanguinary blighter is arskin' for a sacrifice! I knows wot 'e's drivin' at! I fought in the Boxer war. Lydy — this 'ere ain't no plyce for two peaceful Anglo-Saxons!" He dragged her away. "Wot'll we do?"

"The door!" She pointed at it.

"And then wot?"

"Carry on, Mr. Higginson!"

"You're a brick, Miss Campbell!"

"And you're a peach, Mr. Higginson!"

He gave a gallant flourish.

"I always did like Yanks, Miss Campbell."

"Sure I am one?"

"My word — ain't you? Can a duck swim? If you ain't a Yank, then George Washington was an Eyetalian!" And

Marie could have hugged him for the remark.

They crossed to the door, opened it carefully, listened, looked. There was no sound. Then they stepped out into another corridor, bright-lit with swinging yellow lamps. It was really more than a corridor — more like a long hall, very high, with a vaulted ceiling. Up to a height of seven feet the walls were covered with stucco, white on white, ivory and snowy enamel skillfully blended with shiny white lac, and overlaid with a silver-threaded spider's web of arabesques, as exquisite as the finest Mechlin lace, and of Sanskrit quotations in the Devanagari script, showing that the temple had been built many, many centuries earlier, in the golden days when Hindu priests first brought the peaceful words of the Lord Gautama Buddha from across the Himalayas and before the Mongols twisted the gentle message according to their tortuous, mazed mentality. The upper part of the walls, too, must have been decorated by ancient Indian craftsmen. For above the white stucco was a procession, a panorama of conventionalized Hindu frescoes — an epitome, a *résumé* of all Hindustan's myths and faiths and legends and superstitions.

The tale of a nation's life, Asia's civilization and faith — yes, and crimes and virtues and sufferings, here, in front of them, and Higginson was strangely silent, while a thought came over Marie that here she was an intruder, not physically but mentally.

"What can we do?" she asked out loud. "Hobson's choice, don't you think, Mr. Higginson?"

"Right-o!"

So they walked on, down that everlasting corridor, with all Asia's gods jeering at them from the wall paintings, and looking left and right for a door, a window or some other avenue of escape, when very suddenly Marie was startled into complete immobility.

DIRECTLY in front of them the corridor came to an end, or, rather, it broadened out, swept out into a circular hall, the walls covered with slabs of delicate marble carved so that they looked like sculptured embroideries, with splendid Pekingese furniture of black teakwood, a profusion of enameled-silver ornaments, and the floor covered with huge Ming rugs of orange, gold, and imperial yellow.

"Gawd!" whispered Higginson.

Marie was near fainting. She steadied herself by clutching frantically the sailor's strong arm.

And yet the thing which had stirred them so profoundly was only a face — that of an old man, wrinkled, brown, immobile on a scrawny neck, which was like the slimy stalk of some poisonous, incredible jungle flower, the body, arms and legs wrapped in layers of thin muslin, sitting upright on a great chair of carved rosewood that was filled with a profusion of pillows in embroidered imperial Chien-lung silk.

A hard face to picture, to describe, as Marie saw it there, suddenly, with a saraband of purple shadows bringing it into stark relief — it would take the hand of a Rodin to clout and shape the meaning of it, the taint of death, the flavor of dread tortures which surrounded it like a miasmic haze. The face of a sensual, plague-spotted, latter-day Roman emperor it seemed to her, blended with the unhuman, meditating, crushing calm of a Chinese sage — heavy-jowled, thin-lipped, terribly broad across the temples, and with an expression in the pin-points of the black eyes like the sins of a slaughtered soul. All Marie could see and feel was the existence of those features in front of her — grotesque, monstrous, unhuman — and she wanted to shriek — she wanted to beat them into raw, bleeding pulp!

Perhaps the whole sensation, the whole flash of emotions lasted only a moment. Perhaps it was contained in the fraction of the second it took her and the sailor to pass from the corridor, properly speaking, into the hall. At all events, suddenly she was herself again, and she could tell by Higginson's tautening biceps beneath the pressure of her fingers that he, too, was regaining a semblance of composure.

She now jerked her wits into a fair imitation of nerve-control and, side by side with Higginson, took a few steps forward, slowly and deliberately, until she was within a few feet of the face. And then, all at once, it lost its stark immobility. The thin lips trembled and curled. They laughed — yet it was not exactly a laugh — rather a harsh, ghastly, scraping sort of cachinnation.

"Wot ho!" cried the sailor, with hysterical, forced gaiety. "I thought as yer were a bleedin' mummy, me lad!"

And then the lips opened over toothless gums and pronounced words in good English:

"Ah — Miss Campbell!"

Her answer came stammering, ludicrously inadequate:

"Oh — you — you know — who — I —?"

"Who you are? Of course. Am I not the *Chuen to yan* of this temple — of all our sacred brotherhood? I know a great many things — some of which I should know — and some of which," — again he laughed thinly, mockingly — "I should not know. And I am glad, very glad indeed, that you decided to come here to me of your own free will. Your reward will be resplendent. I punish — yes — harshly. But I also reward — generously!" And the thin lips held a tremendous, rather heroic earnestness.

Marie's mind worked with the instantaneous flash of a camera-shutter. This, then, was the *Chuen to yan*, she said to herself, the man — whatever the words meant — whom the Manchu woman had accused with her dying breath, of whom Judge Winchester had spoken. He was quite evidently the man in back of all this trooping, coiling maze of mysteries and intrigues. Then she considered that the *Chuen to yan* had assumed she had come here of her own free will. Here was a card ready to hand, a trump-card if she played it well, and she *would* play it. She was only afraid of what the sailor might do, might say. And so she spoke very quickly.

"This man," she said, "came with me. He is my confidential servant."

She waited, tensely expectant, wondering if the lie would hold good, immensely relieved when the Chinese waved the sailor's presence aside with his hand.

"Yes," he said; "some of these coarse-haired barbarians are quite trustworthy." Marie pressed firmly on the sailor's arm as she heard a belligerent rumble in his throat. "It is strange." He pointed to the pillow at his feet. "Sit down here, child," he continued in a kindly voice.

She obeyed. There was nothing

else to do, she thought. She would have to play her cards carefully, one by one as they came. She looked up at the man, and he stared back at her with black, unwinking eyes.

"You have the thing with you?" he asked.

Again she guessed quickly.

"The Tchou-fou-yao vase?"

"What else is there which might matter to me — to us? Give it to me."

"I have not got it here. You see," — she hesitated — "I did not trust myself to —"

"Oh, yes! You did wisely. It is better to be careful. D'Acosta is no fool. Nor is Sun Yu-Wen. Where is the vase?"

"Send some reliable servants with me — afterward some soldiers — and I'll lead them straight to the hiding place."

"Immediately!"

His left hand reached up, about to strike a gong above his head. But she interrupted him.

"Wait!" she said.

"Why?"

"First — tell me — you spoke of reward — a generous reward —"

He smiled sardonically.

"Greedy, eh? *Hayah!* Children are greedy — and women — and sparrows —"

Marie laughed frankly. Here was a chance at repartee after her own heart.

"Can you blame them?" she countered. "If women don't look out for themselves, certainly the male of the species will not."

He laughed too.

"A lesson you learned in America, eh? Perhaps — by the Buddha — a wise lesson. And so you —"

"Yes," smiled Marie; "first the reward."

"What shall it be?" he asked. "Gold or —"

"Power!" said Marie in a whisper, wondering if she had played trumps.

"Power?" The man stared at her. "You are true to your blood. And suppose I give you power, how will I know that I can trust you? Have we of the sacred brotherhood," — he drew up his shriveled, age-worn body — "the sacred brotherhood which we, still, though the coarse-haired barbarians once called it the Boxers, name by its ancient and honorable title," — he whispered it with eerie, sincere reverence — " 'the Society of Augustly Harmonious Fists' — have we of the brotherhood, have the dead patriots who belonged to other, similar brotherhoods ever been able to trust you — the people of your blood?"

Marie looked up. "The people of your blood," the man had said — and what had he meant?

"But —" She stopped, uncertain how to proceed without showing her ignorance.

"You have always been our enemies," the man continued. "You came as foreigners, conquering barbarians! You never assimilated with us — with the black-haired race. You do not look as we do. You do not dream and aim as we do. As barbarians you came; as bararians you remained — whatever you call yourselves, Manchus, Tatars, Turks or what-not! Once, perhaps, you were Asiatics — but you mixed your blood during the many centuries you lived in Russia, in Germany, in the West — and as foreigners you came among us. Thus," — the man seemed swept on by a tremendous, bitter sincerity of purpose — "you always stood by the other foreigners when they invaded China, and robbed and killed and enslaved —"

"No!" Marie interrupted him. "You are wrong. They did not come to murder and rob. War — yes — it could not be helped. But they came to China to bring civilization and trade — because they take an interest in the destines of China, of Asia —"

"So?" sneered the *Chuen to yan.* "I have been told that it is dangerous for the yellow man if the white man takes an interest in his affairs There is Hong Kong; there is French Indo-China; there is — *hayah!* — they came to trade, to ah — civilize. And they remained to rule, to rob! But you must forgive me. I am rude, tactless. For you yourself are a Westerner — you are white."

"Am I?" Once more Marie decided to play boldly.

"Decidedly."

"And yet the Southern republic claims me as a subject."

"A political trick — nothing else."

"But a trick founded on fact! For there was my mother —"

"Bah!" cut in the *Chuen to yan.* "She was a foreigner — if not in citizenship, then in blood. And so was your mother's father; so was your uncle. Foreigners all! Enemies! What if your uncle, as did your mother's father and his father before him, did prefer the ancient Mongol title? What if he did like to hear himself addressed as the 'Ssu Yueh,' 'Chief of the Four Mountains'?"

MARIE LISTENED, intensely interested, as the mysterious scroll of her mother's family history was unrolled before her eyes.

"What of all that?" continued the Chinese. "His real name was Mavropoulos. He used it when he traveled in Europe, when he intrigued against us with Russia and Germany and France and the rest of the Western powers, and when he went north to intrigue with the Manchus, the aristocrats —

foreigners like himself. And he sided with the foreigners until he died, while we of the south tried — Buddha, how we tried! — to save China, to make her independent. And so —" he made a slicing gesture "— he was killed, and even in death he tried to cheat us. There were only two of those Tchoufou-yao vases that held the ancient symbol of dominion. One he had; the other belonged to your mother, his only relative, and your father took it away when he left China after your mother's death. Your uncle destroyed the one that belonged to him just before he died — smashed it into a dozen pieces so that nobody could read the hidden message pictured on the inside." He laughed. "Your uncle did not know; he never guessed that Destiny was on the side of Canton — that you would come back to China in the hour of China's need, the ancient symbol in your possession —"

The girl was carried away by the *Chuen to yan*'s passionate outburst, and it was the sailor's warning cough which brought her to a realization of her imminent danger. By this time, one of the other guards must have found the Tatar soldier whom Higginson had knocked down, or the man must have regained consciousness. There was very little time to be lost.

"You are wrong," she said in a clear, steady voice. "At least, where I am concerned. I shall return the vase to you. Send for some of your soldiers, so that they can accompany me and —" pointing at Higginson "— my servant to the hiding-place."

"Good — by Buddha and by Buddha!" The Chinese struck the gong.

The girl smiled,

"I forgot! I should like to ask one favor."

"Name it."

She indicated her thin charmeuse frock, her bare head.

"I came directly from dinner," she said, "on a sudden impulse. And my servant, too — he is still in his working-clothes —"

"The Buddha once remarked that vanity is woman's most human illusion," he replied, with a laugh. "Very well. Over there," — he pointed to a huge chest in the corner — "you will find what you want."

AND WHEN, a few minutes later, half a dozen stalwart Chinese soldiers, led by an officer, entered, Marie and Higginson were transformed, at least in externals, into fair imitations of two Chinese, in embroidered robes, mutton-pie caps and neat, black-velvet slippers with padded soles. The *Chuen to yan* turned to the captain of the guard with a flow of Chinese monosyllables, but Marie interrupted him quickly.

"By the way," she said, "there's one thing I would like to tell you —"

"Yes?"

"D'Acosta and Sun Yu-Wen —"

"A Turk and a Manchu! Dogs both!"

"Yes — but clever dogs. They have lots of people in their employ, haven't they?"

"They employ many spies. Why?"

"Well, it I were you, I would tell those soldiers not to walk alongside of me and my servant, but to follow us at quite a distance. No use drawing attention to us — to show the way to d'Acosta's and Sun Yu-Wen's spies —"

The Chinese bowed.

"A cobra and a woman for shrewdness!" he remarked admiringly. "You are right."

Again he spoke to the captain, who saluted and walked up to Marie, drawing a handkerchief from his tunic, while a soldier stepped up to Higginson.

"You will be blindfolded on your way to the street through the temple," said the *Chuen to yan*. "A necessary precaution, you. understand?"

"Yes," said Marie.

"I don't care," whispered the sailor, "as long as I gets out o' this 'ere Temple of 'Orrors."

Thus, blindfolded, Marie and Higginson were led through a number of corridors, upstairs and down, out of the temple. Out on the street the captain of the guard removed the blindfolds.

"Lead," he said. "We follow."

"Right-o!" replied Marie.

"Right bloomin — o!" echoed the sailor; and they walked on, the soldiers following at a distance of sixty steps beneath the violet vault of the dying night.

Just as they turned the first corner, they heard a shout from the direction of the temple — a loud shout that echoed and reverberated, sharp, ominous. It tore through the gloom of the dying night like the point of a knife, but was swallowed the next moment by a hunched mass of sounds as, here, there and everywhere, the doors of the houses opened and the early-morning working population poured out.

Not yet morning; but already China, never asleep, ceaselessly working to feed its ever hungry, never-satiated maw, was preparing for the morning task.

Blue-bloused coolies moved through the streets in an endless procession, each sure of his aim and object. There were men riding in two-wheeled carriages, surmounted by vaulted silk covers; others, rich merchants, drove in low victorias crowned with embroidered canopies. Came

peasants on foot, on mules, on don-keys: fruit-venders, their fiery-colored produce piled high on balanced baskets, and it was finally, just as Marie and Higginson neared the second corner, that they saw their chance. The street here narrowed greatly as a Taoist temple jutted out, with a bizarre massing of pagoda towers and sharp angled walls that were a mass of color, pink, mauve, blue, and yellow, lit by a huge paper lantern to the left of the entrance, which proclaimed in Mandarin ideographs that this was a *li-pai,* a place of worship.

At that moment, the cortege of a funeral was passing, and as the soldiers stopped temporarily to give way, Higginson and Marie, for the same reason, pressed close against a wall.

At the head of the procession came fantastically dressed servants bearing standards, insignia of rank and artificial flowers, all glittering brightly in the light of many torches; other servants rubbed bronze gongs with scarlet devil-sticks. Then came a priest, who mumbled long-winded verses from the *"Ching-Kong-Ching"* and then, garbed in white, the chief mourner, directly in front of a crimson-covered catafalque. They all walked slowly, ceremoniously, but without the slightest indication of piety. Why should they? Canton is old. China is old. Many had died; many more will die. And the women in the mourners' coaches at the tail-end of the procession seemed to know it.

For they chattered and laughed, and leaned from the carriages, exchanging highly spiced compliments with the crowd.

At the very end came a number of empty coaches. They doubtless belonged to the deceased's guild-brothers, Cantonese burgesses, who, having thusly honored the dead, remained in their warm rooms. By the time these vehicles appeared, the torch-bearers had already turned the corner, and the street was again in darkness. The soldiers were screened from the two huddled against the wall by the line of coaches, and Marie, after a quick word in Higginson's ear, opened the door of one and slipped inside, the sailor following. And so, crouched on the floor of the carriage, they were carried past the soldiers, away from the Temple of Horrors, out into the heart of Canton.

"Out again, in again!" whispered Marie.

"Right-o," rejoined the sailor. He closed his eyes. "Wyke me up when we gets to Piccadilly!"

THE CORTÈGE ambled on for about ten minutes, and then, thanks to the practical side of the Chinese nature, the two got another chance. For while it is a laudable deed to honor a deceased guild-brother by sending empty carriages in sign of mourning, there is no use of piling up expenses. So, within sight of the cemetery, and since the gatekeeper levies toll on everybody and everything that passes beneath the sacred portals, the empty coaches remained without, and presently the drivers climbed down from their boxes, tied the horses and mules, and sought refreshment in a little tavern a couple of blocks away.

By now, the sun had risen still

higher, but — and for this the fugitives were grateful — a thick mist had rolled up from the river. They looked warily about, and left their hiding-place when they found that they were alone.

"I know this 'ere town like a book," Higginson said proudly. "This is what the chinks call the K'ung-ti, the Deserted Quarter!"

It was an appropriate name. For, surrounded on all sides by a packed, greasy wilderness of populous streets, it was a hopeless mass of ruins. At the farther end of the street was a tall wooden monumental gate.

"At the time of the Boxer trouble," the sailor went on, "them local Canton ruffians murdered 'ere a whole bloomin' lot of whites, and then this 'ere block of 'ouses was destroyed, as a sort o' punishment. A lot them chinks cared! They build new 'ouses." He looked for a cigarette and a match, found them, lit up, and looked questioningly at Marie Campbell. "And now, lydy, wot?"

"Let's get a move on,"

"Where to, would yer suggest?"

She thought rapidly. She had no idea where she might find d'Acosta or Sun Yu-Wen. But she recalled that the dying Manchu woman had told her about the "friend" to whom she should go, and he, she had figured out, must be Prince Pavel Kokoshkine; she recalled, too, the American consul having told her where the Russian lived — on the other side of the river, not far from the Nan-Hai prison. She gave Higginson the address.

"Know the place?" she wound up.

The sailor inclined his head ruefully.

"I knows most prisons in this 'ere dump," he said, " 'cause o' them chinks frequently and unjustly mistyk-in' me most innercent actions. It ain't far. Let's go down to the river."

"Where is it?"

He pointed at the monumental gate.

"Just through there and down the 'ill. Syfe enough. There ain't no 'ouses there."

THEY REACHED the river in safety, just where there was an anchorage for boats and launches. With the sailor leading, they made their way to a spot where, tied to a low thornbush, was a native boat, a sampan. They waited for a few seconds, wondering if the fisherman who owned it was anywhere about. But there was no sound, not the faintest sign of life. Marie stared across the river — it was a symphony of drowsy murmurs and fleeting, veiled shadows.

Safety lay there, if anywhere, she thought. She said so to the sailor. He shook his head dubiously.

"We'll see in 'arf a moment," he replied, "as the josser remarked when 'e put 'is last 'arf-crown on a rank outsider."

Higginson jumped into the sampan, which tilted and careened dangerously. He stretched out a hand and helped Marie in, then untied the rope with a sailor's skill. They were off, the man rowing at a good clip, putting the full weight of his shoulders to the oars, while the girl sat in the stern, directing the course with the quaint, square Chinese rudder. A hard pull it was; for the river, bloated by the spring monsoons, was a turbulent yellow giant. Twice she changed seats with Higginson when his arms got numbed. Steadily the southern shore slipped away from them, while they bore down on their course, dead toward the promontory which, Higginson said, was their goal. Near shore their task became more difficult. For a wind had sprung up which moved heavily against them, trailing gray sheets of rain-laden clouds. It made the light sampan bob to windward, and they had their work cut out to keep on a steady course.

Finally, they reached the far shore and walked up the hill that rose before them.

"'Ere you are!" said the sailor, pointing straight ahead. "Me old friend — the Nan-'Ai prison!"

"Looks more like a temple to me."

"Used to be one — before them practical-minded Southern chinks turned it into a jail."

She saw the fantastic, exaggerated contour of the pagoda roof, burnished, enameled in spots, mirroring the rays of the sun a thousand fold, like countless intersecting rainbows. From the window near the roof a shaft of light stretched out like a long, osseous yellow hand.

Higginson walked steadily on, with the girl following. So far they had not met a single human being, but, as they neared the top of the hill where the pagoda-prison opened to the road with a huge gate, they were halted by the snick of a breech-bolt and a raucous voice — evidently a challenge — in Chinese. But Marie let out a whoop of joy when the sentinel stepped forth from behind a tree, rifle in hand, for, in spite of his Chinese uniform, there was no doubt that he was a European.

"Hello!" she cried. "I am glad to see you,"

The man smiled. But he shook his head. *Nie! Nie!*" he replied. "No Englees! Russky — Russian —"

"Wot d'yer mean 'Russian?'"

asked the sailor. "Can't yer talk the king's bloody English?"

"Nie." The man laughed.

"Why, yer poor benighted Bolshevik —"

At once, as he heard the one word, the soldier's smile disappeared and gave way to expression of wolfish ferocity. He picked up his rifle and broke into a flood of excited Russian.

Higginson jumped back.

"'Ave a 'eart!" he cried, "Ain't yer got no sense of humor, yer silly josser? I didn't mean to call yer a Bolshevik, Honest to Gawd I didn't!"

Marie stepped between the two men, smiling brilliantly at the Russian.

"Me — want — see — prince," she said, very loud, and in that broken English which people, for some mysterious psychological reason, will employ when speaking to small children and large foreigners. "Savvy?"

"That oughter fetch 'im," commented the sailor admiringly.

"Nie," replied the Russian.

"Look here!" The girl returned to the attack. "See — Prince — Kokoshkine!"

"Ah!" A light of understanding eddied up in the man's eyes. "Pavel Alexandrovitch?"

"I — want — speak — to — him — savvy?" She gesticulated wildly to make the man understand. "Get me? Kokoshkine — Prince Kokoshkine —"

"Da, da, moya dorogoya!" The Russian smiled. "Yes, yes, my dear!"

It was evident that the man understood. He whistled shrilly. A few minutes later another soldier came from a little outbuilding, which seemed to be the guardhouse.

The first gave him rapid instructions in Chinese, and turned, motioning to the two fugitives to follow him.

"Rather early to be about," said Higginson, as they passed through the gate; " 'ardly four bells. I 'ave an, idea as 'ow 'is 'ighness will still be in the arms of Murphy."

But, in spite of the early hour, they found the inner courtyard, a huge, stone-paved affair, crammed with human life, soldiers as well as civilians. The soldiers were hard at work, drilling, mostly in sober brown uniforms — Chinese with a sprinkling of Tatars. But some of the officers were Europeans, evidently Russians, and still in the uniforms of the czar's army.

"Heavens! I thought the war was over," said Marie.

"It ain't over — ever!" replied Higginson, with sudden seriousness.

They passed some batteries practicing drum-fire with blank shells, and a troop of Tatar cavalry, who came on, straight, lances at the carry, thundering across the hard-baked drill ground, their horses mostly new, shaggy mounts, not yet broken to the roll and sob of the guns.

Finally, they crossed the great parade ground, and, through another metal-studded gate, passed into an outer hall, where a liveried Chinese servant received them.

The soldier spoke to him, and the other bowed and departed, to return shortly afterward, accompanied by a tall Russian, dressed in a general's uniform — a very handsome man, dark, clean-shaven, with a short, softly curved nose and straight black eyebrows which divided his gray eyes from the high forehead. He wore on his tunic the Cross of Saint Vladimir.

"I am Kokoshkine," he said, clicking his spurred heels. "And you — *mademoiselle*

"I am Miss Campbell — whom you

invited to dinner tonight. But — would you mind offering me breakfast instead? I am positively starved!"

Kokoshkine smiled. He bent over her hand and kissed it.

"You are just in time," he replied. "I was about to sit down to my morning meal." His English was perfect, with hardly a suspicion of Slav purr; and Marie, quick at reading character, as quick at making up her mind in human relations, liked him at once. He turned to the soldier, speaking in Russian, and then asked Higginson to accompany the other. "Hungry, eh? Could you do with a steak?"

"My word!" came the enthusiastic reply. "Could I do with fifty bloomin' steaks!"

"And a whisky and soda?"

"Dook," — the title was conferred honestly — "them is the first kind words I 'eard since I landed in this 'ere 'eathen town!"

Higginson pulled at his forelock and followed the soldier out of the room, while Kokoshkine held open the door to the next apartment, where the table was already set — very exquisitely, with delicate Chinese eggshell porcelain, Russian silver samovar and tea-glass, and a profusion of flowers, in strange contrast to the martial simplicity of the room, the military maps on the walls, the soldier's kit here and there on table and chairs.

"Another cover!" he ordered the soft-slippered Mongol servant.

A few minutes later, sitting across from Prince Pavel Alexandrovitch Kokoshkine, Marie did justice to a hearty Russian breakfast with a hearty American appetite. Occasionally, out of sheer, unthinking human liking and sympathy, she smiled at her host, who smiled back and who, when thrice she put down fork and cup, saying, "I want to tell you — ask you —"stopped her with a gesture.

"There is no hurry, Miss Campbell," he said. "Eat — rest yourself. Are you in trouble?"

"Yes."

"I thought so. We'll straighten it out for you — never fear!"

She believed that he would.

Several times the breakfast was interrupted by officers, Chinese and Russians, who came in, made reports, and were sent off with short, crisp words of command, and also by the sound — from a large maneuver field at the other end of the promontory, the prince explained to her — as the batteries there did target practice with blank shells.

"Peaceful sort of life you are living here!" she remarked in one brief interval of silence.

He smiled.

"I don't care for it myself. Being a soldier, I naturally hate war. But I must be prepared to — to —" He hesitated.

Marie forgot her own quandary as she remembered what she had heard about this man, the imperialist, the former officer in the czar's army, now drilling Cantonese troops, in the service of these Southern Chinese radicals, whose ideals must have been the very opposite of his own. With American directness she cut in on his hesitation.

"You are an aristocrat, a czarist, aren't you?"

"The czar is dead, *mademoiselle*."

"All right. But you are still an aristocrat."

"Decidedly."

"Then why do you —"

"*Mademoiselle* — please — we will not discuss my personal affairs. You came here, I take it, to talk about your own affairs."

She was a little nettled.

"Oh, very well," she replied. Then, quite suddenly, her slight ill humor disappeared. After all, the man was right. She had been rash, tactless. "I beg your pardon," she said, smiling at him frankly,

"Oh — I did not mean to —"

"But I do beg your pardon. Really — truly! I should not have asked you. And now," — finishing her last glass of tea — "I want to tell you —"

"Do, Miss Campbell!"

"I am in a frightful mess, and Liu Po-Yat told me to come to you — at least, I guessed it was you she meant."

"Oh — then she spoke before she died?"

"You know that she —"

"Was murdered? Yes, Miss Campbell. I know —" he smiled "— a great deal — pardon — of what affects you."

"Seeing that my father is not here to correct my language, I suppose I may say what is on my mind — and express it exactly the way I feel?"

"Of course,"

"Very well. You've said a mouthful, Prince!" And while he laughed, she went on: "I would have been tremendously disappointed if you had not known all about me. Why should you have been the one exception in Canton? Why should you have been slighted. Everybody else here knows all about me — except my little self. Moses d'Acosta, Sun Yu-Wen, Monsieur Pailloux, Judge Winchester, the

Chuen to yan in the Temple of Horrors —"

"Oh," he exclaimed, utterly surprised, "you know those last two?"

"I just came from there."

"What?"

"I had such a pleasant interview with them."

"And — they let you go, Miss Campbell?"

"No, I just went. That's why I am here — breakfasting with you."

"Tell me —"

"I hardly know where to begin." But she told him all that had happened to her, as well as most of her suspicions and deductions, finally taking the *North China Gazette* clipping from her purse. "Here is the thing I told you about," she ended. "Can you make head or tail of it?"

He took it, read it, then looked up.

"You said something about d'Acosta's saying it referred to your uncle's death and came out in the *North China Gazette*. Is it quite clear?"

"You call that clear?" said Marie. "What's it all about?"

"Well," he rejoined, "I really know a great deal about Chinese lore. Let's dissect this sentence by sentence. Now, the first two exclamations of the article: 'Omniscient Gautama! Far-seeing, all-seeing Tathagata!' Taken with what it says afterward, as well with what actually happened, the man who caused this to be printed in the *Gazette* —"

"My uncle?"

"Yes. By this double exclamation he tried to express two overlapping thoughts — one of death and the other of life, one spiritual and the other materialistic. First, he appealed to the Buddha, the eternal deity. But by using the word 'Gautama,' he demonstrated that he was addressing the Buddha in his reincarnation of Lord of the Dead, thus showing that he himself did not expect to live much longer. On the other hand, by using the decidedly more worldly 'Tathagata' appellation of the same Lord Buddha, he endeavored to show that, although in the shadow of death, he was still sufficiently interested in materialistic affairs to appeal to the living, not to all living beings, but only to those who were 'far-seeing, all-seeing,' and by this he meant those who would see far enough to understand the thing which was all-important to him. Clear so far, is it?"

"Oh, yes — after you play dragoman."

" 'How multiform the consolation of Thy Word!' " continued the Russian, "This, too, is couched in mystic, esoteric language of Chinese theology, so that it may only be deciphered by the initiated. It means that the writer is not afraid of death or of what the future may bring — 'consolation,' don't you see? While, 'How marvelous Thy Understanding' refers again to the Buddha as well as being another reference to the living, those among the living to whom he is making this appeal, in the shadow of death — of murder, as he knew it would be, as it did turn out to be. And the last sentence contains the final appeal —"

"To the Buddha?"

"No, Miss Campbell; to one among the living — to you!"

"How do you know?" cried the girl.

"By one word in that last sentence: 'Mara.' It is the name of one of the feminine deities of the Buddhist heaven, comparable to Fate. But it is also —" He smiled. "Miss Campbell," he went on, "doesn't 'Mara' remind you of something?"

"Why —" She considered; then

suddenly. "You don't mean, by any chance, my own name — Marie?"

"Exactly! Marie — that's what your father called you. But your mother's name was Mara, and 'Mara' she called you. She died a few days after you were born, and your father left, a broken, sorrowful, embittered man. He had loved your mother much. Oh — it had been such a romantic meeting, such a sweeping love and passion! And all the obstacles he had to overcome! Your mother's family and clan objecting — but, finally, your father won out. They were married. Then she died, and he took you back to America." Perhaps, with that superstitious Scottish mind of his, he was afraid of the name 'Mara' — and changed it to 'Marie.'"

"How do you happen to know all this?"

"Part of my duty," he replied.

"Duty?" — wonderingly.

"Yes. Political duty. And your father never told you a word?"

"He hardly ever mentioned my mother — the memory seemed to hurt him."

"Nor of China?"

"Only when I left home, when I told him I was coming here. He asked me to take along the little Chinese vase. It seemed to him like a sort of talisman."

"It is," said the prince gravely. "A talisman of dominion — of ancient power and prophecy. Power — dominion — bitterly contested!" he added grimly, as again, from the outside, came the roar of the batteries at target practice, a huge salvo belching up, stopping abruptly, then followed by another burst of sound waves like a giant beating a huge metal drum.

A moment later a giant, ruddy-complexioned Tatar came in. He was booted and spurred, dressed in a loose white tunic, the insignia of high military rank embroidered over his heart in purple and silver. The Russian introduced him to Marie.

"Feofar Khan, the Tatar general." He continued in a whisper, "One of your uncle's best friends and, by the way, a relative of yours."

"Oh!" Marie looked up, interested.

"Very distantly. Both your mother's family and his own claimed descent from Genghis Khan, the Central-Asian freebooter who once conquered China in a moment of enthusiasm. Not very popular with the Chinese — these Tatar gentlemen."

"So the *Chuen to yan* told me."

The prince turned to Feofar Khan, who talked to him in rapid Mongol monosyllables, again bowed to Marie, saluted and withdrew.

"Am I interfering with your work?" asked the girl.

The prince appeared to be a little nervous. But he shook his head.

"No, no!" he said. "I've plenty of time — nearly half an hour. In the meantime — what we were talking about — why, it may, in fact, help me to —" He interrupted himself. "We were speaking about the Tchou-fou-yao vase, weren't we?"

"Yes. And my uncle's last message." She pointed to the clipping. "Tell me one thing: Surely my uncle must have realized that I would not be able to interpret this cryptic message of his — even if I did chance to run across it?"

"As to your happening to run across it, tell me — when did you leave America?"

"The middle of August."

"Your uncle died — was killed a few days after you left. After you left,"

the prince repeated significantly. "He knew that you were coming here."

"How did he know?"

"All these years he never lost track of you. You were his only blood kin, remember, the last descendant of his ancient clan. He knew you were coming to China, and assumed that you would see the papers as soon as you arrived. People pounce upon the papers after an ocean voyage. And the *North China Gazelle* prints a special monthly edition to meet travelers on landing. That's where this clipping is from."

"I remember how the people grabbed those papers up in Hong Kong."

"You see, Miss Campbell? And as to your being able to decipher the message, well, a dying man will clutch at a straw. Your uncle, the last few months of his life, was surrounded by enemies. He did not dare write. He did not dare express his final message in words which his enemies might understand. But everybody in China knew that he was one of the world's leading authorities on Buddhistic legends and frequently made translations of them for English papers. And so, surrounded by enemies, nearly alone, helpless, desperate, knowing that death was near, knowing, furthermore, that you were on your way to China, he clutched at a straw."

"Straw is right!"

"Perhaps, of course, he also depended on his friends to help you decipher it. Miss Campbell, I was your uncle's friend, I could not help him — he was way out there in Urga, in Outer Mongolia — still, I was his friend —"

"And — my friend?" she asked impulsively, holding out her hand.

He took it in both his, raised it to his lips and kissed it.

"Yes," he said. "And I am very proud that you call me friend — very proud indeed!"

He looked at her. A moment her gaze held his. Then she dropped her eyes. She blushed slightly — hated herself for blushing — as she felt a strange, sweet tightening about her heart. She forced her voice to be dry and quite matter of fact as she asked the next question:

"Tell me — how does it happen that everyone here — I mean d'Acosta, Sun Yu-Wen, Pailloux, the Cantonese authorities — is all so well informed about me? Why — d'Acosta actually discovered that I liked the caviar they served aboard ship."

"I know that he did." The prince laughed.

"Didn't you send some to Mr. d'Acosta for the dinner he invited me to last night?"

"Guilty, Miss Campbell."

"Don't apologize. It was first-rate. Still — why do they all know about me?"

"Won't you get it through your charming little head that you are really a very important personage in China?"

"Only in China?"

"Also in the eyes of at least one Russian."

"Thank you, kind sir!"

"You see, Miss Campbell, they are all playing for a gigantic stake here. So they employ spies, confidential correspondents. Take me, for example, I knew exactly when you left America —

a friend of mine over there cabled me —"

"Who?"

"A young American with whom I became very chummy a few years ago in London when he was assistant secretary of the American embassy. Clever chap — very brilliant member of your own intelligence service — quite in sympathy with our party here. Chap called Van Zandt."

"You don't mean Tom Van Zandt?"

"The same."

"Incredible! Footless, dear old Tom! Why, his main interest in life seemed to be the color of his spats, and his one claim to distinction a jade cigarette-holder ten inches long!"

"A great Manchu duke gave him that cigarette-holder," said the prince, "because he helped the duke out of some grave political trouble."

"Tom," she repeated, shaking her head, "who couldn't say 'boo' to a goose!"

"That's one way of fooling the world," explained the prince. "Van Zandt told me often that he considered his spats and his tiny mustache and the vacant stare in his eyes among his chief assets in the intelligence service. People, just naturally, think him a fool — and so they tell him things. You see," — he consulted his watch — "you came here well advertised." He rose and buckled on his sword.

"Why did they all wait so long until they interviewed me about the Tchou-fou-yao vase?"

"At first we were not sure if you had it."

"Who are 'we'?"

"D'Acosta, Sun Yu-Wen, and myself."

"The three of you are friends, then?"

"Very great friends — in a way. We even work for the same object — the same general aim. But there are differences of opinion — perhaps of ideals. I have no time to explain now." And, while he saw to the loading of a brace of cavalry pistols, he went on, "A few days after your arrival, we sent a confidential agent to your hotel, a woman, she took a position as maid —"

"Liu Po-Yat, the Manchu?"

"Exactly. She told us as soon as she found out that the vase was in your possession. Even then we were careful. For we were not sure if you were familiar with the trinket's significance. Also, we wondered if the other party —"

"The *Chuen to yan*'s brother-hood —"

"Yes. We wondered if they had approached you, had perhaps come to terms with you — by — pardon me — bribery or perhaps threats, or skilful diplomacy. Pailloux had an idea."

"That bearded Frenchman seems to be a traitor."

"Evidently, But things in Canton were coming to a head. We dared wait no longer. The three of us decided to risk it, to come to you, to ask you for your help and trust in spite of Pailloux's advice —"

"You did not come together?"

"No. According to our old three-cornered agreement, given the — oh — difference in ideals, each proceeded independently of the other —"

"A Far-Eastern idea of the Three Musketeers, eh?" She laughed. "All for all — and each one for himself! And Mr. d'Acosta got there first. He chose his moment well. He knew that I owed a large hotel bill —"

"Oh, yes," Kokoshkine smiled "He is a shrewd Levantine — a clever financier." He slipped the brace of pistols into his belt.

"Why these murderous preparations?" asked Marie Campbell

"Events are developing rapidly, gravely. A moment ago, when Feofar Khan came in, he told me that the *Chuen to yan* and Judge Winchester have found out about how you fooled them. Listen!" He pointed through the window whence, suddenly, the artillery practice having, ceased, there brushed in a great flourish of hoarse-throated trumpets — those three-yard-long, thin-snouted, straight-stemmed Chinese war-trumpets — blaring in a half-chorus, first hanging desperately on a high, shrill note, then suddenly tumbling an octave and roaring a bassoon-like charge in unison like a herd of enraged bulls. He picked up his military field-glasses, adjusted them, peered through them, and gave them to the girl. "Over there," he said. "On the other side of the river. Look!"

And she beheld there, minute but distinct through the powerful lenses, a large body of soldiery.

"There are other garrisons in this town," said the prince, "besides the one which I command — those over there are Prince Tuan's men, Mohammedan ruffians from Kansuh and the west." She saw the bright cluster of banners round the squadron commander, saw the horses and their riders pushing through the clouds of dust which floated high above them. She noted the bright crimson of their tunics and the blackness of their turbans, saw more men run up, carbines in hand, swing themselves rapidly into high-peaked saddles and gallop away in different directions.

"War?" demanded the girl.

"No. At least — not yet I told you — didn't I? — that you are an important personage here. These troopers are being sent out to search the town for you, high and low. They will do their utmost. They must have the vase — *and* you. Today, if possible. And there is little they will stop at. They may actually invade the foreign quarter, the Shameen, and then —" he shrugged his shoulders "there will be trouble. That's what Feofar Khan told me a while back. The *Chuen to yan* sent me orders to join them with a troop of horse."

"And — are you going to obey?"

"Yes."

"But — you — a European — an imperialist, how can you?"

A strange expression came into the gray eyes.

"Miss Campbell," came the enigmatic reply, "I have my own philosophy in life. And one of my maxims is that, even if you are the most devout Christian in the world, you cannot attempt to save your life by reciting the New Testament to the tiger who is about to pounce on you — nor that you can keep faith with the jackal, who could not keep faith with you. Never mind — I'll explain it to you some other time," — he kissed her hand — "when we shall be even greater friends than we are today."

A Cossack orderly entered, received an order in purring Russian and withdrew. Pavel Kokoshkine turned to the girl.

"About the vase?" he asked. "It is in the hotel safe, you said?"

"I left it there."

"And have I your permission to take it?"

She pondered for a moment, remembering her father's words, that she should not use the vase unless she absolutely had to. And again she felt the sweet tightening about her heart as she looked at the Russian and then, quite suddenly, with a sublimely feminine lack of logic, she decided that the moment had come of which her father had spoken.

"Yes," she said. "Take the vase."

"But — you don't know how I shall use it — what I am going to do with it?"

"Oh —"

"You trust me, Miss Campbell?"

"Yes."

"And — perhaps — you like me?"

"Very much indeed."

"I am glad." He tightened his belt-buckle. "You see," — he said it very simply — "I love you — you don't mind my telling you?"

She did not reply at once. She had felt that this was going to happen. Finally she looked up, and said,

"I am so glad you love me."

"You — you mean —" His voice cracked.

"Yes, dear," she replied to his unfinished question, and she walked up to him, her face uptilted, her lips slightly open, and, as he still hesitated, she lifted her hands and buried them in his thick curly hair. She drew him down to her and kissed his lips. Then she blushed, receded rapidly, hid her embarrassment in flippant, frivolous words:

"Don't you ever dare tell me that I proposed to you!"

A moment later the door opened and Feofar Khan came in.

"Ready?" he asked.

"Ready, General!" replied the prince.

The Tatar bowed to the girl, then addressed his superior officer.

"What about Miss Campbell?" he asked.

"That's what is bothering me," said the other. "I am afraid to leave her here, and of course I can't take her along,"

"I am awfully sorry I am such a nuisance," smiled Marie, and, after Ko-

koshkine had explained to her that he had decided to take with him only those troopers whom he could trust absolutely, leaving the garrison in the hands of his Chinese men, that, on the other hand, he could not leave her here with the same Chinese soldiers, radicals every one of them, who, given the *Chuen to yan*'s many spies, might discover her identity and whereabouts, she said quite calmly that the only thing for him to do was to take her along.

"Impossible!" cried the prince.

"On the contrary — quite possible," said Feofar Khan. He bowed to Marie. "Miss Campbell," he said, "I am a much married man. I have taken nearly the full quota of four which the Koran permits the true believer. And yet —" He smiled.

"A proposal of marriage?"

"Strictly temporary. Will you, for the time being, join the number of my wives?"

"Safety in numbers!"

"Even so," objected the Russian, "the situation remains the same — the Chinese might suspect —"

"Being Chinese, they will never guess at the simplicity of utter audacity," said Feofar Khan. "On the other hand, being Asiatics, even these Southern radicals will draw the line at suspecting or searching the palanquin supposed to contain an inmate of my harem. Then in town, if we should have to, I have some Tatar friends who will take care of her."

Marie laughed.

"I never imagined that there could be so many gorgeous thrills in the world," she said.

"My apartment is across the hall," continued Feofar Khan, "I have with me some women servants from my own country, entirely trustworthy.

They knew and worshiped your uncle. Come — we have not much time to lose."

He took Marie to his apartment and gave rapid instructions to three ruddy-complexioned old Mongol women. They laughed and salaamed. He left; and a few minutes later Marie returned, looking for all the world like a Tatar girl of the far-western plains — that hardy race born and bred on horseback — in a coat of heavily quilted silk that reached half-way to her knees, riding-boots, high-heeled and rowel-spurred, loose breeches of untanned leather, conical head-dress, and her face covered by an orthodox Moslem horsehair veil.

"Breeches!" She laughed. "How shocked my father would be if he knew!" She surveyed herself in the mirror. "Rather becoming, don't you think?"

"Keep the costume," Feofar Khan said "It is yours."

"Thanks! I shall wear it when I get back to New York — at the very first fancy-dress ball given by the junior League. I'll be a riot!"

Meanwhile, in the outer courtyard, the Russian, Tatar and Manchu troopers and officers were assembling as a giant Circassian captain brought the army-whistle to his lips, strapping on carbines and revolvers, others bringing out the horses, with a babel of cries in purring Slav and harsh Mongol. Confusion, impatience, a crackling of steel, a minister thumping of kettledrums, but finally order and discipline by the time that Prince Kokoshkine and Feofar Khan came into the courtyard, where their orderlies were standing by their horses' heads.

Not long afterward there was the rhythmic thud of a dromedary's padded feet and grumbling, spitting, protesting, the grotesque animal came into sight, a gaudy palanquin litter slung to the left of the great hairy hump, while the driver, Feofar Khan's body-servant, was clinging precariously to the arrangement, half side-saddle and half chair. Came Marie, her eyes gleaming excitedly through the meshes of her veil, and escorted by Higginson, who, judging from his uniform, had by this time given up his seafaring vocation to take service in Prince Kokoshkine's European contingent.

Feofar Khan salaamed deeply before Marie. He lifted her up into the palanquin litter and closed the thin curtains of yellow silk, but not before he had improved the occasion by assuring her loudly in his native tongue, so that all the Mongol soldiers might understand, that she was the latest addition to his harem, his youngest and best beloved wife.

Then there came a bugle-call and the cavalcade moved out of the courtyard with a jingle of spurs and sabers, Prince Kokoshkine riding on the left of the palanquin, Feofar Khan on the right, and so they rode down the hill and skirted the banks of the Pearl River, which they crossed farther down-stream with the help of half a dozen great flat ferryboats.

All the way across, as they entered Canton proper, as they rode through the native streets, they heard the bull-like roar of Chinese war-trumpets. Panic was licking the town with a tongue of flame. The crowds, hardly knowing why, were beginning to grow uneasy, nervous. They rode down the street of Excellent Purity, past the Temple of the Monkey and the Stork.

On its threshold stood a gaunt priest, holding a tall pole with a red banner high in his hands.

"*Pao Ch'ing Mien Yang!*" he shouted, with the full force of his lungs. "Death to the works of the foreigners and honorable loyalty to China!" His voice throbbed with fanatic, horrible sincerity.

"*Pao Ch'ing Mien Yang!*" Here and there, in the throng of coolies and merchants, isolated voices took up the cry, and Prince Kokoshkine spurred his horse more closely against the dromedary's heaving flanks.

"Don't be afraid, Marie," he whispered up through the curtains, rising in his stirrups.

She smiled bravely.

"I am not worrying, dear," she said.

"*Pao Ch'ing Mien Yang!*" cried the gaunt priest of the Temple of the Monkey and the Stork.

"*Pao Ch'ing Mien Yang!*" whimpered an almond-eyed Cantonese servant in the Shameen, as he set his white master's breakfast-table with minute care.

"Kindly eschew political discussions — at breakfast, Wong," said his master, who happened to pass through the dining room, and also happened to be Moses d'Acosta. "What is the trouble?" he asked.

"No savvy," came the reply in pidgin, with the stereotyped words of all Chinese when they do not wish to speak the truth, and, once more the gentle, patient servant, "Bleakfast leady."

D'Acosta smiled.

"Eat it yourself," he said. "I am going to take mine at the Grand Hotel." And he left the house and turned down the street.

He swarms of blue-bloused coolies on their way to work. They seemed strangely tense, talking among themselves with a low humming like that of a thousand angry bees.

Walking on, d'Acosta met Mademoiselle Droz, the exiled Parisian vaudeville actress, out on her morning constitutional.

"You seem out of sorts, *mon p'tit*," she said. "Any special reason?"

"Yes."

"Namely?"

"This is China — and we are white."

"Nothing new in that. We have always been white — and this has always been China."

"That's just what I am kicking about."

"Oh?"

"Yes. Don't you think there is something disconcerting in being waited on by those who you know are waiting on murder and sudden death?"

"Did your boy try to kill you?"

"No. He is fond of me, and a decent lad."

"Then —"

"He is a Chinese. He may slit my throat tomorrow, in spite of all his liking for me."

"Why don't you leave China if you don't like it? You have plenty of money."

"Money? Bah!" He was quite sincere. "There are also my ideals."

"Ideals?" She gave a cynical laugh. "Ideals are like nuts. In time the kernel

rots — and they become hollow. Eat them when they are fresh — then get new ones."

"You are too French for me this morning, *mademoiselle.*"

"And you too Oriental. *Au revoir, mon p'tit!*"

"*Au revoir!*"

He walked on to the hotel. There the atmosphere seemed surcharged with electricity. The Chinese waiters whispered uneasily among themselves, and even the most supercilious, race-conceited European clerk at breakfast grew a little pale as he remembered tales he had heard from old-timers about the Boxer outbreak.

What made the Europeans uneasy was the fact that Pailloux, the hotel manager, was not about. When Moses d'Acosta entered the dining room, a dozen men rose and surrounded him.

"What's all the trouble? What is happening?"

D'Acosta brushed them away with a gesture of his hand.

"Nothing is happening, gentlemen — except your own cowardice. Cowardice made the Boxer trouble possible." And he walked away, sat down, swallowed a cup of black coffee and asked the Chinese head waiter to send for Pailloux.

"He has not been home all night."

"Oh?" D'Acosta was surprised. "All right — I'll talk to the assistant manager." The latter confirmed the information. He added that Pailloux and De Smelt, the house detective, had left the hotel shortly after dinner the night before, taking Miss Campbell with them.

"Are you sure?"

"Positive. I helped her into the carriage."

"Where did they go? Any idea?"

"No — except that they drove into the native town."

"Hm." The Levantine shook his head. "I am going up to my apartment." He kept a suite at the hotel. "Kindly send or telephone to Mandarin Sun Yu-Wen and ask him to join me immediately."

"Very well, sir."

Moses d'Acosta went to his rooms, He must have furnished them in a moment of homesickness for his native Constantinople, his native Levant. For there was nothing here to remind one that this was China, It seemed rather an epitome of the Moslem Near East with its somber black-on-black shadows trooping densely on an ancient Kermanshah rug; a flowery Tabriz; and a camel-brown, wool-piled Turkoman carpet, with the sudden, stammering lilts of sunshine dancing in through the high, grilled windows.

There was peace here, and it enveloped him almost physically. With a little sigh of satisfaction he sat down cross-legged on a huge pillow and lit a water-pipe blazing with emeralds and hard Jeypore enamel. But when, not long afterward, a servant announced Mandarin Sun Yu-Wen, d'Acosta became immediately the perfect Mongol host. For he knew the other well; they were friends in spite of their differing ideals and philosophies, and he knew how the old Manchu appreciated being shown the slightly stilted etiquette of his own race by a foreigner.

So, in spite of the fact that time and haste just now were important elements, he did not hurry his ceremonious Peking greetings as Sun Yu-Wen entered.

The mandarin seemed nervous, uneasy; but he, too, adhered strictly to the rules of conduct as written in the

Book of Ceremonies and Exterior Demonstrations.

Both men bowed deeply.

"Please deign to enter," said d'Acosta,

"How should I, the very little and insignificant one, deign to enter, O brother very wise and very old?" came the correct self-deprecatory reply.

Three times the invitation was repeated, to be met three times by the same answer, and finally, profusely apologizing, the mandarin entered, closed the door, and bowed again, sucking in his breath.

"Walk very slowly," said the Levantine.

"No, no!" countered the mandarin to show his humbleness and unimportance. "I shall walk very quickly, O brother very wise and very old!"

The other extended an arm and indicated the pillows.

"Please deign to choose a place for your honorable body," he said. "Take the west side — the side of august honor."

"Every place is too flattering for me, the very small and insignificant one."

"Won't you deign to drink?" continued the Levantine, after both had sat down.

"Thank you. I shall drink, if at all, from a plain wooden cup with no ornaments."

"No, no!" exclaimed the other, "You shall drink from a precious cup of transparent green jade with three orange tassels." He clapped his hands; the servant entered, brought tea and sweets and cigarettes, and it was then that the two strangely mated friends spoke of what was on their minds.

"You have heard about Miss Campbell?" asked d'Acosta.

"Yes," replied the Manchu, with all the bland peacefulness of the Buddha who sees the world crumbling into dust but shows no trace of emotion.

"What do you think will happen, Sun Yu-Wen?"

"That is on the Buddha's knees. Ahee!" The Manchu sighed.

The other made an impatient gesture.

"Suppose — if you will pardon me saying so — we hustle the Buddha a little and give him a push in the right direction."

The mandarin, frankly Mongol, and therefore frankly irreligious, was nowise shocked.

"Can we?" he smiled.

"At least we can try."

"How, my friend? You don't know, eh? Nor do I."

"But — to give up —"

"What else is there to do? Listen!" He pointed at the window. "The trumpets are roaring. By this time the *Chuen to yan*'s jackals are all over town. And then?" He folded his hands calmly across his obese body. "We be important men, you and I. These many years we have been almost sacrosanct. But even the fleetest horse cannot escape its own tail. My friend," he added, "perhaps my spirit, released from his fleshly envelope, will soon jump the Dragon Gate and kowtow deeply before the spirits of my honorable ancestors."

"You seem to relish the prospect," came the heated rejoinder. "I don't. And, as for Miss Campbell, and, also, the vase —"

"She hid the vase," interrupted the mandarin.

"How do you know?"

"Simple deduction. Last night she was a prisoner. If she had had the vase on her person, they would have found it."

"How do you know they did not

find it? That is just what I believe and what I am afraid of. It is the possession of this vase which is making the *Chuen to yan*'s brotherhood and all this riff-raff of Southern radicals so dangerous, which. Is causing all the trouble."

"No! If they had found the vase on Miss Campbell, they would not mind her having escaped."

"Oh — escaped, has she?" D'Acosta was astonished as well as relieved.

"Yes."

"Sure of it. Sun Yu-Wen?"

"Absolutely. My spies told me. Therefore, I repeat, since she did not have the vase, she has hid it, and that is why all these Southern jackals are nosing the ground. And they will find it. They will search everywhere. The little jackals will lick blood, will like the taste of it. It will mean death — for many — in Canton, death — for all — in the Shameen!"

"Logical enough. There remains one hope — one man — Prince Kokoshkine."

"He left the barracks early this morning," said the Manchu, "on the *Chuen to yan*'s orders — my spies brought me word,"

"He — he obeyed the orders?"

"What else could he have done? He cannot fight all Canton."

"Did he take all his cavalry with him?"

"No. Only his Russians, Tatars and Manchus. I have not yet heard from all my spies. I left instructions at my house to bring me word here. They will doubtless report by and by. We will wait — there is nothing else for us to do." He sipped his tea, then looked up, very grave, "D'Acosta," he went on, "we have been friends — we three — you and I and Pavel Kokoshkine. We — all three — have worked for the same aim, the peace of Asia, which means, perhaps, the peace of the world. Our methods have differed. For we belong to three different races, Slav, Jew, and Mongol. You have believed in building with the power of money, of finance, of big business, to make China so independent out of her own resources that she can resist the world economically — and thus command respect. I cling to the philosophy of my ancestors and also, being not altogether a fool, to certain more constructive maxims. I believe in the power of diplomacy, the wonderful diplomacy of the old monarchy, the Manchu régime, which found its pinnacle and its pride in the late dowager empress. Thus it has been my idea always to bring back the monarchy and, with it, peace. And Kokoshkine, the soldier, believes that peace can only come through war or the threat of war. That is why he has taken service under the Cantonese government, to lead them, to become all-powerful, to undermine with their own troops the influence of the *Chuen to yan*'s brotherhood, then to strike when the moment was ripe. We failed — you and I and the Russian. All our three methods —" he smiled very gently "— have proved useless, barren. Finance, diplomacy, forces — useless — all three, all three!" He sighed. "We differed, when really even to differ was only a waste of time."

"And yet," rejoined the Levantine, "we three agreed on one thing — the power of superstitions and ancient traditions. The greatest power here in China!"

"Yes," admitted the other; "the power contained in that vase. And there, too, we have failed. If the vase be lost, then lost is its power to us. And if it falls into the hands of the *Chuen to yan*'s brotherhood — My friend, I have already instructed my relatives in Peking to bury my body in a charming spot, on the side of a hill, with an exquisite view over the fields, so that my spirit after death may thoroughly enjoy itself. There is no hope, for you, for me, for Pavel Kokoshkine. If the latter turns against his Cantonese master, then the odds are too high — they will crush him. If he does not turn against them, then presently the *Chuen to van* will kill him as one too powerful, too influential, as soon as he has sucked him dry of military knowledge and tactics. It is over. The book has been read. The grape has been pressed." He drew an opium-pipe from his loose sleeve, rose, and took the smoking paraphernalia from a small lacquered table in the corner of the room. "Have I your permission to take a few whiffs of the black smoke — to make the end more sweet?" he asked; and, when the other inclined his head, "Thank you, old friend!"

Delicately he kneaded the brown poppy cube against the tiny bowl of his pipe, then dropped it into the open furnace of the lamp and watched the flame change it gradually into amber and gold. The opium boiled, sizzled, evaporated. The fragrant smoke rolled in sluggish clouds over the floor, and Sun Yu-Wen, having emptied the pipe at one long-drawn inhalation, leaned back, with both shoulders pressed well down on the pillow, so as better to inflate his chest and keep his lungs filled all the longer with the fumes of the kindly drug. A slow smile overspread his placid, butter-yellow features. He stared at the rolling opium clouds. The noises of the outer world, the tumult and the riot, the crackling of steel and hate, the roaring of the Chinese war-trumpets seemed very far away; and he was already floating on the fantastic, grotesque wings of poppy-dreams when the Levantine shook him by the shoulder. He sat up, rubbed his eyes.

"Yes?" he asked dreamily.

"Tugluk Khan is here."

Immediately the mandarin became fully conscious, pushed his opium-pipe away with a regretful gesture, and smiled at Tugluk Khan, his chief spy, a Moslem Tatar from Chinese Turkestan, dressed in the orthodox blue of a Cantonese coolie, who stood before him with clasped hands.

"What news?" he demanded.

"I passed Prince Kokoshkine's troop of riders below the corner of the Loo Man-Tze Street," replied the other. "Feofar Khan was with him."

"They saw you?"

"I was in a crowd of coolies, I did not dare speak. But I touched the bridle of his horse, asking for alms as if I were a beggar, and as he bent down to curse me, I whistled two shrill notes, as do the long-limbed rice-birds of our own west country. Allah grant that he heard and understood!"

"He did not speak?"

"Wait, master! For there is one strange thing of which I must tell you. Feofar Khan has his youngest wife with him."

"Youngest wife?" cut in the mandarin. "Ridiculous! I know that Tatar reprobate. He loves soft hands and melting eyes. But he has three wives already, each as old and shriveled as the devil himself, and each henpecking our brave general with the strength of her tongue. They are jealous of each other. But against a forth wife they would make common cause. He would not dare marry again. Besides, I saw him only two days ago. He was not married to a young wife then. And a Tatar wedding takes seven days to celebrate.

"But I heard, master!"

"What?"

"What he said to her. She was in a palanquin slung to the flank of a dromedary, with Feofar Khan riding on one side, Prince Kokoshkine on the other. And, after I whistled the call of the rice-bird, Feofar Khan rose in his stirrups and spoke to his young wife, through the curtains."

"What did he say?"

"He called her 'Blood of my Liver' and 'Pink-breasted Pearl,' and —"

"Never mind those Tartar terms of endearment. What else did he say?"

"He begged her — the narrow-footed one —"

"Wait!" interrupted the mandarin. "Tell me — aren't you Tartars proud of your women's short, broad feet?"

"Yes. But Feofar Khan did call her narrow-footed! He begged her pardon for exposing her to the rough tumult of the streets, and added that soon she would be at rest in more fitting surroundings, in the house of his second cousin, Hunyagu Khan."

Sun Yu-Wen looked up, startled.

"At rest — in the house of Hunyagu Khan — did he say that?" he demanded.

"Yes, master."

The mandarin laughed, while the Levantine looked on in astonishment.

" 'Trust the snake before the devil, and the devil before the Tartar.' " He quoted the ancient proverb. "Good, good, my Tugluk Khan!" He tossed the latter a purse filled with gold coins. "You have done well. Rest yourself. Go downstairs to the kitchen and ask the cook to give you of his best. I shall send for you when I need you."

He dismissed his spy and turned to Moses d'Acosta, every bit of lethargy gone from his placid face.

"My friend," he said, "it appears that I was wrong, after all, about my spirit jumping the Dragon Gate. For the end is not yet!" He started toward the door. "Come!"

"Where to?" asked the Levantine.

"To the house of Hunyagu Khan."

"But," came the objection. "I am not worse than the average coward. Still, for the two of us, marked men both, to go beyond the Shameen — with the *Chuen to yan*'s jackals roving everywhere —"

Again the mandarin laughed.

"You own this hotel. Ever consider its location?"

"I have. And right now I don't care for it. It is too near the outer wall which divides the Shameen from the native town, in the direct danger-zone."

"For which praises be to the Lord Buddha!" said the Manchu. "You see — of the native town, just on the other side of the outer wall which surrounds the Shameen. His back courtyard runs parallel with yours. You understand?"

"I do — now!" exclaimed d'Acosta. "Seems to me that Feofar Khan sent a message after all."

"He did, indeed. He asked us to meet him, or if not him, then his youngest wife — the narrow-footed one — in Hunyagu Khan's house. Narrow-footed — a white woman, don't you think?"

"Miss Campbell?"

"Right you are."

They left the hotel and stepped into the back courtyard, a small enclosed place, above it the back of the hotel rising and presenting a windowless expanse of whitewashed bricks. The only opening was a narrow door, behind a screening cluster of bushes, which led into the kitchen. But, from snatches of talk that drifted up from there, they knew the cook and his assistants were just then fully occupied. For, true to his master's instructions, Tugluk Khan was just then bullying the personnel of the kitchen to his heart's content.

D'Acosta looked round warily.

"All right," he said. "Here's for Hunyagu Khan's house!"

The Shameen wall was perhaps ten feet high and crowned with a stone coping, but a couple of feet from the ground there was a narrow ledge from which they could reach the top. The Levantine, thin and lithe, swung himself up first, then lent a helping hand to the Manchu, whose girth was not meant for violent exercises. For a moment they balanced on the wall, then let themselves drop on the other side. They got up, crossed the courtyard, and knocked at the back door of Hunyagu Khan's house, who, true to his clannish breed, employed only Tartar servants. They entered, and shortly afterward Hunyagu Khan came from an inner apartment.

He kowtowed before his guests and gave them a hearty welcome.

"Yes," he said, after they had told him why they had come; "you are doubtless right. Wait here. My servants are close-mouthed and trustworthy. My house is yours, and so is my feeble strength. No, no; do not thank me! I am but the lowly dust beneath your charming and exquisite feet."

He clapped his hands. A servant entered, received his orders, and returned with steaming cups of tea and cigarettes. They sat down. And, while outside the great yellow city was coiling like a snake about to strike, while the war-trumpets roared louder and louder, while Moses d'Acosta looked on, wondering, slightly impatient, the two Mongols talked gently and lengthily of other, unworldly matters, with the dignity of men at whose back three thousand years of unbroken racial history and pride were sitting in a solemn, graven row.

"Yes, yes," said Sun Yu-Wen in answer to one of Hunyagu Khan's remarks; "it is mentioned already in that delicate tome called 'Ku-Luang's Commentary' that —"

The voice droned on, and Moses d'Acosta was falling into uneasy sleep when he was suddenly wakened by a great tumult outside, a neighing of horse, a jingling of head-stalls, a crackling of steel, a thumping of kettle-drums, and curses, shrieks, cries — and, clear above the mad symphony, a rough voice shouting a hectic torrent of words, a crazy mixture of terms of endearment and full-flavored Oriental abuse.

"Feofar Khan!" said Hunyagu Khan. "I know his voice — and his choice of language."

"Little pink-and-blue sweetmeat! Little melon seed of much delight!" shouted Feofar Khan above the din of steel and jingling bridle. "Oh, narrow-footed one!"

Moses d'Acosta inclined his head.

"Yes," he said; "Feofar Khan is continuing the telling of the message," while outside the latter went on, bewailing the sending of cruel, stony fate which had forced her, his youngest wife, for love of him to leave the "fat and warm security of the harem, to launch herself upon the bitter, bitter waters of adventure and fatigue and extremely bad roads.

"Ahee!" shrieked the Tartar general. "And to have swine-fed Kansuh ruffians, to have the very sweeping of the Canton gutters crack low jokes at me and my beloved narrow-footed one to the detriment of my nose!"

"Listen," said another voice.

"I shall not listen! All I could I have suffered, like the gentle, patient man I am! But to have you — the great chief whom loyally I served — to have you doubt me!" — and a sound very much like weeping.

"But what do you want?" asked the other voice.

"I want a safe asylum for my youngest wife, here in the house of my kinsman. Permit me to take her into the house, to introduce her to my cousin, to beg him for hospitality —"

"I told you that we are in a hurry, that —"

"Yes, great master; you told me — at least, you gave me to understand — that you do not entirely trust me — and it is that which hurts most. And all because of that great and most evil grandson of a cockroach, Sun Yu-Wen, and that unbeautiful and illegitimate descendant of many piglings, Moses d'Acosta —"

The other voice cut in again, sharp, high:

"Feofar Khan, I do not mistrust you. Nor is it my intention to interfere in your domestic affairs. It was foolish of you to bring your wife along —"

"I love her, O great chief!"

"Foolish just the same. All right. She has my permission to go into Hunyagu Khan's house. No," — quickly — "she can go alone and explain matters to your cousin. You will stay here with me, as will Prince Kokoshkine. I need you both."

"Who is that speaking?" asked the Levantine, and a servant whom Hunyagu Khan had dispatched through a side door came in and replied that it was the *Chuen to yan*.

"The *Chuen to yan*'s soldiers are knocking at the gate," he reported. "They have a woman with them."

"Heavens!" exclaimed d'Acosta. "This is the front room — they'll find us here —"

"Where?" asked the mandarin.

Hunyagu Khan laughed.

"I am a Moslem.," he said, "and, I trust, orthodox. There is always safety and privacy in an orthodox Moslem's house — if he be broadminded enough to forget at times his orthodoxy. Follow me."

They crossed the room at a rush, another, and yet another, while in the distance they heard the outer gate open, heard the rough accents of Cantonese soldiers, and, finally, at the end of a hall, their host pulled apart a gaily flowered curtain.

"My harem," he said. "Come! Let's forget for the time Moslem prejudice and etiquette!"

They entered quickly, amid great laughing and giggling and chattering and. clanking of jewels and rustling of loose silk trousers, as their host's wives and daughters and female slaves rushed about, staring for a moment wide-eyed at the male visitors, then rapidly adjusting their face-veils and fleeing precipitately into a back apartment. Hunyagu Khan left, to return a few moments later, ushering in a veiled woman clad in the height of fashion of the Mongolian plains.

"The narrow-footed one!" he introduced and laughed, while the newcomer took off her face-veil, showing the smiling face of Marie Campbell!

"Hello, everybody!" she said, and to the Levantine: "I always did pity Oriental women — today more than ever. My word — these veils are stifling, and hardly hygienic, I should judge!" She sat down on a divan. "I am famished and thirsty and, since my father isn't here to kick the ceiling, I'm simply dying for a smoke."

Moses d'Acosta held out his cigarette-case. She lit up, leaned back comfortably, and blew three perfect smoke rings.

"Your nerves seem to be still in working order," commented d'Acosta.

"Have to be! I am a remittance-woman, am I not? And your hotel — why — the prices you charge — if your guests didn't have iron nerves, they'd die of heart-failure when they see their bills! Which reminds me. Last night, I rushed off suddenly from dinner. I owe you and Mandarin Sun Yu-Wen an apology. But when you mentioned that Tchou-fou-yao vase again — I couldn't stand it any longer."

"Yes," smiled the Manchu; "and it seems that you ran into a great deal of trouble, Miss Campbell." He sighed. "What did I tell you last night? Oh, yes — I told you that it is strange indeed how the fate of the many millions depends always from a woman's jeweled earrings. Miss Campbell, have I your permission to speak once more about the little Tchou-fou-yao vase?"

"Go ahead," laughed the girl.

"You have it?"

"I hid it."

"Will you give it to us?"

"*Us?*" she echoed. "Last night there seemed to be a difference of opinion between you and Mr. d'Acosta."

"Last night the danger was not as imminent as it is today." And he explained to her how he, Moses d'Acosta and Prince Kokoshkine were friends, each working for the same aim, the peace of the world through China's peace, how they had differed on the question of method, but how all three knew that superstition was the greatest power in China. "Superstition and tradition!" he wound up. "In this land of ancient superstitions, ancient traditions! Contained in two little vases —"

"One of which my uncle broke to pieces. Oh, yes — Pavel told me —"

"Pavel?"

She blushed slightly. "Prince Kokoshkine, I mean. You can tell me more about the vase later on. In a hurry to get it, aren't you?"

"Yes, Miss Campbell."

"Very well. The vase is in the hotel."

"Impossible!" exclaimed the Levantine.

"I had the hotel searched — even your rooms."

She laughed.

"Nice, honest host you are, aren't you? I shall complain about you to the Hotel Men's Association as soon as I get back to New York. But there is one place you forgot to search."

"Namely?"

"The little safe in Pailloux's private office. I slipped it in time on the second shelf, way back amid a lot of old papers I did it on a woman's instinct."

"Blessed be woman's instinct!" said the Levantine. "It's a much more powerful weapon than man's logic." He was out of the room, and a moment later, looking from the window, they saw him cross the back courtyard and swing himself across the Shameen wall into the hotel ground.

While they waited for his return, the mandarin told her about the power and influence of the little vase — and a queer tale it was, intensely Chinese, intensely Asiatic, reaching into the dawn of legendary antiquity, stretching on, through the gray, swinging centuries, into the present era. For it appeared that, hundreds of years earlier, at the time when Chi Huang-Ti, the ruler of the Chinese feudatory states which laid the foundation of the Celestial Empire, began to build the Great Wall of China and to fortify old Peking as the only means of stopping the marauding Mongol horsemen, a sainted priest was given two tiny vases by a wandering monk — the Buddha himself, the legends told — with the injunction to guard them well. For whoever possessed these vases, Chinese or foreigner, would by the very strength of them have dominion over China. The stranger — monk or living Buddha — had pointed out on the inner surface of the vases a miniature painting of China's ancient divinities. They were all there, very tiny, but all-powerful; and, since the Chinese are intensely practical, the sainted priest had been given two vases, in case one should be broken or lost. The vases, the double emblem of dominion, had gone from century to century, from hand to hand, from dynasty to dynasty. When Genghis Khan, the great Mongol conqueror, had come out of the bleak Hsing-an Mountains to subjugate China, he had taken the vases, had paid homage to them, and after him his grandson, Kublai Khan, all the cruel Mongols of the Yuean dynasty, the Mings, and the Manchus. The Manchus, too, had passed, and it was many years before her death that the dowager empress, obeying a dream, had sent the vases to the far west, to the Ssu Yueh, the chief of the Four Mountains, for safekeeping. Had come the revolution, the republic — "and," Sun Yu-Wen wound up, "you know the rest."

"Is this little emblem really so powerful?"

"Absolutely! No Chinese, not even the most modem, the Westernized and scoffing and atheistic, would dare disobey its hidden command."

"And — I suppose," asked the girl, "no Chinaman would dare risk its destruction, now that my uncle has destroyed the duplicate and only one is left."

"You are right, Miss Campbell."

Then, when she was silent, her face cupped in her hands, evidently deep in thought, he asked gently.

"What are you thinking of?"

"Of Pavel Kokoshkine. Out there," — she pointed to the window, whence came, louder and louder, the riot and tumult of the crowds, the loud braying of trumpets — "riding through the streets by the side of the *Chuen to yan*, helpless —"

"Force was his belief. Steel and bullets They failed him."

"As diplomacy failed you — and finance failed Mr. d'Acosta, and —" she slurred, then smiled "— I wonder if you were perhaps right about — how did you put it? Something about all the world dangling from a woman's jeweled earrings, wasn't it?"

"Doubtless I was right," said the Manchu.

"I am beginning to agree with you. And do you know why?"

"No."

"Because at times there is an idea —"

"In the jeweled earrings, Miss Campbell?"

"No. In the feminine brains behind the jeweled earrings. You'll forgive me — won't you? — if I pat myself on the back."

She laughed, but when, a few moments later, Moses d'Acosta returned and gave her the little vase, she grew serious. Dominion — she thought, as her fingers touched the cool bit of porcelain — dominion and power in this small piece of glazed clay! She looked at it, wondered. What had caused her mother to give the tiny thing to her father on her deathbed, as she must have done? A spirit of prophecy? She shrugged her shoulders. However, it had happened. She rose, and put on her thick horsehair face-veil.

"I am going," she said.

"You are — what?" The two men's astonished voices came simultaneously

"Going."

"Where?"

"To the Temple of Horrors." And she cut through their excited buzz of expostulations with: " Send some of Hunyagu Khan's servants with me — Buddhists. I don't suppose all his people are Moslems. While I am gone, communicate with the *Chuen to yan* — can you?"

"Yes," said the Manchu. "One of my spies is quite near. But —"

"Tell the *Chuen to yan* I have the vase. Then bring him with you to the Temple of Horrors. And — Pavel Kokoshkine — don't forget to bring him, too, whatever else you do."

"But what do you expect to do?" demanded Moses d'Acosta.

"Are you a poker player?"

"Yes."

"Very well. I am going to draw four cards — with the hope that I'll accumulate a royal flush."

Not many minutes afterward, accompanied by half a dozen of Hunyagu Khan's stalwart Tatars, who had received orders to obey her implicitly, she was out on the Canton streets, and to her dying day she never forgot the next quarter of an hour — the tumult, the riot, the crowds of excited coolies, the *Chuen to yan*'s jackals scurrying everywhere, like scorpions, searching, searching — for her. She never forgot the ever-rising shouts of *"Pao Ch'ing Mien Yang,"* "Death to the foreigners," the insane fervor of the throngs, the incredible, trembling elation of hate. What was it all about? The crowds did not care, did not know. But it swept over them like a typhoon, and steadily they seemed to crystallize their one purpose — the Shameen — the hated foreigners there! And the mob gathered strength and volume, rolled on relentlessly, and it took all the physical force and all the diplomacy of the *Chuen to yan*'s picked agents to keep them from their purpose. "Not yet!" the *Chuen to yan* had ordered. "We will not fight the foreigner — not unless we have to. Search! Find! You must find!"

Marie was grateful to her retinue of Tatars. They cut through the throng as a knife cuts through cheese, shouting insults and defying words at everybody, and belaboring with a beautiful impartiality the backs and thighs and heads of merchants and peasants alike.

"Oh, thy right!" they yelled, as they brought down their long, brass-tipped staves. "Oh, thy left! Oh, thy face!" suiting the swing of their sticks to the part of Chinese anatomy which they were striking, "Give way, unmentionable ones! This is a great lady on her way to sacrifice to the spirits of her honorable ancestors!"

Pushing, fighting, striking, Marie in the middle, they pressed on, and finally gained the Temple of Horrors. There the crowd was a little less dense. The door was open. Marie looked. She saw inside, wreathed in incense smoke, the dread statues of horror, and, at the farther end, the one representation of sweetness and gentleness, a great statue of the Goddess of Mercy. There were a number of yellow-robed priests in the temple, but they gave way when the Tatars told them that this was the wife of a great Mongol chief come to pray.

So, preceded by her escort, Marie entered the temple. She crossed its full length until she came to the statue of the Goddess of Mercy. It stood on a gilt lotus pedestal above a long sweep of steps. Upon these she knelt and prayed, prayed fervently to the God of her childhood, prayed and waited, minute after minute, the tiny vase clutched tightly in her hand.

Presently, as if from a great distance, she heard voices and footsteps. She turned, saw the *Chuen to yan* enter the temple, accompanied by a number of high priests, and behind them, driven on by soldiers' musket-butts, Sun Yu-Wen, Moses d'Acosta and Prince Pavel Kokoshkine, their hands tied behind their backs. She waited until they had crossed half the length of the temple. Then she rose and called out in a loud, clear voice:

"Here! I am here!"

And suddenly she rushed up the steps that led to the statue of the Goddess of Mercy, stood there, the vase in her hand; and while the priests rushed about like angry bees, crying excitedly: "A sacrilege! A sacrilege!" her own voice came ringing, high and strong.

"I am speaking to the *Chuen to yan*, the chief of the Society of Augustly Harmonious Fists!"

The *Chuen to yan* stepped forward and looked up at her. For a moment there came again that blighting fear she had felt when she had looked upon those features for the first time. But she controlled herself immediately. She was playing for a great stake, she told herself, and she held the winning hand. She was sure of it.

Still he gazed up at her.

"Ah!" he breathed, just the one word, mockingly.

"I am here."

"So I notice."

"And," — she opened her hand, showed a rapid glimpse of the tiny vase — "I have the vase, the Tchou-fou-yao vase — the ancient emblem of dominion and power!" When the priests heard the word "Tchou-fou-yao," something like a shiver ran over them and they kowtowed deeply. "I give you the choice," she went on.

"What choice?"

"Either I put the vase here, at the feet of the Goddess of Mercy, so that it may remain here for all time to come, as an emblem of China's greatness, greatness in the past, greatness again in the future — that it may remain here forever, made sacred by the protection of this goddess." Her words came sweeping, with an intense sincerity of which she had not thought herself capable. "If I do that, then I want your word, your sacred word of honor by whatever you hold holy, that you will make peace —"

"Peace with whom?" the *Chuen to van* demanded, a strange, eerie look coming into his eyes.

"Peace with all the world! No longer the war of intrigues, of gliding words and lies! But peace, chiefly and foremost, with these three men —" she pointed to d'Acosta, Sun Yu-Wen and Kokoshkine "— who work for China, even as you are working. Peace — through compromise! But if you do not do as I tell you, I shall drop the vase. I shall smash it into a dozen pieces, as my uncle smashed the vase he had."

"You would not dare!"

"I would! And you know I would! And then lost for all time the hope of dominion and peace and power! Yes! I would dare — and you know I would!"

There was a moment's complete silence; then, from the throng of priests, who had caught the meaning of the words, a cry went up — not a hundred cries, massed and blended into one, but just one cry, such as one would imagine to follow the death of the last hope, the last faith, the last promise from the face of the earth. And suddenly the *Chuen to yan* inclined his head.

"You win," he said very calmly.

For he was a Chinese, an Oriental. A fanatic? Yes. But also a fatalist. Fight the inevitable? And what price was there in that, what pride, what logic and worth?

He turned to the soldiers, gave curt orders, and a moment later the bonds of the three prisoners were cut.

It was the Manchu who spoke first.

"*Chuen to yan,*" he said, holding out his hand, "let us forget what has passed. Let us work together — in the future — the four of us! Was it not Confucius himself who once said that the superior man gives in, but aids to achievement, while the inferior man remains stubborn and leads to ruin?"

"Yes," replied the *Chuen to yan*; "the four of us."

"Oh, no!" laughed Marie, coming down the steps of the pedestal. "Not the four of you! Only three."

"Why?" asked Moses d'Acosta.

"Because one of the four is coming home with me — to America." Again she laughed and slipped her hand through Prince Kokoshkine's arm. "Pavel," she said, "would you mind cabling to Tom Van Zandt as soon as it's safe to go back to the Shameen and ask him to be your best man?"

"Gladly!"

"And another question: Are you awfully proud about that title of yours?"

"Not a bit, dear. Why?"

"Well — you see — it appears that father never became naturalized, and that, through my mother, I am a Chinese subject. And so it's up to you to become an American citizen. And you can't do that if you stick to your title!"

And they laughed and kissed, while the Goddess of Mercy looked down upon them with her painted, eternal smile. 🌐